A NEW CASE FOR MYCROFT

"He was shot right through the heart," Jake said, "although there are those who said he didn't have a heart. Damned good trainer though."

"No one heard anything?"

Jake shrugged. "The stables are quite a distance from the house and with the weather . . ."

"Tire tracks? Shells? Anything? A man can't be murdered and a horse vanish without leaving some trace."

"If the police have anything," Samantha said, "they're not publicizing it."

"And why take Sir Beauregarde?" Penelope asked, knowing the answer even as she spoke the words. Loomis had been training a potential Arabian national champion. The competition in the Arabian business was fierce and intense. A national champion commanded huge stud fees. Potentially, millions of dollars were at stake over the long run. "Horse lovers wouldn't do that, would they?"

Jake shrugged. "It's a business. The recession hurt the Arabian industry and hurt it bad. It wouldn't be the first time a horse has been killed for the insurance money."

"There's more," Samantha said. "Horace Melrose has a rather large loan from my bank. A good part of the collateral Horace put up is a half-million-dollar insurance policy on Sir Beauregarde. Unfortunately, the policy doesn't cover acts of God or foul play."

"Insurance investigators will be all over this case," Jake said, "making sure the policy is null and void. Unless . . ." He glanced at Samantha, smiling reassuringly. "Unless you find the person who killed Jack Loomis. Find the killer and we find Sir Beauregarde, save the Great Empty Creek Arabian Horse Show, and keep the bank out of financial hot water."

"You'd better stay for dinner," Penelope said in keeping with a Warren household. "I'll order Chinese."

AMANDA HAZARD MYSTERIES
BY CONNIE FEDDERSEN

DEAD IN THE CELLAR   (0-8217-5245-6, $4.99)

DEAD IN THE DIRT   (1-57566-046-6, $4.99)

DEAD IN THE MELON PATCH   (0-8217-4872-6, $4.99)

DEAD IN THE WATER   (0-8217-5244-8, $4.99)

Available wherever paperbacks are sold, or order direct from the Publisher. Send cover price plus 50¢ per copy for mailing and handling to Penguin USA, P.O. Box 999, c/o Dept. 17109, Bergenfield, NJ 07621. Residents of New York and Tennessee must include sales tax. DO NOT SEND CASH.

Garrison Allen

STABLE CAT

KENSINGTON BOOKS
Kensington Publishing Corp.
http://www.kensingtonbooks.com

KENSINGTON BOOKS are published by

Kensington Publishing Corp.
850 Third Avenue
New York, NY 10022

First Kensington Hardcover Printing: June, 1996
First Kensington Paperback Printing: July, 1997
10 9 8 7 6 5 4 3 2 1

Printed in the United States of America

For Good Friends and Lunch Pals
Barbara, Cathy, and Linda

THE CAST
Mostly In Order of Appearance

Empty Creek, Arizona, aka Empty By God Creek and Don't You Forget It! The strangest little town west of the Mississippi.

Sir Beauregarde Revere of Dunbarton Lakes, aka Beau. A magnificent, very horny Arabian stallion who has the potential to become *the* national champion. Through a peculiar chain of events, Beau falls in love with an older filly.

Jack Loomis. Beau's trainer.

Abigail Wilson. An apprentice trainer.

The Great Empty Creek Arabian Horse Show. It is a respected precursor to the Scottsdale Arabian Horse Show. The champion stallion crowned in Empty Creek is the odds-on favorite for Scottsdale.

Penelope Warren. Our redoubtable heroine and sole proprietress of Mycroft & Company, Empty Creek's mystery bookstore, who finds herself in the midst of an unexpected pre-midlife crisis.

Mycroft, aka Big Mike, Mikey. A twenty-five-pound Abyssinian alley cat from Abyssinia who finds the world much too interesting to have a crisis in any of his nine lives, so long as there is a plentiful supply of lima beans to eat, pretty women for cuddling, and the occasional visit with *Murphy Brown,* that sleek calico who lives down the road.

Samantha Dale, aka Sam. President of the Empty Creek National Bank and a member of the board that puts on the horse show each year.

Jake Peterson, aka Big Jake. President of the horse show board of directors and a pretty awful poker player.

Harris Anderson III, aka Andy. Penelope's devoted and often bemused boyfriend and editor of the *Empty Creek News Journal.*

Chardonnay, aka Char. A gentle six-year-old Arabian filly who lives with Penelope and Big Mike. She loves peppermint candies and long rides into the desert.

Red the Rat and *Daisy.* Empty Creek's desert rat and eternal optimist. He has to be optimistic after searching for a lost gold mine for upward of thirty years now. Daisy is the latest mule to share his life.

Matilda Bates, aka Mattie. Beau's former owner and now a well-preserved temptress who has Red the Rat right square in the

sights of her Winchester Model 94 rifle. Mattie is a crack shot
and will not hesitate to use the 30–30 to prod Red to the altar
(after a good bath, of course).

Horace Melrose, aka That Rich, Pretentious, No-Good Jerk. Beau's
current owner.

Maryanne Melrose. The soon-to-be former Mrs. Horace Melrose.
She is suing that rich, pretentious, no-good jerk for everything
he's got.

Nora Pryor. Single Mom and author of *Empty Creek: A History
and Guide.* She interrupts work on the second edition of her
book to help her daughter prepare for competition in the Great
Empty Creek Arabian Horse Show.

Regina Pryor, aka Reggie. A sixteen-year-old beauty who was for-
tunate enough to inherit her mother's wondrous strawberry
blond hair and the sexiest voice north of Nogales. Reggie is
passionate about horses and Dirk Tindall.

Dirk Tindall. A junior at Empty Creek High School and the star
quarterback who is leading the usually hapless Gila Monsters
to the school's first winning season in twenty years.

Elaine Henders, aka Laney. Penelope's best friend and Empty
Creek's prolific writer-in-residence who pens sultry and highly
erotic romance novels set in old Arizona. This redhead, as ravishing as any of her frequently ravished heroines, utilizes a
number of mail-order catalogs in her research.

Wally. Laney's live-in cowboy companion and always agreeable research assistant. Penelope just loves the way Wally crinkles his eyes laconically.

Alexander, aka Alex. A diminutive Yorkshire terrier and Mycroft's best friend. He lived quite happily with Laney and Wally until Laney decided he needed a companion.

Kelsey, aka Kelsey, No! Kelsey, Stay! Kelsey, Be Nice to Alexander! Alex's nemesis. She has a vertical leap of three feet and is destined to flunk out of obedience school—twice. She thinks the world revolves around her presence. Big Mike has her number though.

Cassandra Warren, aka Storm Williams, Stormy. Penelope's younger sister who has starred in such epic motion pictures as *Amazon Princess and the Sword of Doom*.

John Fowler, aka Dutch. Stormy's fiancé and chief of the Empty Creek Police Department. Although he is hopelessly in love with Stormy, Dutch sometimes thinks the Warren sisters will be the death of him.

Lawrence Burke and *Willie Stoner, aka Tweedledee* and *Tweedledum*. They are the only two members of the Empty Creek P.D.'s Robbery/Homicide Bureau. They have a love-hate relationship with Penelope and Big Mike, a fondness for jelly donuts, and an amazing ability to arrest the wrong person—or cat.

Debbie, aka Debbie D, Dee Dee. She doesn't need a Super Bra to look super. Her glorious attributes have been termed "national treasures" and Red the Rat once recommended their registration as "deadly weapons."

Sam Connors. A police officer and former boyfriend of Penelope's. They might still be going together had Mycroft not . . . Still, all worked out for the best as Sam and Debbie are now a devoted item, much to the dismay of Debbie's many suitors at the . . .

Double B Western Saloon and Steakhouse. The place where Debbie works as Empty Creek's favorite cocktail waitress. The Double B is the habitual meeting place for Empty Creek's curious collection of eccentrics.

Kathleen Allen. A part-time assistant at Mycroft & Company, a part-time college student, and a full-time inspiration for lurid verse commemorating *her* bosom. Penelope *used* to think that Kathy was quite sane.

Timothy Scott. Kathy's roommate, lover, and Empty Creek's deranged poet laureate of the above-mentioned bosom.

Lora Lou Longstreet. The free-spirited owner of The Tack Shack, a supply house for all things horsey and good gossip.

David Macklin. A part-time artist for the Empty Creek P.D.

Mr. Richard Raymond and *Ms. Susan Vaughn*. Insurance investigators for Amalgamated Equine Surety, Inc.

Cackling Ed, aka That Horny Old Doofer. A demented senior citizen.

Anthony Lyme-Regis. A tweedy English gentleman and a director of television commercials.

Lola LaPola. A newly wed television reporter who fits right in with the other nuts who reside in Empty Creek. They now live next door to Stormy and Dutch with an assortment of animals and *the* pillory in their bedroom, which never fails to remind them of how they fell in love.

The President's Ball. Held the night before the opening of the Great Empty Creek Arabian Horse Show, it is one of the highlights of the social season.

The Chorus. Composed of assorted horses, humans, and other critters including bunny rabbits, a rattlesnake, the odd coyote or two, *the* Robert Redford and *the* Jane Fonda, various horse owners, trainers, and handlers, an astrologer, a cuckoo clock, and a hot walker used for exercising horses.

PROLOGUE

Had the judges of the Great Empty Creek Arabian Horse Show been present to see Sir Beauregarde Revere of Dunbarton Lakes, a magnificent black Arabian stallion of sixteen hands, they would have been momentarily impressed with his decorum. He stood at attention in his twelve foot by twelve foot enclosure, showing no inclination to restlessness or unruly behavior. The judges, too, would have been influenced by Sir Beauregarde's physical refinements of satinlike hair, neat erect ears, the fine structure of his head, and the gracefully curved tail. No fault would have been found with Beau's other qualities either. He was strong and muscular, intelligent and possessed of a personality befitting a potential Arabian National Champion.

Had those judges been present, Sir Beauregarde would doubtless have been crowned with a champion's ribbon and cup forthwith. Unfortunately, they were not, but their absence proved to be of little consequence, for Beau broke the championship mold by turning and delivering a massive kick—with both hind feet—to the door of his enclosure.

In short, Sir Beauregarde Revere of Dunbarton Lakes was pissed, as well as bored, lonely, and more than a little horny. He craved the companionship of other horses, preferably a nice filly of a certain age suitable for breeding.

A second kick was no more effective than the first. The door would not give. Beau glared momentarily at the offending structure that barred his path to freedom and then, with a nervous, restless snort, he relaxed, accepting the inevitable, and went back to dreaming of better days when he had run free with other colts, frolicking happily and racing about on long, unsteady legs.

He stared through the tiny window in the door, but there was nothing to be seen in the dim light cast by the single bulb illuminating the area outside his cell. A steady rain pummeled the roof and Beau cocked his ears to listen, still yearning for freedom, even if it meant being out in the wet and cold.

Beau stood quietly until his reverie was broken by alien sounds in the night. The argument was loud, although brief, and ended with the sharp report of a gunshot—loud and reverberating in the confines of the barn, but quickly muffled by the steady rain outside.

Beau whinnied nervously and listened, but there was only silence and the faint scent of blood. He had heard human arguments before. Usually, they preceded the opening of his stall and a vigorous workout, punctuated by the fearsome crack of the trainer's whip. Beau waited, but as time passed, he slowly relaxed again, disturbed only by the strange odor, growing stronger in the chill night air.

Finally, the door at the far end of the barn creaked as it slid back on its runners.

A thin flashlight beam bobbed as it made its way along the

various stalls to stop at Beau's enclosure. He whinnied softly in greeting at this strange break in routine. He shook his head and whinnied again as the door slid open.

"Hey, Beau, how about a carrot, old boy?"

Beau munched happily while a gentle hand patted his neck. He chewed on a second carrot while the warm rug was placed over his big body and a third before accepting the halter without resistance. Beau was more than ready for a little adventure.

"Okay, Beau, there's more where that came from, but we have to go now."

Beau followed the lead, snorting and balking slightly as he was led on a wide berth around the body slumped on the floor of the barn. The blood scent receded quickly once outside and Beau waited patiently while the barn door was closed, savoring the rain and the chilled air that smelled of freedom. They walked for some distance through the darkness, plodding through the mud where the boots of a human and the hooves of a champion stallion left their marks, only to be quickly erased by the rain.

Beau clambered willingly up the ramp into the horse trailer. Again, he waited patiently and stumbled only slightly as the pickup truck lurched forward, wheels spinning briefly in the mud. Then, he settled down to enjoy the unexpected but most welcome ride. Anything was better than his stall and the tedium of training.

The possibility that he might be on his way to a glue factory apparently never occurred to Beau.

CHAPTER ONE

Penelope Warren was in a world-class funk and didn't know how to get out of it. Well, actually, she did know how to ease her restless dissatisfaction with life in Empty Creek, Arizona, but was undecided whether to run off to Africa again, ship over in the United States Marine Corps, or take up sky diving—all rather impractical options considering the presence of Big Mike, her longtime friend and feline companion. Although Big Mike—a twenty-five-pound Abyssinian alley cat from Abyssinia—might like sky diving, Penelope was positive he wouldn't like the Marine Corps, and if they went back to Africa he would miss his many friends, probably even Doctor Bob, his vet with whom he had a love-hate relationship.

Besides, Penelope had been there, done that, at least for the first two options, having already served four years in the Marine Corps right out of high school, much to the dismay of her parents and the delight of Cassandra, her little sister, before collecting three degrees in English literature in rapid succession. The pleasure of Muffy and Biff, her parents—their real names were Mary and Jameson—at watching the president of Arizona State University bestow the Doctor of Philosophy degree upon their daughter was quickly dampened when Penelope announced at ceremony's conclusion that she was off to Ethiopia to teach English at some remote college as a Peace Corps Volunteer.

It was there one evening, as Penelope sat on the porch with a gin and tonic watching the sun set over what the old British colonials used to call miles and miles of bloody Africa, that a tiny squalling kitten fell from the bougainvillea, practically into her lap, barely missing the gin and tonic. Although his eyes had not yet opened, the fledgling lion hissed ferociously and bared tiny fangs at the sudden disruption in his life before settling contentedly into the pocket of Penelope's windbreaker. She quickly named him Mycroft for Sherlock Holmes's elder—and smarter—brother, although as he grew into Big Mike, she realized that he would never be a candidate for admission into the Diogenes Club.

When Penelope's Peace Corps service drew to a close, there was no question of leaving Big Mike behind, so she spent a week in Addis Ababa distributing *baksheesh* and gathering the necessary documents and official stamps to take Mycroft home.

"But, madam, this is a lion," each new official protested. "You cannot export lions."

At each stop, Penelope smiled sweetly and offered a small consideration in the form of ten Ethiopian dollars.

"Ah, yes, but this is a domestic cat. Of course, domestic cats may be exported."

At week's end, Penelope was nearly broke and wishing she owned the rubber stamp concession in Ethiopia—Mycroft's departure papers had forty-seven different stamps on them by the time they were ready to board the Ethiopian Air Lines (its initials stood for Every Airplane Late) flight to head for home.

Damn, I miss Africa, Penelope thought. Big Mike probably did, too. He had ruled the college campus fearlessly, instilling terror in wild dogs, jackals, and even the ubiquitous hyenas. Perhaps Africa would be better than sky diving. But there were times when she missed the Marine Corps, too, except for reveille.

Still, there were other responsibilities and considerations as well. Penelope did not want to part with Chardonnay, the sweet-tempered Arabian filly who shared the small ranch with her and Mycroft. And, of course, there was the little matter of Mycroft & Company, the mystery bookstore she owned and operated—quite successfully, too.

And Penelope could just imagine dear Andy's reaction if she suddenly announced, "I've reenlisted in the Marine Corps and I'm off to Okinawa." Even Andy's usual unflappable self would be flapped with that one.

No, there was nothing for it, but to accept grim reality. Carefree youth had deserted her major big-time. Even the fact that it was football season and both of her favorite teams—the San Diego State University Aztecs and the Empty Creek High School Gila Monsters—were so far undefeated could not assuage her melancholy.

"I'm old," Penelope groaned.

"You're thirty-five," Kathy Allen said without looking up from the books she was arranging on a shelf. "That's not old."

"How would you know? You're barely old enough to buy a drink legally." Penelope turned to stare morosely out the window as the bird in the cuckoo clock above the fireplace mantel emerged to announce the hour and comment on her state of mind. Penelope would have cheerfully ripped the little bird's head off if it hadn't been a gift from her mother.

The unseasonal rain didn't help her mood either. The normally bright and crystalline skies above Empty Creek had been drab and sullen for days, adding to Penelope's discontent, and giving lie to the creek that provided the town's name. Empty Creek was now a rushing torrent, threatening to overflow its banks, to say nothing of Empty Creek Road where the water surged along the gutters, spilling over to the sidewalks.

Lights from the business establishments on the other side of the street were but faint glows, lonely beacons in the gloom. Penelope could barely read the big canvas sign hanging over the main drag, bravely proclaiming, despite the elements, the eminent arrival of the GREAT EMPTY CREEK ARABIAN HORSE SHOW.

"At least, it could stop raining," Penelope complained.

"I wonder how Mrs. Burnham is coming with the Ark?" Kathy asked.

Penelope rolled her eyes. The steady downpour had caused Mrs. Elaine Burnham, Empty Creek's very own town crier, to enter Mycroft & Company the previous day and announce, despite considerable scriptural evidence to the contrary, that another Flood was at hand and that it was time to start packing up the animals two by two, preferably in alphabetical order. Mrs. Burnham's mind tended toward somewhat addled tidiness.

Penelope responded to this proclamation rather mildly, considering her state of mind. "I suppose that means we start with Mr. and Mrs. Aardvark and that poor Zebra couple must bring up the rear again."

"Exactly!" Mrs. Burnham cried, opening her umbrella while still inside the bookshop in defiance of all established superstition and then forcing it through the door, giving it a distinct list to the right. Penelope had watched Mrs. Burnham march away down the street, splashing determinedly through the puddles in her sensible brown oxfords.

Big Mike responded to Mrs. Burnham as he always did, turning over in his sleep before the crackling fireplace, ears twitching. Mrs. Burnham's voice always reminded him of an irritating, chirping little bird that should be put on the first stagecoach out of town. Besides, Big Mike knew that he and Murphy Brown, his sometime paramour, were boarding first. Cats always took precedence over aardvarks, whatever they were, and everything else for that matter.

"I swear, Mikey, that woman . . ."

Mikey growled softly, which Penelope translated as, Leave me alone, but holler when the Ark sails.

Now, Penelope turned away from the window and said, "Blah."

"That's enlightening," Kathy responded.

"Don't be impertinent."

"You're driving me crazy," Kathy said. "You're driving everyone crazy. Read a good book."

"I can't find anything that appeals to me."

"Go to a movie then."

"Ditto. Life as I once knew it is over."

"Oh, god," Kathy groaned. "What are we going to do with you?"

Kathy's plaintive question was answered later that afternoon when Samantha Dale, president of the Empty Creek National Bank and Big Jake Peterson, president of the board of directors for the Great Empty Creek Arabian Horse Show, shook the rain from their umbrellas and raincoats and hurried to warm themselves before the fireplace.

"Hi, Kathy," Samantha said with a smile. "Is Penelope here?"

Unfortunately, Penelope, who had exchanged staring out the window for staring into the fire, had suddenly announced that she was taking Big Mike and her midlife crisis away for the rest of the day.

"Penelope went to visit Stormy," Kathy said quickly, only a little flustered at the entrance of two of Empty Creek's preeminent personages.

"Darn," Samantha said. "And it's important, too. Do you think she'd mind if we interrupted?"

"I don't think so. Penelope needs a good interruption. She's having a midlife crisis."

"Good Lord. She's hardly into her thirties."

"That's what I keep telling her, but she doesn't listen."

"Wait until she's my age."

"You're not old," Kathy protested.

"That's sweet of you to say, but I'm forty-two and feeling every day of it right now." Samantha turned to Big Jake. "Well, shall we . . ."

"She needs a good man," Jake blurted.

"Penelope has a good man," Samantha said.

"I meant you."

"That's another discussion entirely," Samantha replied, not at all unkindly or puzzled at the abrupt pronouncement. Big Jake, probably the shyest man in Empty Creek, had been acting strangely in her presence for weeks.

"Can I offer you something?" Kathy asked hopefully. "I just made a fresh pot of coffee. Please."

In the greater scheme of Empty Creek life, Kathy was not lacking for strong and positive feminine role models. Penelope, of course, was first in Kathy's pantheon of local heroines, followed closely by Storm Williams, Empty Creek's reigning queen of B movie stardom and, in real life, Cassandra Warren, Penelope's younger sister. But there was always room for Samantha Dale on Kathy's pedestal.

Most of Empty Creek's denizens thought Samantha—Sam to her very special friends—was the smartest and prettiest bank president in the forty-eight contiguous states. That had not always been the case. When she had been hired some five years earlier to pull the bank out of its financial doldrums, there had been fierce resistance to her appointment from many who thought the board was simply beguiled by her beauty. But as the bank grew and its assets multiplied, Sam breached the macho frontier mentality of her detractors—all men, of course—and won their confidence and approval. Now, any complaint or snide comment about Samantha constituted fighting words.

"Please," Kathy repeated. Besides worshiping Samantha, Kathy had a curiosity as healthy as Big Mike's. She was dying to know what was going on between Sam and Big Jake. That was a new development of which Kathy thoroughly approved, but she was much too polite to inquire. Besides, Mrs. Burnham would have all the details soon enough and announce them to the world at large.

"Well, I think we have time for coffee, and as long as we're here, what new novels can you recommend, Kathy?"

Stormy lived on Crying Woman Mountain, a dark hulk looming over Empty Creek, and named for an Indian maiden's spirit who could be heard weeping on occasion. Samantha and Big Jake were quiet on their way up the mountain, each for their own reasons.

Big Jake's massive paws tightened on the steering wheel as he berated himself for blurting out that Samantha needed a good man. She did, of course, but that was not the kind of thing to be said in a politically correct society. A degree of subtlety was now necessary in the eternal dance between the male and the female of the species, nuances that Jake did not possess. Big Jake sighed, a considerable feat considering the tenacity of his grip on the steering wheel. Samantha's perfume was driving him crazy.

Samantha pretended to examine her purchases, a half-dozen paperbacks on her lap that promised all sorts of murder and mayhem. The irony was not lost on Samantha considering the nature of their mission but, in truth, she was distracted by the smell of Big Jake's cologne. Polo, she thought. She had noticed it before. After all, they had known each other for years—at the Chamber of Commerce mixers, at Rotary luncheons, serving together on the board of the Arabian show, during various business transactions—but it was not until this very morning, when Big Jake marched into her office with Horace Melrose in tow, that she had realized something was about to happen between them.

Isn't it interesting the way a crisis will bring two people together? Samantha thought as she awaited Jake's next gambit.

"Good Lord, what brings you two out on such a day?" Stormy exclaimed. "Come in, come in."

"We're looking for Penelope," Jake said.

"Kathy said she was here."

"She was, but she left. She's having a midlife crisis."

"We heard. That's so silly. Just look at what she's accomplished. The Marine Corps, the Peace Corps, a PhD, successful businesswoman, to say nothing of her uncanny ability to solve crimes. All I ever did was get an MBA, married, divorced, and work."

"Try and tell her that."

"I will. Do you know where she went?"

"Laney's. She said a writer would be far more understanding than an actress. She was mumbling something about sky diving. I told her to shape up."

"Well, I guess we'll just have to go out there."

"Not until you warm up," Stormy said. Both Stormy and Penelope had been firmly indoctrinated into their mother's philosophy that no visitors ever went away from a Warren household without being plied with great quantities of food and drink. "Would you like coffee, or something stronger?"

Since Big Jake had already added a dollop of bourbon to the coffee back at Mycroft & Company, he opted for stronger, a little something more to keep the chill away. Samantha accepted a glass of cabernet sauvignon and successfully resisted Stormy's attempt to trot out the entire contents of her larder for hors d'oeuvres.

While Stormy fussed in the kitchen, Jake went to the fireplace, less to warm himself than to admire the huge, larger than life, movie poster of Storm Williams in her role of *Vanessa Diamond, P.I.* Samantha quickly followed, brushing against Big Jake's arm, very neatly diverting his attention away from the beautiful and voluptuous woman on the poster. It was enough to deal with Stormy's beauty in person without having to compete with the glamorous version as well. Fortunately, Stormy was ga ga over John "Dutch" Fowler, the Empty Creek police chief, despite the fact that he had received his nickname as a result of once arresting a man with an apparent fetish for wooden shoes.

Big Jake looked down on Samantha and smiled. Sam thought he might have kissed her if Stormy hadn't chosen that moment to return with their drinks.

"When does it come out?" Samantha asked, nodding at the poster.

"Next month."

"We'll have to have an Empty Creek premiere. Spotlights and everything."

"Oh, shucks," Stormy said modestly. "It'll probably disappear like all the others." In her guise as Storm Williams, Penelope's little sister had starred in a series of action adventure movies remembered primarily for the heroine's bare breasts and otherwise scanty clothing.

"You were great in *Amazon Princess and the Sword of Doom*," Jake said, much too gallantly in Samantha's opinion.

"Thank you."

"Why did you take another name?" Jake asked. "Cassandra's a very nice name."

"Myron Schwartzman, my agent, was in love with burlesque queens when he was younger. I think I'm supposed to be Tempest Storm. His favorite was Irma the Body, but I wasn't about to go through my career as an Irma, with or without the body."

"I remember Irma," Jake offered. "She was great. There was this thing with tassels, or was that someone else. . . ."

"Well, we better get on our way," Samantha interrupted. "We have to catch up to Penelope."

"Dutch told me what happened. I didn't even get a chance

to tell Penelope. Serves her right. I assume that's why you're looking for her."

"A bad business," Jake said.

Driving back down Crying Woman Mountain, Samantha took a Kleenex from her purse, slid across the big seat of the pickup truck to Jake's side, and rubbed briskly at the mist on the windshield.

"By God, Samantha Dale, I meant what I said back at the bookstore. You need a good man."

"Do you know any applicants?" Samantha asked, smiling tolerantly, believing it was the whiskey talking now.

"Well, yes, I do, and it's not that twerp Horace Melrose."

"I only went out with him once," Sam protested. "That was enough."

"Always knew you were smart," Big Jake said pulling off into a view area and turning off the engine. The view would have been magnificent had the weather not been so wretched.

"Well, would you go out with me?"

"Yes."

"Really?"

Samantha smiled and nodded shyly. "Now what was that about tassels . . . ?"

Had Harris Anderson III, editor of the *Empty Creek News Journal*, not been so preoccupied with Penelope's midlife crisis, he probably would not have forgotten to call the police department for the daily crime report. And then, too, he might have noticed Big Jake's pickup in the cutout where Samantha Dale was smiling again and saying, "This is the first time I've ever been kissed *before* the first date."

But Andy was, indeed, distracted and so he sped by in one direction not knowing that he was already way behind in the race to find Penelope as Big Jake, somewhat reluctantly, started the engine and headed off in the opposite direction.

Alexander, a diminutive Yorkshire terrier with the heart and bark of a German shepherd, and Mycroft's best friend, was having his own midlife crisis, one brought on by a most unwelcome addition to the household he shared with Laney and Wally. Even the brief visit from Penelope and Big Mike had done nothing to alleviate the situation because, quite simply, he had been ignored.

Alexander was still sulking when Samantha and Big Jake arrived at Laney's only to find they had missed Penelope and Big Mike. Again.

The object of Alexander's dissatisfaction was an eight-week-old Yorkshire terrier who had taken over the household. The puppy yipped and slobbered and skidded around happily in her position as center of the universe.

"She's darling," Samantha cried. "What's her name?"

"Kelsey."

"Cute," Big Jake said trying not to step on the little dog as another coat of slobber was applied to his cowboy boots.

"Really," Laney complained, "Penelope's having a midlife crisis and I wind up with a new dog. There's something wrong with this scene. I told her to have a good game of Dance Hall Girl and the Gunfighter."

Samantha, having read all of Laney's sultry, very inventive, and extremely erotic romance novels set in old Arizona, wasn't about to ask the rules of Dance Hall Girl and the Gunfighter, not in front of Big Jake, at least not on what was turning out to be a very strange first date.

"Well, Kelsey seems very nice," Samantha said.

"Alexander hates her."

"He'll get used to her."

Alexander, who was sitting in his box, face to the wall, ignored by all, doubted *that*.

"All right," Laney said clapping her hands together, "what can I get you?"

"Nothing, really," Samantha said. "It's getting late and we really have to talk to Penelope."

"Well, she's probably at home. I was going to tell her everything, but she just rushed off. It's just what she needs to snap out of it."

"You know?" Samantha asked.

"Everything but the person or persons unknown who did it. The desert telegraph has been busy today."

Penelope and Mycroft, blissfully unaware of the caravan following their trail through the byways of Empty Creek and the surrounding desert, built a huge fire in the living room fireplace. Rather, Penelope did the actual work while Big Mike supervised. And then, while Big Mike stretched, turned, and stretched again, in preparation for a good nap, Penelope clambered on the couch, bouncing uneasily on the thick cushions before standing on the firmer arm of the couch.

Sergeant Penelope Warren, USMC, Force Recon, the elite of the elite, was ready to jump. The fact that she had come no closer to Force Recon other than briefly dating a first lieutenant in that unit bothered her not at all. She knew she would have been a great Recon Marine.

Looking down from the door of the aircraft, the vast panoramic desert beckoned. The air rushed through her hair. Without the slightest tremor in her heart, Penelope closed her eyes and stepped through the door into space.

Since her first parachute jump was made from a height of approximately four feet, Penelope found the experience less than satisfying. Still, she performed a credible PLF—Parachute Landing Fall—rolling over on the living-room rug, gripping the risers expertly to spill the air from her chute.

Mycroft, distracted from his nap preparations and alarmed by the thud of his friend's landing, approached cautiously, ready to apply first aid or mouth-to-mouth resuscitation if necessary. Apparently, however, nothing was broken for Penelope sat up and hugged Mycroft. "Mikey, Mikey, Mikey," she said. "What *are* we going to do?"

Big Mike probably thought that a good bowl of lima beans—he had a passion for lima beans—was just the thing to alleviate a crisis, but he had the good sense not to suggest it while Penelope was inexplicably jumping off the couch. When in doubt, purring was always most restorative. So he started his motor.

Penelope was sitting at the vanity, peering intently into the mirror counting wrinkles. She was up to four when she realized the lines appeared only with a smile or a frown. Disappointed, she leaned forward and began a quest for gray hairs in her long blond hair that was more often than not pulled back into a ponytail. Her quest—unsuccessful—was interrupted by the doorbell. Pleasantly surprised, Penelope ran through the house and flung the door open to greet her temporary saviors.

"Sam. Jake. What are you doing out in this weather?"

"You haven't heard, then?" Sam asked.

"Bad business," Big Jake said, shaking his head. "Jack Loomis has been murdered and Sir Beauregarde horsenapped."

"What happened?" Penelope cried. "When? How? Why?"

Sam smiled brightly. "That's what we want you to tell us."

CHAPTER
TWO

L ola LaPola had the story on the early news. For her stand-up, the pretty television reporter stood beneath an arch-way sign that announced it was the entrance to the HMM Winged Victory Arabian Ranch. Behind her the long driveway was framed on both sides by immaculate white fencing.

"Famed horse trainer Jack Loomis was shot and killed some-time early this morning," Lola said staring grimly into the cam-era, "and Sir Beauregarde Revere, the Arabian stallion he was grooming to be a national champion, stolen."

The report cut away from Lola to a stable with a door open on an empty stall with the stallion's name above it. "It hap-pened here, just outside Sir Beauregarde's stall. The body was discovered at six A.M. by Maryanne Melrose, wife of Horace Melrose who owns the ranch and employed Loomis."

The television screen split to show stock still photos of Loo-mis and Sir Beauregarde.

"Maryanne Melrose is said to be suffering from shock and was unavailable for comment."

The screen cut back to a close-up of Lola. "The police are continuing their investigation, although sources close to the department say there are no firm leads in this shocking death. This is Lola LaPola reporting from Empty Creek and now back to you in the studio."

Murder was Penelope Warren's stock in trade. The shelves of Mycroft & Company were heavily laden with fictional accounts of bloody deeds, ranging from the classics of *Hamlet* and *Crime and Punishment* to the magnificent television productions on video such as *Prime Suspect*, with all the varying gradients in between. She stocked true crime accounts, too, for those among her customers who preferred their mayhem grounded in fact, although Penelope rarely read them herself, finding the human capacity for violence and cruelty to one another incomprehensible in its reality of greed, anger, and the senseless taking of life. Fiction, however horrific, was better.

Now Penelope's midlife crisis was a distant memory as she reacted to the death of a man she had known, although only slightly. She had seen him around town, of course, usually in the Double B Western Saloon and Steakhouse where he was a solitary figure at the bar. Tall and lanky, Jack Loomis had a hard-lined face and even harder eyes, smiling only occasionally in his loneliness. Penelope felt grief and sorrow at his death, as she would for any man or woman, even a stranger, and for the human condition that could kill a man in his prime.

"You better tell me about it," Penelope said. She listened intently to Samantha and Jake, although she was a little piqued at not having learned of the early-morning discoveries sooner. What good was it being the future sister-in-law of the police chief if you were the last to hear of a murder and the disappearance of the most famous horse in Empty Creek?

"He was shot right through the heart," Jake said, "although there are those who said he didn't have a heart. Damned good trainer though."

"No one heard anything?"

Jake shrugged. "The stables are quite a distance from the house and with the weather . . ."

"Tire tracks? Shells? Anything? A man can't be murdered and a horse vanish without leaving some trace."

"If the police have anything," Samantha said, "they're not publicizing it."

"And why take Sir Beauregarde?" Penelope asked, knowing the answer even as she spoke the words. Loomis had been training a potential Arabian national champion. The competition in the Arabian business was fierce and intense. A national champion commanded huge stud fees. Potentially, millions of dollars were at stake over the long run. "A rival stable?"

"You know what the Arabian business is like," Jake said.

"Cutthroat."

"That's a mild description. The bad publicity could destroy the horse show."

"But murder and kidnapping Sir Beauregarde? Horse lovers wouldn't do that, would they?"

Jake shrugged. "It's a business. The recession hurt the Arabian industry and hurt it bad. It wouldn't be the first time a horse has been killed for the insurance money."

"There's more," Samantha said. "Horace Melrose has a rather large loan from my bank. A good part of the collateral Horace put up is a half-million-dollar insurance policy on Sir Beauregarde. Unfortunately, the policy doesn't cover acts of God or foul play."

"Insurance investigators will be all over this case," Jake said, "making sure the policy is null and void. Unless . . ." He glanced at Samantha, smiling reassuringly. "Unless you find the person who killed Jack Loomis. Find the killer and we find Sir Beauregarde, save the Great Empty Creek Arabian Horse Show, and keep the bank out of financial hot water."

"You'd better stay for dinner," Penelope said in keeping with a Warren household. "I'll order Chinese."

It was easier said than accomplished. The order had to be constantly amended and increased because of a steady stream of new arrivals.

Andy was the first to splash in, exclaiming, "I've been looking all over for you," a sentiment echoed by Stormy and Dutch as they rushed into the house without knocking.

No sooner did Penelope have the new arrivals settled in front of the fireplace with drinks than Alexander and Kelsey announced Laney and Wally with excited barks. Penelope sighed and went back to the telephone. There were worse things that could be done than holding a wake for Jack Loomis. "It's me again, Mr. Kee."

Andy smacked his forehead in disgust when he found out he had been scooped on the Loomis murder, although there was nothing he could have done, since it was Monday and the *Empty Creek News Journal* was published only on Thursdays and Saturdays.

Everyone pestered Dutch for more details on the investigation, but there was little he could add. "We don't know anything," he said. "Yet."

Wally and Jake went out for more beer and wine.

Laney and Stormy huddled in a corner, poring over the Ravishing Redhead's latest naughty lingerie mail-order catalog. Both women were much too shy to shop in person.

Samantha set the table.

Mycroft gave Kelsey a lesson in manners, whacking the Yorkie puppy across the nose, sending her crying to Laney. Alexander looked on with satisfaction. He had learned long ago that one doggie kiss was tolerated by Big Mike, two was stretching it, and three was definitely cruising for a scratched nose.

Penelope corraled Dutch. "Need I remind you that Mycroft and I are honorary members of the Empty Creek Police Department?"

"I was trying to impress your sister."

"You did. Now impress *me*."

"I can stand on my head."

"So can I," Penelope said. "At least, I think I can still do it."

"I can spit farther than you."

"I doubt it."

"I can. . . ."

"No, you can't," Penelope interrupted. "Come on, Dutch, give."

"God, I hate it when you do this."

"Larry and Willie don't have a clue. Right?" Larry Burke and Willie Stoner made up the Robbery/Homicide Bureau of the Empty Creek P.D. Over time, the dislike between Penelope and Mycroft and Tweedledee and Tweedledum had mellowed into a grudging respect.

"Motive?" Dutch said. "Yes. Horace Melrose wants the insurance money. A rival trainer could have done it. Another ranch could have taken the damned horse." Dutch sighed. "Suspects? Yes, all of the above and more. Clues? Zero. Loomis was shot at point-blank range. Probably a forty-four caliber. The rain and the mud screwed everything else up. We really don't know anything. Yet."

"Cowboy gun. Probably not a woman then. Too big. You see, you've eliminated half the population right there."

"You could shoot a forty-four."

"So I could. We'd better only eliminate a fourth of the population then."

"You're going to get involved, aren't you? Again."

Penelope nodded. "As a favor to Samantha."

"What's her interest?"

"She's on the board of directors for the horse show. You know that. Sam and Jake are worried about the bad publicity. They want the show to be a success."

"That's all?" Dutch asked suspiciously.

"Horace Melrose used Sir Beauregarde as collateral on a loan from the bank."

Dutch shook his head. "Sometimes, I wish I'd stayed in Los Angeles. Mostly, we always knew who the bad guys were." He looked around the room, rather sadly, Penelope thought. "Here, the bad guys always seem to be your friends and neighbors."

"To absent friends," Big Jake said raising his glass.

Penelope wondered who mourned and who might be gloating tonight as she, too, lifted her glass in memory of the recently departed.

The others followed suit. "Absent friends," they echoed although none had counted Jack Loomis among their friends.

"Why didn't anyone tell me sooner?" Penelope complained, waving her chopsticks at the assemblage.

"We tried," her sister pointed out, "but you were too busy growing old and decrepit."

"I called," Dutch said.

"We chased you all over town," Big Jake said.

"Well, what took you so long?" Penelope asked, noting that Samantha blushed at the question. "Jake, you must be a very slow operator."

Not anymore, Samantha thought. "We had to make a stop," she said.

Finding herself alone with Laney in the kitchen, Samantha asked, "How *do* you play Dance Hall Girl and the Gun-fighter?"

Laney tossed her thick mane of red hair and smiled wickedly. "It's really quite simple. Amanda Prentice—she's the dance hall girl in my new novel—is playing poker with Bret Hardison—he's the gunfighter—but when she has the best hand of the night, Bret keeps raising her until she's out of money. That's when she bets . . ." Laney paused dramatically. "Her honor."

"Does she win?"

"Oh, no. She has a full house, aces over kings, but Bret has a straight flush. Did I tell you she's very beautiful and comes from a good family down on its luck? She's only working in the saloon to support her widowed mother and her little brothers and sisters."

"I should have known. And does Bret take advantage of poor Amanda?"

Laney shook her head. "He's a Southern gentleman, from a

fine old Virginia family that lost everything in the Civil War. He was a cavalry officer with J.E.B. Stuart and very gallant. When Amanda loses, she slowly pushes back from the table, stands on weak, trembling legs, looks him directly in the eyes, and says very bravely, 'It seems I am now at your disposal, sir.' "

"How terrible."

"Yes, but Bret says, 'It was a pleasure playing poker with you, ma'am.' He bows, kisses her hand, and stalks out."

"Leaving poor Amanda . . ."

"Desperately in love."

"I can hardly wait to read it. I hope Bret marries Amanda in the end."

"Oh, he will, but there are a great many trials and tribulations facing Amanda yet. She's framed for murder by the big cattle rancher who wants her family's land. Bret rescues her from the gallows at the last second and they ride out of town with the noose still around her neck. You don't have to do all that, of course. Wally and I never get past the poker game part. He has a very credible Southern accent when he has his way with me. You should try it with Big Jake."

"Is it that obvious? He only asked me out for the first time today."

"He's staring at you with big calf's eyes. You could do much worse."

"I did once."

"Didn't we all?"

"I'm going down to feed Chardonnay," Penelope said, looking out into the darkness during a break in the weather. She slipped into a gray duster, a coat still favored by a great many erstwhile cowboys while riding the modern range.

"I'll go with you," Samantha said, taking her raincoat from the coatrack.

"Like that?"

Despite the weather, Samantha's elegant business outfit— gray skirt, white silk blouse, red blazer, matching pumps—was unruffled, looking as though she were just beginning the day, not ending it. "If you have some old boots . . ."

Penelope rummaged in the cabinet beneath the kitchen sink, emerging with a pair of knee-high rubber boots.

"Perfect," Samantha said, kicking her pumps into a corner.

The two women sloshed down the muddy path to the barn. Fifty yards beyond, the no-longer-empty Empty Creek was a raging torrent, threatening to overflow its banks. Inside, Chardonnay whinnied and tossed her mane in greeting. Penelope produced and unwrapped a peppermint candy that the horse took gently from her hand and munched contentedly. "What can I say?" Penelope offered by way of explanation. "She likes peppermint candies. Mikey likes lima beans. I don't know any normal animals."

"I don't know any normal people," Samantha said. "I used to, but not since coming to Empty Creek. I dated Horace Melrose once, when he and Maryanne were estranged. Thank God, they got back together. He was too pompous for me."

"I don't know him," Penelope said as she filled a pail with various healthy horsey concoctions. "Would he have his own horse kidnapped?"

"Why? In order to collect on the insurance policy, Sir Beauregarde would have to be killed in such a way as to leave no evidence for the insurance investigators to find. There's no payoff if the horse simply disappears. None of it makes any sense."

"It never does until it does," Penelope said. "Whatever that means."

Samantha laughed. "Now *that* makes perfect sense."

When they returned to the house, Lola LaPola had apparently just finished interviewing Dutch for the late news. The camera crew was filming her cutaways, those innocuous shots of the reporter nodding intently as she pretended to listen to Dutch's responses—already uttered—that would later be edited into the footage.

Finished, the crew turned their attention to leftovers while Lola looked hopefully at Penelope and Samantha. Both women smiled at the young reporter but shook their heads. A year before when Lola had first covered a story in Empty Creek—an abortive robbery at Samantha's bank—she would have demanded an interview. Since her incarceration in the pillory at the Empty Creek Elizabethan Springe Faire, however—at Penelope's order in her role as Queen of the Faire—Lola had fallen in love with the young bailiff who took her into the Queen's custody, mellowed considerably, and taken up residence in Empty Creek with the very same bailiff. And incidentally, Lola thought Penelope was the greatest thing for matchmaking since computerized dating services.

Lola discarded her microphone and crossed the room. "How are you?" she asked. "It's been ages."

"We saw your report," Penelope said. "Very concise."

"Thank you."

"You were very good," Samantha agreed.

"Are you going to be involved?"

"I suppose so."

Samantha and Big Jake were the first to leave.

"I'll be in touch tomorrow," Penelope said. "Better yet, can we meet for lunch? I have a lot of questions, but I don't know what they are yet."

Samantha looked to Jake. "Noon at the Double B?"

"Never going to pass up lunch with two lovely ladies, no matter what the circumstances."

The others soon followed, departing amidst a flurry of sisterly kisses, embraces, and handshakes, with a few throaty barks tossed in to speed things along, although Alex was given permission for a sleep over with Big Mike.

The impromptu wake for Jack Loomis was over.

The rain started again as Big Jake pulled into Samantha's driveway. They had been quiet all the way home, each lost in thoughts about the day's events.

"Would you like to come in for a nightcap or coffee?" Samantha asked. "Perhaps a soft drink?"

"Something soft would be nice."

They ran for the house.

After hanging up their raincoats and pouring diet colas, Samantha said, "I'm just going to change. Make yourself comfortable. I won't be a minute."

When she returned, Samantha found Big Jake sitting in one of two matching easy chairs separated by a table and a lamp, although there was an adjoining and perfectly good couch available.

"I hardly ever see you dressed informally," Jake said.

"You like?" Samantha twirled for him. "It's just old jeans and a sweater."

"You're beautiful."

"Well, thank you, sir."

Samantha went to the sound system and slipped a disc into the player before going to sit in the other chair.

The gentle voice of Johnny Mathis filled the room.

"We used to dance to these songs in high school with all our hormones raging."

"Do you think Penelope will be able to help?" Big Jake asked, missing his cue.

Damn!

"Oh, I think so," Samantha answered. "She's been very good in the past."

"I hope so. I don't have much confidence in Dutch's two detectives."

"They don't have much practice in big cases."

"Well, he should just hire Penelope."

"I think *we* just did. Informally anyway."

When Johnny began singing "Twelfth of Never," Samantha said to hell with it. She thought it just about the most beautiful love song ever written. "Dance with me," she said.

"I can't," Big Jake said staring morosely at the carpet.

"Why not?" Samantha asked. "Are you a Baptist?"

"I don't know how."

Whew!

"Is that all? Well, I'll just teach you."

"This is number four," Andy said.

"Four what?" Penelope asked dreamily. She was curled up on the couch before the fire, legs tucked beneath her, between three of her favorite people—her head resting on Andy's shoulder on one side as she gently ruffled a purring Mycroft's fur on the other. Alex was on Andy's lap.

"The fourth murder investigation you've been involved in."

"Yes, I suppose it is."

"It goes without saying that you'll be careful?"

"Not to worry, dear heart."

Andy nodded gravely and then started doing those things that warmed Penelope's blood and disturbed the slumbering Big Mike and Alex.

"Well, at least your midlife crisis is over."

"What midlife crisis?" Penelope sighed happily. "Mmm. I'll give you an hour to stop that."

Long after going to bed, Samantha lay awake, the memory of Jake's good-night kiss and the lingering scent of his cologne alternating with thoughts of murder and Jack Loomis's body lying on a cold slab in the morgue.

As she turned over for the umpteenth time, Samantha wondered what it would be like to play Dance Hall Girl and the Gunfighter with Big Jake. He might be very good as a gunfighter. He had those steely eyes. Samantha was positive she could play the Dance Hall Girl to perfection, even without tassels.

But then she remembered that Jack Loomis had those same killer eyes and someone had murdered him in a game far removed from Laney's harmless sexual fantasy.

Penelope, too, lay awake, snuggled securely in Andy's arms, his steady breath ruffling the little hairs on the nape of her neck. As always, he had fallen asleep with his hand on her breast, holding her gently. It was uncanny. No matter how much they might toss and turn during the night, Penelope always awakened with the swell of her breast overflowing Andy's hand, unconsciously telling her he would always be there to take care of her, although she was perfectly capable of taking care of herself. Penelope liked the intimacy, thinking it sweet and one of Andy's more endearing qualities.

Mycroft was in his usual place. When finally admitted to the bedroom—there had once been an unfortunate accident with a previous lover of Penelope's—Big Mike had burrowed his way beneath the blankets to sleep between them, as if announcing once again that Andy shouldn't get too accustomed to monopolizing Penelope's attention. Alex was content to sleep on top of the covers.

Above, the rain beat steadily on the roof, coming down now harder than ever, beating furiously against the windows in sporadic forays, rattling the glass in their panes, all grim and frightening reminders of a man's death. "Rain, rain, go away," Penelope whispered, "come again another day." But she found no comfort in the old nursery rhyme.

CHAPTER THREE

"I hate horses."

"You know what horses are? I'll tell you what they are. Manure factories. That's what horses are."

"Do you know how many run-down stables and stupid ranches there are in a twenty-mile radius of Empty Creek?"

"Zillions. That's how many. Maybe bodzillions."

"Dutch says we gotta check every one of them."

"Hi there. Anybody seen this stupid horse?"

"My mama didn't raise me to go looking for a missing horse."

"We're detectives in Robbery/Homicide. This ain't the Missing Horse Bureau."

"Dumb damn horse."

"Where's the stupid cat anyway?"

"Want a jelly donut?"

It was as close to expressing affection for Penelope and Big Mike as either detective was able to come. Penelope had listened to their joint tirade—rather benevolently, she thought, considering the day was not going at all the way she would have planned it.

First, she was up much earlier than customary. Ever since that first reveille at Parris Island—reveille hell, it was the middle-of-the-damned-night—Penelope had an aversion to early rising and now firmly subscribed to the Moss Hart theory that anything worth seeing would still be there in the afternoon. She had tested the theory and found it true, visiting Westminster Abbey, the Tower of London, the British Museum, Notre Dame, the Eiffel Tower—all well after the people who thought rising with the dawn a virtue.

Kathy, however—who usually opened Mycroft & Company—had an early class in John Milton, a requirement for graduation and so opening the bookstore fell to Penelope. It wasn't Kathy's fault. Penelope blamed the college authorities for scheduling Milton so early. How could anyone intelligently discuss man's first disobedience and original sin at nine o'clock in the morning?

And she missed Big Mike. It just wasn't the same at the Robbery/Homicide Bureau without Mycroft burrowing through the In and Out baskets, knocking files to the floor, and otherwise tormenting Larry Burke and Willie Stoner.

But Mycroft was mad at her, blaming Penelope for a little mishap. After some grumbling—Big Mike was also a championship caliber sleeper—he had joined her and Alexander in the Jeep for the ride to work. Since the Jeep was parked in the garage when it rained, there had been no problem avoiding the rain on the way to work.

There was no garage at Mycroft & Company. On the bright sunny days that were Empty Creek's norm, Big Mike simply leaped from the Jeep and, very stately, ambled into his daytime domain. But Mycroft hated water as much as he hated missing his sleep, perhaps more. Had Alexander not slept over, there might not have been a problem.

But he had and there was.

In an effort to make only one trip through the continuing downpour—despite weather forecasts to the contrary—Penelope slung her purse over her shoulder, opened the umbrella, gathered tiny Alex under one arm and Big Mike under the other. Juggling cat, dog, umbrella, and purse was difficult, but not impossible. It was when she attempted to give the Jeep door a back-footed kick to close it that she lost her balance, dumping Big Mike and Alex most unceremoniously into a deep puddle, thereby giving some truth to the old saying that it was raining cats and dogs.

The ensuing squalls and barks were hideous to the ears. Penelope was positive representatives of the SPCA were rolling Code Three—red lights and sirens—to rescue the poor little creatures from her evil clutches when she finally managed to get the door open.

Alexander readily accepted her apologies as she dried him off. But Mycroft leaped to the very top shelf in the back room and refused to come down, glaring malevolently at the cause of his misfortune as he performed his own ablutions. Although Mycroft was a Capricorn, he possessed the Cancerlike capacity for carrying a grudge. He was still sulking, even refusing the temptation of lima beans, when Kathy arrived after her class and freed Penelope to pursue a murderer and horsenapper.

"He ain't sick, is he?" Burke asked, refusing as usual to refer to Mycroft by name. He touched the scars on his cheek where Mycroft had once given him a good crack, enraging Burke so much that he became the first cop in history to arrest a cat for obstruction of justice.

Penelope shook her head. "He's mad at me. I dropped him in a puddle."

"Good," Burke said helping himself to another jelly donut, "serves the big fur ball right."

Penelope yawned. On another occasion, she might have remonstrated with Tweedledee, but she could carry a grudge, too. After all, she hadn't planned to drop Mycroft in the puddle and she had apologized. He *could* be such a big fur ball at times.

"Sure you don't want a jelly donut?"

Penelope yawned again, noting perceptively that Burke and Stoner had matching jelly stains on their shirts. "No, thank you. I will have some more coffee."

Tweedledee beamed. "Good, ain't it? I like the vanilla mocha combination."

Penelope hated the vanilla mocha flavor, but it *was* coffee of a sort. "Why all the concentration on Sir Beauregarde?"

"That's another thing. What kind of dumb name is that for an Arabian? Oughta be called Sheik Bin Ali Mutt or something."

Although positive the only sheik Tweedledee might be conversant with was a condom, Penelope persisted. "Why the horse?"

"Because we ain't got nothing else. Rain washed everything away."

"Inside the stables, too? There must have been something."

"Jack Loomis," Tweedledum said helpfully.

"Besides him."

"Boot prints. Big boots for men, little boots for women. Hoof prints. Lots of both."

"What about motive? Who wanted Jack Loomis dead?"

"We're working on that. Going through his address book. Not much there either. People he worked for mostly. No girl-friends. Doesn't seem like he was a popular fella. Not like me and Willie here. We made a copy for you. It's in the file with the rest of the stuff."

"Better take a picture of the horse with you."

"Just in case."

Penelope gathered up the files and the glossy photograph of Sir Beauregarde. "Thanks, guys."

"You find anything, you let us know first."

"Of course."

"Don't step in any horse puckey."

Tweedledee and Tweedledum guffawed loudly, but it turned out to be sound advice.

Desperately in need of yet another infusion of strong black coffee, Penelope arrived for her luncheon appointment at the Double B Western Bar and Steakhouse early. The Double B's coffee was known far and wide for its ability to curl toenails and make hair stand on end. In addition, there were no frills and it was good. What kind of cop drank vanilla mocha anyway?

At this lull between the breakfast and lunch crowds, the Double B was nearly empty. Red the Rat, recently returned from yet another quest for a lost gold mine, occupied his customary stool at the bar, sipping one of the Double B's famed and fiery Bloody Mary's and admiring the twin attributes that gave Empty Creek's favorite cocktail waitress her nicknames of Debbie D and Dee Dee, referring to the alleged cup size of her large and perfectly shaped breasts that one wag or another had called "national treasures" and that Red said should be registered as deadly weapons.

"Hey, Red," Penelope said. "Almost didn't recognize you, all slicked up."

It was true. On his usual forays into town and the Double B, Red smelled about the same as his usual companion, Daisy the Mule, and guaranteed the stools on either side remained empty. Today, however, Red was freshly scrubbed, his thinning hair slicked back, gray beard neatly trimmed, and he wore brand-new jeans and shirt.

"Debbie, what do you think of Red?"

"Almost took my breath away. Sam better watch out or I'll run off with Red." Debbie's beloved, Sam Connors, was a member of Empty Creek's finest and, simultaneously, the reason Mycroft was no longer admitted to Penelope's bedroom during amorous moments and why Debbie did not have a cat. One session as a scratching post had been quite enough for Sam.

"Where's Mycroft?" the desert rat asked blushing at the unaccustomed attention.

"Pouting."

"Well, shame on him. What happened?"

"I dropped him in a puddle of water."

"Good thing he didn't take your ear off."

"I didn't mean it."

"Damaged his dignity," Red the Rat said sagely. "No man likes his dignity damaged."

"Most men don't have any dignity," Debbie said.

Red snorted and started his own pout. Now, *his* dignity was damaged.

"Penelope. Over here."

Penelope turned and saw Nora Pryor sitting at a corner table. Taking her coffee, Penelope crossed the room. "What are you doing here so early?"

"I'm meeting Matilda Bates. After what happened to Jack Loomis . . . Well, he was working with Reggie and with the horse show so close . . . I'm hoping Mattie will take over. Reggie really wants to do well at the show. She was devastated when she heard."

Penelope sat down. "Mattie's very good I hear. I bought Chardonnay from her.

"Perhaps I should talk to Reggie," Penelope continued. "She might be able to tell me something about Jack Loomis. Would you mind?"

Like everyone else in Empty Creek, Nora knew of Penelope's proclivity for successfully investigating cases of violent death. "I wouldn't mind. Reggie's strong and already bouncing back. Dirk Tindall is keeping her mind focused on other things. She's madly in love with him. Are you going to the game Friday night?"

"Wouldn't miss it." Dirk Tindall was the star quarterback of the Empty Creek High School Gila Monsters, leading the team to their first winning season in eleven years. Only a junior, Dirk already had college scouts drooling over him. "I didn't know Reggie and Dirk were dating."

"Oh, they're not. He doesn't know she exists."

Now, Nora Pryor was a heartbreaker. She possessed long, wondrous strawberry blond hair that fell to the middle of her back and the sexiest voice north of Nogales according to those who were aficionados of such things, which was most of the men in Empty Creek. In addition to her other attributes—a pretty, freckled face, a slender body with small firm breasts, shapely legs, and an infectious laugh—Nora was also *the* local historian of note and author of *Empty Creek: A History and Guide to the Environs,* now in its third printing.

Although she wasn't present, Penelope knew Regina Pryor was a fifteen-year-old version of her mother. In short, a heart-breaker-in-training.

"I can't believe Dirk would miss Reggie. She's beautiful."

"And smart. Like her mother. But sadly, Dirk is enamored of a certain head cheerleader."

"The one with the legs that go to forever?"

"Exactly."

"Men." Penelope glanced back at the bar. Red the Rat was still pouting, although rather halfheartedly as Debbie smiled at him.

Matilda Bates entered the Double B, saw Nora and Penelope, and marched across the room. Although the years of working outside in sun and wind had taken their toll, Mattie was still a striking woman, perhaps in her midfifties, tall and slender with her dark hair just beginning to show streaks of gray. An accomplished horsewoman in her youth, Mattie had a number of trophies gathered at various shows, including the big one at Scottsdale. Now, she lived quietly outside town on a small ranch, boarding horses for others, raising the occasional Arabian for sale to those who could pass her muster (like Penelope), and teaching those youngsters she deemed worthy and willing to work hard for championship goals. Mattie had run off two useless husbands at the barrel of her 30–30 Winchester Model 94 and outlived another that Penelope knew of.

Nora rose, as though student greeting teacher. "Thank you for coming."

"Hello, Nora. I didn't know you were going to be here, Penelope."

"Oh, I'm not, really. I'm waiting for Samantha and Big Jake."

"That Loomis business, I assume."

Penelope nodded. "Sam and Jake asked me to look into it."

"Jack Loomis was mean to the horses entrusted to him. There are trainers and then there are trainers. There's no reason to be cruel."

Penelope knew Mattie's view on horses well. She practically had to sign vows of perpetual kindness before Mattie would allow her to buy Chardonnay.

"Who is that delightful creature at the bar?" Mattie asked abruptly as she sat and looked about the large room.

"That's Red the Rat. You *know* him."

"That's Red? My goodness, what a difference a bath makes."

"Or two or three."

"I think I'll just have a word with Red before I leave. Inquire after Daisy."

"You raised Beau, didn't you?" Penelope asked. "And sold him to Horace Melrose?"

Mattie took her eyes off Red, somewhat reluctantly, Penelope thought. "That was before I knew Jack Loomis would be the trainer. Otherwise . . ."

As the Double B began to fill, Penelope claimed her table. The Double B was a favored watering hole for the denizens of Empty Creek. If you sat there long enough, anyone you might want to see would pass through. It was not uncommon for the mayor to adjourn late-running city council meetings to the

Double B. Many a business deal had been struck at the long bar or one of the dining-room tables. Romantic entanglements often began—and sometimes ended—on the small dance floor.

The back room was given over to the pool playing crowd. The clickity-clack of the pool balls was a constant refrain from the lunch hour until last call. Another crowd gathered at the bar to watch whatever sporting event might be in season, although pickings were slim on a weekday afternoon. Today, Pete the Bartender had the television sets at either end of the bar tuned to the tractor pull reruns. Penelope thought briefly of asking him to change the channel to the repeat of *Masterpiece Theater*, but there would be an outcry from the Tractor Pull devotees watching avidly.

And then Samantha and Big Jake hurried through the door, rain dripping from their coats and the shared umbrella.

"I brought a copy of the insurance policy," Samantha said after the exchange of greetings and the ordering of white wine for all.

"Good. That's one of the questions I didn't know I wanted to ask."

Penelope glanced through the exclusions of the policy. It did not cover intentional destruction of the animal unless it was imperative for humane reasons or death because of surgery unless carried out by a qualified veterinary surgeon and in an attempt to save the animal's life. Sir Beauregarde's death because of a malicious act by the insured, employees, or agents was excluded, as was death by nuclear fission, nuclear fusion, or radioactive contamination. There were the usual exemptions for war, invasion, acts of foreign enemies, hostilities, civil war, rebellion, revolution, insurrection, riots, strikes, and civil commotions. Death resulting from jettison from aircraft or watercraft was excluded in a paragraph of its very own.

"This seems rather standard," Penelope said glancing up at Samantha and Jake.

"Keep reading," Samantha said. "There's a theft and unlawful removal clause."

Penelope read on. "But this says the company is liable for theft, death resulting from theft, death or permanent loss of possession directly resulting from unlawful removal, even malicious or willful castration by those responsible for such unlawful removal."

"Now, turn the page."

Uh-oh.

There it was in big and ominous letters.

*BUT IN NO EVENT DOES THIS EXTENSION COVER...

" 'Section A,' Samantha recited closing her eyes wearily, 'Any loss arising from; mysterious disappearance; escape; or voluntary parting of possession or title to the animal (or animals) as a result of the insured (or others to whom the animals have been entrusted) being induced by a fraudulent scheme, trickery, or similar false pretenses. Section B, Consequential loss.' I've read it so many times. . . ."

"It does seem to cover any possible scenario if Horace Melrose was involved in some scheme."

"Or Loomis," Big Jake interjected. "Beau *was* entrusted to his care."

"But if he was *just* stolen . . ."

"The company is liable," Samantha said, "after ninety days."

"But the insurance investigators are already concentrating

on Section A," Jake said. "They're all over Horace and everyone who works or worked for him."

"I better get out there this afternoon."

"The rain's supposed to clear."

"This is interesting," Penelope said reading from an additional page. " 'This policy covers Sir Beauregarde if during the policy period it becomes permanently impotent, infertile, or incapable of servicing mares.' "

"*If* Beau is recovered," Samantha said, "and *if* he becomes a national champion, everyone is covered for the loss of stud fees in the unlikely event he is no longer fertile."

"It sounds so clinical. Horses are people, too." Penelope turned to Big Jake. "Did you service Samantha last night?"

"Penelope!" Samantha protested as her cheeks turned crimson.

Big Jake spluttered, turned a rather bright red himself, gathered their glasses, and rushed off to the bar for refills, although Debbie was standing right there at the next table.

"Well, you know what I mean. I wouldn't like to think of myself being . . . serviced."

"Actually," Samantha said, "it sounds kind of kinky, in a nice sort of way."

Penelope giggled. "It does, doesn't it? Andy, it's time for my three-thousand-mile service. Don't forget to change the oil and water."

"Did you see Jake's face?" Samantha contributed a few giggles of her own.

"You should have seen your own face."

"I wasn't expecting *that*."

"Well?"

"Well what?"

"Did he?"

"Penelope! It was our first date. Sort of."

"I just think you and Jake make a good couple. I'm happy for you and I hope you get serviced real soon."

Penelope and Samantha were still giggling when Big Jake returned.

"It's all right," Samantha said. "Penelope promised to be good."

"I did not."

Jake shook his head helplessly.

"I, we, really appreciate your doing this for us," Samantha said. "Lunch is on me."

"No, lunch is on *me*," Jake said. "No arguments. From either of you." At least, he could control *that* aspect of the day.

"Where's Big Mike?" Samantha asked in a belated attempt to help Jake recover his senses.

Penelope sighed and told the story once more.

Big Jake looked very relieved at the change in subject.

As the Double B slowly emptied after the lunch-hour rush, Mattie Bates was seated next to Red the Rat, a hand resting casually on his arm, laughing delightedly at something he said.

Well, well, well, Penelope thought. The latest pairing of mare and stallion. There seems to be a lot of that going around.

She pushed through the door and blinked in the bright sunshine.

Finally.

Now, perhaps Big Mike will forget about the little accident and help me find a murderer.

CHAPTER
FOUR

As Penelope crossed the street to Mycroft & Company, she saw the bookstore's namesake sitting in the window looking very regal—and dry—as he peered out at the passing scene. When Penelope entered, Big Mike jumped gracefully from the window and came to her, meowing loudly. Penelope translated his criticisms easily. Where have you been? Why did you leave me behind? I missed my beer at the Double B. Let's get going. We have a murder to investigate and a horse to find. At least, that's what Penelope thought Big Mike was saying. The sun's appearance had evidently restored his good humor.

"That's all he's done since you left," Kathy said, "sit in the window and complain. Laney came by for Alexander. Said she'd see you later. Mrs. Burnham wants to know the latest. You're to call her immediately. Dutch called with the autopsy report. Jack Loomis died of a gunshot wound to the heart. This is certainly an interesting place to work. Oh, and by the way, I sold some books."

"Good for you."

"Well, someone has to keep the place going while you're off looking for killers."

The huge tents were going up adjacent to the covered main arena where the Great Empty Creek Arabian Horse Show would be held—with or without Sir Beauregarde. The Empty Creek version of equine heaven couldn't compete with the big Scottsdale show. With perhaps five hundred horses entered into the various competitions, it was one-third the size of the nationally renowned Scottsdale event, but Empty Creek was a respected precursor to the big one down the road later in the Arabian year. The horses and riders who won at Empty Creek were invariably elevated to front runners for Scottsdale.

Sitting in the empty stands, Penelope and Big Mike looked down at the arena. In two weeks, the stands would be filled with Arabian enthusiasts whooping their approval at a particularly excellent demonstration of the communion between horse and rider. Bars on either side of the arena would be dispensing everything from beer to the finest champagnes. Those men and women who included the show on their social calendar would dress accordingly—the women more so than the men, bringing out their expensive jewelry and elegant dresses purchased especially for the occasion.

It was normally the finest whoop-de-do of the year for Empty Creek, beginning with the President's Ball on the Thursday evening before competition opened, if you called a foot-stomping, shit-kicking, old-fashioned Western hoedown a President's Ball—and most people in Empty Creek did.

The show itself encompassed the main arena and a number of surrounding arenas where the various competitions would be played out—classic Arabian, English pleasure riding, Western pleasure riding, trail horse, working cow horse, stock horse, jumping, dressage, native costume, lady's side saddle, equitation.

During the weekend of the show, the big tents on either side of the main arena housed food courts and a variety of vendors showing the latest in horse wares. Even Temptress, a shop specializing in alluring and seductive lingerie, had a booth at the show. The Temptress catalog was one of Laney's favorites.

"Hey, lady, you're not supposed to be in here."

Penelope and Big Mike turned to find a burly workman gesturing at them.

"Why not?" Penelope inquired pleasantly.

"You might get hurt. Insurance wouldn't like it. Only supposed to be workmen in here."

"But all the work is going on outside," Penelope pointed out, quite reasonably to her mind.

"Don't matter. You want a job, I'll put you to work. Then, it don't matter. You can stay. Have to lose the cat, though."

Having stopped at the arena to commune with the atmosphere of the Arabian horse world and to put herself and Mycroft in the proper frame of mind for investigating that insular little microcosm of Empty Creek life, Penelope was more than a little irritated at the interruption. Still, she replied politely, "No thank you. I have a job and he's with me."

"I'm Billy Tubbs, the foreman on this job," he said clumping his way across the bleachers to sit beside Penelope. "Want a toot?" he asked pulling a flask from a jacket pocket.

Penelope smiled and shook her head. "I've got work to do."

"We're an equal opportunity employer," Billy Tubbs said after a long hit on the flask. "Got your Afro-Americans, got your Hispanics, got your Native Americans, got your Asian

Americans. Got damn near everybody but a woman. She quit yesterday. Hired away right out from under my nose. Get a good woman and everybody wants her. Taking over a construction crew down to Carefree. Sure you don't want a job . . . or a toot?"

"I'm still working."

"Looks to me like you're just sitting here with a cat. Damned big cat, too."

"We're thinking."

"Libraries are for thinking."

"Not when you're looking into a murder."

"Hey, I know you now," Tubbs said. "You're that detective lady I read about. Helps the po-lice out when they got their heads stuck somewhere they shouldn't oughta be."

"Penelope Warren." She offered her hand. "And this is Mycroft. Big Mike when he's working."

"Proud to know you, ma'am. You gonna solve this murder?"

"We're going to try."

"He was over here the other day. Wanted to make sure the surface of the arena was to his liking. Dirt mighta been okay, but he wasn't to my liking none. Pain in the be-hind. How'd you know he was here?"

"I didn't," Penelope said. "I just wanted to remember the flavor of the show. Get in the mood."

"Kinda like chanting mantras or something?"

"Kind of."

"Well, you chant all you want. Anyone tries to run you off, you tell 'em Billy Tubbs said it was okay."

Driving into the HMM Winged Victory Arabian Ranch with Big Mike in his accustomed spot at her side again, Penelope found it difficult to believe that only last night Lola had stood in the rain reporting the skimpy details of Jack Loomis's murder and Beau's disappearance. While Arizona storms were often fierce and prolonged, the desert could be very forgiving at times. Already, the sun was burning away the ravages of two days and nights of rain. The house at the end of the driveway and the buildings beyond gleamed in the bright afternoon.

No one answered the Melrose doorbell, so after listening to the faint chimes inside fade out for a third time, Penelope and Big Mike went around to the back of the house.

The discussion from behind the fenced pool and patio area was brief, loud, and one-sided, and Penelope heard only the last salvo. It was enough, however, to convince even Tweedledee and Tweedledum that all was not happy in the Melrose household.

"I want a divorce."

Hearing the determination in Mrs. Maryanne Melrose's voice, Penelope also immediately decided that the M for Maryanne in the HMM Arabian Ranch name wasn't long for this particular spot in the world. Or, if her divorce attorney was any good at all, the H for Horace was likely on its way out.

"I mean it this time," Maryanne Melrose said concluding the debate to her satisfaction.

"I'm sorry," Penelope said over the fence.

"Don't be. He's a pompous little jerk."

"I meant I was sorry for intruding. I didn't mean to eavesdrop."

"Oh, that doesn't matter either. Everyone will know soon enough. I'm going to take him for everything he's got, including the Corvette."

. Her timing was impeccable and punctuated by the screech of tires as Horace Melrose sped away in a lime green car.

"Come on in. Would you like some lemonade?"

Maryanne Melrose pushed sunglasses back on her head and rose to greet Penelope. She was tall, slender, tanned, and carried herself with an air of aloofness. She was dressed in jeans and a man's western shirt hanging loose.

Having seen the back of Horace Melrose disappearing into the house, Penelope realized the western shirt was much too big to be his. The fact that Maryanne wore only one large gold hoop earring, reminded Penelope of Stormy's memorable role as Wild Liz, Pirate Queen, in a somewhat historically confused costume drama. But then most of Stormy's films were confused in one fashion or another.

Maryanne poured a glass of lemonade for Penelope before going into the house for a saucer of milk for Mikey. Since he'd missed his ration of nonalcoholic beer at the Double B, Mycroft lapped the milk thirstily and then, pretty much of a lady's man anyway, thanked Maryanne for her hospitality by curling up in her lap. Having his own inscrutable methods for interrogating witnesses and suspects, he promptly fell asleep.

Penelope firmly believed that Mycroft had spent fully two-thirds of his life curled up in one woman's lap or another. Normally, that didn't bother her but with a covey of guilt birds still hovering about, blaming her for dropping Mycroft in the puddle, Penelope was a little jealous. Perhaps Big Mike hadn't completely forgiven her yet. A bribe might be in order, something along the lines of a double helping of lima beans.

"Now, how can I help you?" Maryanne asked. "Big Jake said you'd be stopping by."

"Then you know we're looking into Jack Loomis's murder and Sir Beauregarde's disappearance."

"At least, you have it in the right order. Horace doesn't care about anything but Beau."

"Is that what you were fighting about?"

"Poor Jack. . . ." Maryanne pulled her sunglasses down.

Penelope thought tears glistened behind the dark, rose-colored lenses but said nothing.

"No, we were fighting about an accumulation of wrongs, slights, careless words, misdeeds, hurts, hateful things. . . ."

Penelope waited.

"Have you ever been married?" Maryanne asked suddenly, rhetorically, barely giving Penelope time to shake her head. "It's nice at first, but then . . . after a while . . . you become part of the furnishings . . . just another piece of property . . . he starts looking at other women and you don't feel pretty and desirable anymore. . . ." Maryanne shook her head angrily and looked away for a moment. When she turned back with a rueful smile on her face, Maryanne said, "But you didn't come here to listen to my marriage problems."

"You found the body. . . ."

"I couldn't sleep. You know how sometimes it's so nice in the morning, peaceful, with birds chirping, a little chilly, but everything smells so fresh."

Penelope didn't so she pointed out, "But it was raining like crazy."

"Same principle. Anyway, I couldn't sleep so I went for a walk in the rain."

A snatch of dialogue from a half-remembered novel entered Penelope's mind. *Sometimes I see me dead in the rain.* Who said that? she wondered. Was it Catherine in *A Farewell to Arms?* She drove the thought away. "What took you to the barn?"

"Nothing, really. I was just passing by when I saw the door was open. I looked in and . . . it was horrible. Poor Jack."

"Did he have any enemies? Someone who wanted him dead?"

Maryanne shook her head. "I've been through all that with the police. I suppose there could have been someone who was jealous of his success, but I don't know who. Jack pretty much kept to himself. He lived in a trailer at the far end of the property. He did his job."

Penelope nodded. There were worse epitaphs than "He did his job." "Would you mind if we looked around some, the stables, Jack's trailer, that sort of thing?"

"You'll find Abigail, that's Abigail Wilson, at the stables. She is, was, Jack's apprentice. She can tell you where to go. I still can't believe he's dead."

Penelope found Abigail Wilson sitting on a corral fence, watching as a handler led an Arabian through its paces.

"Are you one of the insurance investigators?"

"No."

Abigail waited, looking down suspiciously at Penelope. She was a frail, girlish creature who appeared to be no more than twenty-one, wearing the customary western garb. Her feet looked too small for the big pink boots hooked on the rail.

It was time to trot out an explanation for her presence. With some people it helped to show the badge that identified her and Mycroft as Honorary Members of the Empty Creek Police Department. On occasion, Penelope had been tempted to tell just the teeniest lie and say she was a private investigator—

which she was in a way, only lacking the credentials to prove it. With Abigail, however, she decided upon veracity. "I'm just a gifted amateur," Penelope said, "who has been asked by interested parties to look into the death of Jack Loomis and the disappearance of Sir Beauregarde."

"Who are these interested parties? I'll bet they're more interested in getting Beau back than finding out who killed poor Jack."

"It seems that one leads to the other."

"Jack interrupted the crime in progress and he was killed. It's as simple as that."

"Perhaps."

"What else could it be?"

"I don't know," Penelope replied truthfully.

When Abigail jumped down from the fence, she stumbled slightly and Penelope reached out and grabbed her arm for support. She was surprised at how delicate the young woman was, like a fragile china doll.

"Thanks," Abigail said. "I've been in shock ever since it happened. I'm sorry if I sounded rude. I didn't mean it."

"That's understandable. Something like this is never easy."

"Jack was so good and I was learning so much from him. We were going to be a team. We could have gone anywhere, done anything, after Beau became the national champion. Now, I don't know what to do. Horace said I could stay on for awhile, but there doesn't seem to be much point to it."

"I've heard that Jack Loomis was cruel to the horses in his charge."

"That's ridiculous. He worked them hard, of course, but that's part of what it takes to be a national champion. It's like anything else. The horse has to be completely focused on one thing, that moment in the ring with all the judges watching his every move. Jack didn't do anything that another trainer wouldn't do."

"And what is that?"

"He kept Beau in isolation. Having other horses around upsets the concentration. Special diet. Repetition. Repetition. Repetition. That's not cruelty. It's dedication to the goal."

"Does the horse have any say in the matter?" Penelope asked gently. "Perhaps Beau would have been happier running with the mares."

"Beau was born to be a champion. He knew that. I could tell. Poor Beau. I hope he's all right."

AST and ADF—After the Simpson Trial and After Dennis Fung—criminalists across the nation paid meticulous attention to crime scenes, large and small. One never knew when a sharp New York defense attorney might be lurking, waiting to pounce on the smallest mishap in gathering evidence. It was no different in Empty Creek. Both ECPD criminalists had watched the beleaguered Dennis Fung testify during the trial. Both still awakened from nightmares with cold sweats, fearing the wrath of their chief if they screwed up. Penelope knew what they felt like. Dutch's anger had been turned on her more than once.

As a result, everything that might have the slightest pertinence—and a lot that didn't—to Jack Loomis's death had been gathered, tagged, and properly routed to preserve the integrity of the chain of evidence. This attention to detail meant that there was absolutely nothing left for Penelope and Big Mike to discover.

Fresh straw had been strewn over the stable floor, hiding the blood where Jack Loomis had fallen. It didn't matter. The diagram in the police file showed exactly where the body had been in relation to Beau's stall.

Penelope paced off the confines of Beau's stall, comparing it to Chardonnay's spacious enclosure. She estimated it to be twelve feet by twelve feet, not at all big for a healthy and energetic stallion. "It would be like keeping you in your travel cage all the time," Penelope said to Mycroft. "You wouldn't like that at all."

His answering meow told Penelope that she better not try it.

Dutch had once told her that the legendary Los Angeles homicide detective Jigsaw John said that murderers always made mistakes, dropped something, left fingerprints, some identifying clue. But if this killer had made a mistake, Penelope was damned if she could find it.

The mobile home where Jack Loomis had lived was parked right smack in the desert scrub at the north end of the ranch. The windows, once dusty, were now streaked with dirt from the rains. A residue of fingerprint powder still clung to the doorknob. It was locked.

The lime green corvette skidded to a halt and Horace Melrose popped out, much like a Jack-in-the-box. "What are you doing here? Are you one of the insurance investigators?"

"Didn't Maryanne tell you?"

"We're not speaking. Who are you?"

"I'm Penelope Warren. Samantha Dale and Jake Peterson asked me to look into Jack Loomis's murder."

"Oh, you're the one. Samantha said she knew a pretty good private detective. I wasn't expecting a woman. Or a cat."

"Well, here we are. Woman and cat."

"I hope Samantha knows what she's doing."

"Oh, she does," Penelope said. "So do we."

Melrose looked rather dubiously at Big Mike who was still perched on the hitching rail. For his part, Mycroft was probably trying to decide if the new arrival—who smelled of horse liniment—was a veterinarian about to start poking and prodding at him. With a well-developed aversion to being poked and prodded, Big Mike was ready to defend himself. Fortunately—for all concerned—Melrose turned back to Penelope.

"I've told the police everything I know, which is very little. I didn't do it or arrange to have it done. Loomis worked for me. He was a damned good trainer. I don't know what he was doing in the barn at that hour. I don't know why anyone would steal Beauregarde. I don't see how I can help you. Unless you'd like to have dinner with me."

"No, thank you. Do you have any enemies?"

"Besides my about-to-be-former wife?" he asked bitterly.

"Well, yes."

"Just anyone with a horse to rival Beauregarde."

"How many is that?"

"Three or four locally. More if you go outside Arizona. We're playing for big stakes here. With a horse like Beauregarde . . . there's no limit on potential. With him out of the way, another horse will be champion and I'll be ruined."

Penelope saw his eyes glint with greedy disappointment. "Do you have a list of your potential enemies?" she asked.

"I gave it to the police, but I've thought of a few more since then. Stop by the house on your way out and I'll give you a copy."

"Thank you. One more thing. Do you have a key?" She nod-

ded toward the mobile home where the late Jack Loomis had
lived.

Melrose rummaged through the console in the car and
emerged with a key, holding it out. "Are you sure you won't
have dinner with me?"

"My boyfriend wouldn't like it."

Melrose tossed her the key. "Oh, well."

Penelope watched Melrose drive off, wondering if Maryanne
would get the Corvette in the divorce settlement. She certainly
deserved it.

Together, Penelope and Big Mike prowled through the mobile home. Fingerprint powder was everywhere, but there was
little else to suggest that the place had been searched by the
police. Perhaps Dutch had issued a neatness memorandum.

Jack Loomis had lived without luxuries, subsisting exclu-
sively on beer and frozen dinners as near as Penelope could
tell. He didn't even have a television and his wardrobe apparently consisted entirely of boots, a duster, jeans, and western
shirts, all strikingly similar to the one worn by Maryanne Melrose. Penelope checked the sizes; seventeen-inch neck, thirty-
six-inch sleeves. Jack Loomis had been a big man.

While Mycroft looked for clues under the bed, Penelope
sorted through the items in the nightstand. She wasn't surprised to find a few magazines filled with pictures of naked
women. She *was* surprised to find a pair of heavy shiny handcuffs. They were real police handcuffs, not at all like the toys
that Laney occasionally favored. Gleaming, they had obviously
been wiped clean of prints. But she scooped up some fingerprint powder and sprinkled them anyway. Nothing.

"I wonder why Burke and Stoner didn't take these?" Penel-

ope asked as Mycroft crawled out from beneath the bed to report. She put the cuffs in her purse.

Loomis didn't seem to have read much and the few novels
scattered about tended toward lurid covers and graphic de-
scriptions of overendowed men and women making love in
seemingly impossible positions. But they were not of the kind
to suggest that Loomis liked to use restraints on his girlfriend.
Besides, no girlfriend had surfaced—yet.

After his initial prowl through the mobile home, Big Mike
went back outside. That was a pretty good indication that there
was little of evidential value to be found. But Penelope was
reading a particularly colorful passage about a trapeze and
wanted to see how it turned out. Her ears were crimson when
she tossed the book aside to follow Big Mike, slamming the
door behind her.

That was when Mycroft found a large gold hoop earring
nearly buried in the dirt beneath the trailer.

CHAPTER
FIVE

Regina Pryor and Lady Brenda were a good pair, comfortable together as rider and horse should be in the Arabian Western Pleasure Riding competition. Reggie put Lady Brenda through the paces—the walk, a little jog-trot, into the lope, and finally the hand gallop. The spirited Arabian responded to each new command effortlessly.

"She's good," Mattie said, "but I can show her a few little things to make her even better."

"I think she has an excellent chance to win," Penelope said. She had stopped off to watch after leaving the Loomis trailer. Maryanne Melrose could wait.

Mycroft, who was perched rather precariously on the narrow top rail of the corral, apparently agreed because he was mewing excitedly. Quite an accomplished horse cat himself, Big Mike often went riding with Penelope and Chardonnay, happily ensconced in one saddle bag while his buddy, Alexander, yipped and yapped from the other. The two of them had once appeared in a four-column photo—above the fold, mind you—on

the front page of the *Empty Creek News Journal*. That sort of
thing happened if you occasionally shared a bed with an editor
who had an affinity for both Penelope and weird animals.

The elder heartbreaker beamed with pride as she watched
her daughter finish the workout, dismount gracefully, and hug
Lady Brenda's neck before starting the cooling off routine for
the big animal.

"Someone should have a word with Dirk Tindall," Penelope
said. "I can't imagine what he sees in that cheerleader. I've
never liked cheerleaders myself. They're always so . . . so . . .
cheery."

Nora smiled. "It'll work out the way it's supposed to," she
said.

"You sound like Alyce," Penelope replied. "She's always
saying that sort of thing." Alyce Smith was Empty Creek's resident astrologer and psychic. Penelope liked and firmly believed in Alyce's ability, although the young woman showed a
singular lack of ability in predicting her own destiny, a failing
that had gotten her in trouble on more than one occasion.

"Well, it's true," Nora said.

"What's true?" Mattie asked. She had been intent on watching her two new charges.

"Things work out the way they're supposed to," Nora replied.

"They surely do," Mattie said. "Have you made any progress in that other matter, Penelope? I notice you've been out
here all afternoon."

"A little, perhaps. I'm not sure. Abigail said Loomis was just
doing what it took to make Sir Beauregarde a champion, that he
wasn't cruel."

"Ain't natural, child, what they do to them horses. Ain't natural at all."

Reggie led the bay-colored Arabian up the ramp of the horse trailer and then helped Mattie lift and secure the gate. "I'd ride back with you, Mrs. Bates, but Ms. Warren wants to talk with me first."

"Call me Mattie, child. I ain't *that* old."

"Nor am I," Penelope said quite conveniently forgetting that only twenty-four hours earlier she had been in the throes of a deep depression concerning galloping age.

"Yes, ma'am."

"Oh, Lord. You can dispense with the ma'ams, too." Mattie climbed into her pickup and drove off.

"*Was* Jack Loomis cruel to his horses, Reggie?"

"Never to Lady Brenda," Reggie said, "I wouldn't let him do anything like that."

"Good for you, but how about other horses? Sir Beauregarde, for example."

"Well, not really, but I could tell." Reggie looked down and scuffed the toe of her boot in the dirt. "Sometimes, when I watched him with Beau . . . what a horse . . . he wasn't afraid of Jack, but . . . well . . . Beau hated him. He had a glare in his eyes when Jack was around. He always looked like he wanted to kick Jack in the head. I think maybe Mrs. Bates, Mattie, was right. Jack had been mean to Beau."

"Jack?" Nora questioned.

Reggie shrugged. "He wanted me to call him Jack, like Ms. Warren, Penelope, I mean. He was kind of a flirt."

Nora looked at Penelope. Penelope looked at Nora. Nora asked the question. "Did he . . ."

"Of course not, Mom! Jeez! I'd hit him in the head with a two-by-four if he tried anything like that. All he ever said was that I should come back when I was eighteen and he'd take me to the next level."

"Whatever that means," Nora humphed.

Penelope turned away with a smile, remembering what it was like to be sixteen, still a girl really, but trapped in a woman's body with confused emotions and yearnings.

"Besides," Reggie said, "he was so old."

With a taste for the younger woman, Penelope thought, remembering only belatedly to modify the accusation with alleged, as Andy always insisted until a surmise became fact. "He wasn't *that* old," Penelope said thinking of her own age.

"You know what I mean. I just think a woman shouldn't marry a man more than five years older than she is."

"And I think," Nora said, "that a woman shouldn't be thinking of marriage until she's graduated from college and worked for a while."

"Oh, Mom!"

Penelope watched them walk away. Maybe Dirk Tindall knew what a handful Regina Pryor would be. "That's a no nonsense young lady," she told Mycroft.

Big Mike was apparently reserving his opinion, at least until he'd had a chance to try out Reggie Pryor's lap—or Lady Brenda's saddlebags.

Penelope found Maryanne Melrose still sitting by the pool. The lemonade had been replaced by a bottle of vodka and an ice bucket.

"I didn't expect you back. I've decided to have a drink. Would you like one?"

"No, thanks," Penelope said holding out the earring. "Mycroft found this outside Jack's trailer. It's yours."

"No. Mine is right here. I've been so distracted, I forgot to put it on. I feel so silly, going around all day with only one earring." She patted her shirt pocket and then looked at Penelope with surprise. "It's gone."

"You were Jack's girlfriend."

"I don't know what you're talking about."

"That shirt you're wearing. I'll bet anything it's a seventeen-inch neck with thirty-six-inch sleeves."

"Jack's size?"

Penelope nodded.

"I just wear it to piss off Horace."

"That's all? When a woman wears a man's shirt, it's a very intimate gesture. You don't just go up to someone and say can I wear one of your shirts so I can anger my husband, especially when the husband is also the employer."

Maryanne slid a sheet of paper across the glass tabletop. "Horace left this for you."

"So you did expect me?"

"Yes." Maryanne looked nervously at the house. "Please . . ."

Penelope waited.

Mycroft was back in Maryanne's lap, purring.

Maybe he was playing Good Cat-Bad Cat.

"Please," Maryanne repeated, stroking Mycroft's fur gently.

"You were lovers, weren't you?" Penelope said wondering why she always had to be the Bad Cat.

"Yes, all right, Jack and I were having an affair, but I didn't kill him. I loved him. We were going to get married after my divorce."

"You went to the barn to meet him."

"Yes," Maryanne said sadly, wistfully. "We were going to make love in the hay. Have you ever done that?"

Penelope shook her head.

"It's so romantic. It's nice and warm and even better when it's raining. You just lie there afterward and listen to the rain beating on the roof and feel so safe."

Penelope thought that making love in a haystack might be itchy and scratchy, but she always tried to be tolerant of another's foibles. With friends like Laney, you learned to develop a little tolerance. "Did you think what might have happened if you got there earlier? You might be dead, too."

Maryanne shuddered. "More than once."

"Did he ever tie you up? Or handcuff you?"

"Of course not. What kind of question is that?"

"I found these in his nightstand." Penelope let the handcuffs dangle from her fingers.

"I've never seen them before. Jack was always kind and gentle."

"Then, you won't mind if I take them?"

"Not at all," Maryanne said with as much indignity as she could muster.

Penelope and Big Mike entered the bank just before closing to make a report. Samantha Dale was in her office with a man and a woman, their backs to Penelope and Big Mike. Penelope thought Sam looked worried, but the banker smiled and waved them in.

"I was just talking about you," Sam said. "These are the insurance investigators. Mr. Richard Raymond and Ms. Susan Vaughn. Penelope Warren. And Mycroft, of course."

Mr. Raymond and Ms. Vaughn did not make a good first im-

pression and not only because they looked disdainfully upon
Penelope and Big Mike. Penelope made it a general rule never
to trust a man who wore a pencil-thin mustache, despite Mycroft's fondness for the bawdy ballads of Jimmy Buffett. She
also made it a rule never to trust a woman with thin, pinched
lips. Mr. Raymond and Ms. Vaughn violated both rules, respec-
tively. And there was the little matter of a man with two first
names, although that wasn't as bad as Joseph Heller's Major
Major Major in *Catch 22*.

The second impression was little better, solidifying Penelope's opinion when Ms. Vaughn used her thin, pinched lips to
say, "Get that disgusting cat out of here. I'm allergic."

With Mycroft's flair for the dramatic, he promptly leaped
into Ms. Vaughn's lap. She shrieked and tried to dislodge him.
Mistake number one.

Never easily dislodged if he didn't want to be, Mycroft dug
in, which led to mistake number two.

Ms. Vaughn leaped up and down several times like a buck-
ing bronco, a not inconsiderable feat since she managed to remain sitting—and shrieking—the whole time.

Although Mycroft had never experienced an earthquake
firsthand, he had heard Penelope talk about the Big One often
enough and probably thought this was it and decided even
Mother Earth wasn't about to throw him off.

The few remaining customers and the bank staff rushed to
Samantha's office and watched the spectacle with amazement.
In an attempt to be helpful, a man hollered, "Throw some
water on him."

Mr. Raymond, hearing this not-so-sound advice, rushed out.
But since he didn't know where the water cooler might be

located, he grabbed a fire extinguisher from the wall, setting off
an alarm in the process.

The little crowd gathered around the door parted, as though
for Moses, and Mr. Raymond let fly a second after Penelope
shouted, "No!"

Mycroft took Penelope's shout as his cue to exit the scene,
which he did by leaping straight into the air, executing a graceful pirouette, and landing without even a ruffled whisker on
Samantha's desk where he was able to watch the proceedings
with an unimpeded view and a great deal of amusement. Disgusting, indeed.

"How do you turn this thing off?" Mr. Raymond shouted as
he bathed his now hysterical colleague with foam.

The wail of sirens announced the arrival of Engine Company
Number One and a moment later firefighters and paramedics
rushed into the bank brandishing an assortment of axes, hoses,
additional fire extinguishers—as though Ms. Vaughn needed
more foam—and a stretcher, which she very well might need.

The intrepid firefighters were followed by a uniformed cote-
rie from Empty Creek's finest, including Sam Connors and his
partner Peggy Norton who had once foiled an attempted robbery at this very same bank.

Once Sam Connors saw Big Mike sitting on the desk, he was
tempted to call for additional backup. But when he saw the apparition covered in foam and not knowing how to protect and
serve whoever might be underneath, he collapsed in helpless
laughter.

Unamused, Mr. Raymond cried, "Help," before turning the
nozzle on the crowd that hastily scattered and ducked.

When the fire extinguisher finally extinguished itself by running out of fuel, the only sounds to be heard were Sam Connors

in a choking fit and Ms. Vaughn alternately whining piteously, and screaming bloody murder.

Since they had a casualty to treat, there was no question of a false alarm charged against the bank, although Captain Rufus Murdock, the engine company chief, looked rather suspiciously at Mr. Raymond who had somehow managed to cover himself with foam as well.

"What started the fire?" Captain Murdock asked.

"What fire?" Mr. Raymond said wiping foam from his pencil-thin mustache. "It was the cat."

"The cat was on fire?" Murdock asked incredulously.

"No, the cat was on her lap."

"So it was her lap that was on fire?"

"Is everyone in this town crazy?" Mr. Raymond screamed.

Penelope, who rather thought everyone in town *was* crazy, said, "She frightened him with all that hollering and cavorting around."

"I said we should throw some water on him," the customer who had provoked the entire incident said. "That's the way to stop a dogfight. Turn a garden hose on 'em. Works every time."

"But this wasn't a dogfight," Penelope pointed out, "and the bank doesn't have a garden."

"Same principle, but nobody said anything about a damned fire extinguisher," the customer replied with disgust.

Still screaming and threatening lawsuit, Ms. Vaughn was transported from the scene strapped to the stretcher. After treatment for assorted cat scratches and a tetanus shot, Penelope thought Ms. Vaughn might have to be transferred to the psychiatric wing of Empty Creek General.

"I don't think she was allergic at all," Penelope said when

things had returned to what passed for normal in Empty Creek. "She only sneezed once." It was her final comment on the matter.

"I never knew that a fire extinguisher held so much whatever it is," Samantha said. That was *her* final word on the topic. Then she said, "Let's go to the Double B. I'll buy you a drink. And a double for Mycroft. We deserve it."

Hearing that, Mycroft purred. That was *his* final comment on the episode with Ms. Vaughn, word of which was already rapidly spreading through Empty Creek and its environs, adding another chapter to his already substantial legend.

At the Double B, Big Mike leaped to his accustomed stool at the bar and said howdy-do to a still pretty slicked-up Red the Rat. Samantha ordered Big Mike's favorite nonalcoholic beer and a bottle of the chardonnay Pete the Bartender kept tucked away for special occasions.

Once comfortably settled at Penelope's usual table, Samantha said, "They'd already told me they had no intention of cooperating with you. They have no interest other than to save their company from paying off."

"And that means they are going to concentrate on proving that Horace or his agents stole Beauregarde."

"Exactly."

"Well, then, I won't cooperate with them either. It'll be a race between Mr. Raymond, Ms. Get-that-disgusting-cat-out-of-here Vaughn and Mycroft and me." Penelope smiled. "Far be it from me to tell them that Maryanne Melrose was having an affair with Jack Loomis."

"She was?"

"Said they were going to get married after the divorce."

"Divorce?"

"I guess they don't need to know that Jack Loomis also seemed to have an affinity for younger women either."

"He did? My, you have been busy."

Penelope smiled again. "That's why you're paying me the big bucks. In a manner of speaking. Shall we have another glass of wine, Ms. Dale?"

"Delighted, Ms. Warren."

Another glass of wine was poured.

"But what does it all mean?"

"Beats me," Penelope said.

That evening, Penelope leafed through *A Farewell to Arms*, but she couldn't find the quotation. She had been sure it was Catherine who said it. *Sometimes I see me dead in the rain.* Perhaps it was in the movie. Perhaps I'm imagining it and nobody ever said it. But they should have. It's a good line, if somewhat morbid. Penelope went to the bookcase and replaced it.

"Have you ever made love in a haystack?" she asked.

"No," Andy replied. "Have you?"

"No. Would you like to?"

"Wouldn't it be kind of itchy?"

"That's what I think, but Maryanne Melrose says it's very romantic."

"Well, I'm always ready for a little variety."

"You've been talking to Laney again."

"Well . . ." Andy smiled sheepishly.

"Well?" Penelope demanded.

"She keeps recommending the bondage starter kit."

"You wouldn't dare!"

"No, I probably wouldn't."

"On the other hand . . ." Penelope went to her purse and pulled out the handcuffs.

"Penelope! I'm shocked."

"They're not mine, silly. I found them in Jack Loomis's trailer." She rummaged through a drawer or two. "Aha!" she cried triumphantly. "I knew I had a key someplace."

"Why do you have a handcuff key?"

"Just in case."

Andy watched as Penelope played with the handcuffs, opening one steel bracelet and then the other. "What else did you find?"

"Well, Maryanne Melrose was having an affair with Loomis, but Reggie Pryor says Jack was flirtatious. I think he might have been attracted to younger women."

"Reggie's just a girl."

"Have you taken a close look lately? She's quite the young woman. But anyway, nothing happened. Reggie did say Sir Beauregarde hated Jack."

"How can you tell what a horse is thinking? He's just an animal."

"Mycroft, give him a good whack. Just an animal, indeed."

Big Mike gave Andy an appraising glance, but apparently decided it was too much effort to leave his place in front of the fire. It had been a rather trying day so why bother with exertion when it wasn't really necessary? Andy would come within whacking range sooner or later. Mikey closed his eyes and promptly fell asleep.

"You know what I mean."

"I do not. Animals have feelings and thoughts and emotions. They're just furry people. Right, Mikey?"

Mikey snored by way of reply.

Thus ignored, Penelope idly snapped one cuff shut around her wrist.

"What are you doing?"

"Just testing," Penelope replied. She put her arms behind her back and snapped the other cuff shut. "There."

"There what?"

"Just there." Penelope shook her wrists. "I wonder what Jack was doing with handcuffs? Maryanne said he wasn't kinky that way."

"Well, do you go around telling people that you like me to lick honey off your beautiful body?"

"That's different. Besides, it was only once and only because Laney put the idea in my mind. I was curious. I don't remember you objecting at the time."

"I'm not sure all that honey was good for me."

"Well, if you hadn't gotten so carried away with it."

"The jar didn't come with directions."

Penelope shook her wrists again. "You know, these are real police handcuffs. Just like Larry Burke's."

"You should know."

In that earlier and quite stormy phase of her relationship with the local gendarmes, Penelope had also been arrested and ignominiously handcuffed when Tweedledee was determined to jail Mycroft.

"That's the point. I *do* know. I'll bet the bondage starter kit doesn't come with real handcuffs. They'd be toys, like the ones Laney used on Wally that time and couldn't get them off."

Andy shook his head. "She's a pistol."

"As I remember, that's what Wally said at the time. Still, I wonder why Jack Loomis had real police handcuffs."

"Perhaps he preferred authenticity."

"If that was his motive, he certainly got it." Penelope had suddenly discovered that while it was quite easy to handcuff yourself, it was quite another matter to get loose. "You can unlock me now."

Andy grinned mischievously.

"You wouldn't."

Andy dropped the key into his shirt pocket.

"What if we have visitors?"

Andy shrugged. "We'll just tell them that we're playing police officer and dangerous female criminal."

"You got that from Laney."

"Did not. I made it up myself."

"Laney would be proud of you."

"Yes, I rather think she would."

"And how does the dangerous female criminal get loose?"

"She has to seduce the ruggedly handsome police officer."

"You're not ruggedly handsome. You're tall and lanky and look like Ichabod Crane."

"The ruggedly handsome Ichabod Crane."

"All right, I'll give you that. Now unlock these things."

"Nope."

"Andyyyy! How can I seduce you like this?"

"The beautiful female criminal will find a way."

"At least, give me a sip of wine."

"I can do that." Andy held the wineglass to Penelope's lips.

"Thank you," Penelope said feeling quite helpless.

"You're welcome."

"Okay, come on now. Let me loose."

"Make me."

"Brute."

Faced with the grim prospect of a long prison sentence, the

dangerous—and beautiful—female criminal smiled. When wheedling didn't work . . . well . . . there was more than one way to skin a cat—sorry, Mikey—or seduce a make-believe cop.

Penelope found most of them, but even after reducing Andy to a whimpering shell of his ruggedly handsome self, she wondered what Jack Loomis was doing with real police handcuffs.

CHAPTER SIX

Penelope read Andy's newspaper account over coffee, wishing that she had discovered something that would have given him a fresh angle for the piece. But she hadn't and so Andy had done the best he could in belatedly reporting the known facts of the case to date.

LOOMIS MURDERED, POTENTIAL NATIONAL CHAMPION STOLEN
By Harris Anderson III
News Journal Staff Writer

Famed Arabian trainer Jack Loomis was shot and killed early Monday morning and Sir Beauregarde Revere of Dunbarton Lakes, the stallion Loomis was grooming as a potential national champion, was apparently stolen by the assailant or assailants.

Loomis's body was discovered outside the horse's empty stall at approximately 6 A.M. by Maryanne Melrose, the wife of Horace Melrose, the stallion's owner. Maryanne Melrose, distraught over the discovery, is in seclusion and could not be reached for comment.

Empty Creek Chief of Police John Fowler also would not comment on the murder and theft other than to say, "The investigation is continuing and we are following up on a number of possible clues."

Time of death was set at sometime after midnight. The rain conditions obliterated any traces of the vehicle and trailer presumably used to transport the missing stallion.

Loomis, 42, was a much sought after trainer in the Arabian world, having seen two of his stallions crowned national champions previously.

The Empty Creek News-Journal has learned that Horace Melrose used the missing stallion as collateral on a loan from the Empty Creek National Bank. The bank is named as beneficiary on a substantial insurance policy, although there are exclusionary clauses in the event of foul play.

Insurance investigators are focusing on such possibilities, particularly in the wave of thoroughbred horse killings that has swept the country recently as some owners have hired "hit men" to kill their horses in order to collect on the insurance.

"I resent their [insurance investigators] allegations that I might be involved in some scheme to kill Sir Beauregarde for the money," Horace Melrose said. "I loved that horse almost as much as I love my wife."

Samantha Dale, president of Empty Creek National Bank, admitted to concern over the murder and conditions under which Sir Beauregarde was stolen.

"I am confident, however, that the authorities will find the person or persons responsible for this dastardly deed and return Sir Beauregarde to his rightful owners," Dale said.

Unmarried, Loomis apparently lived a quiet life, residing in a small trailer home at the HMM Arabian Ranch owned by Melrose.

Colleagues cited Loomis's dedication to Arabians and the horses he trained. Abigail Wilson, 23, worked under Loomis as an apprentice. "He was a wonderful man and so talented. I learned so much from him. I feel like I've lost a great teacher," Wilson said.

Sir Beauregarde was expected to contend for the championship at the Empty Creek Great Arabian Horse Show, a forerunner to the Scottsdale show on the road to the national championship.

Jake Peterson, board president of the local show, said that the murder of Loomis and disappearance of Sir Beauregarde had dampened enthusiasm among Arabian enthusiasts everywhere, causing a number of cancellations, but that there were no plans to cancel the event.

"Jack Loomis would have wanted the show to go on," Peterson said. "We intend to do that. The show will open with a moment of silence for Jack and the championship trophy will be presented in his honor."

Oh, well, Penelope thought as she turned to read her horoscope, perhaps I'll be able to give him an exclusive when all is said and done. A scoop would be a very nice present for him.

Penelope and Mycroft spent exactly twenty-seven minutes at the bookstore. From Kathy's point of view, this brief sojourn was more than satisfactory because Penelope, hard on the track of a killer, was just as bad as Penelope having a midlife crisis. In short, Penelope was sometimes unbearable in her single-minded devotion to a cause.

As a result, Kathy allowed Penelope and Big Mike to go off without showing them the latest poetic effort from her beloved Timothy Scott who was carving out a rather specialized literary career by immortalizing her breasts in verse. "Alabaster mounds of pleasure" was among his more notable efforts.

Although Penelope thought Timmy's work showed poetic promise, she had expressed just the other day a desire for Timmy to expand his vision to include some of Kathy's other noteworthy body parts. "You have very nice legs, after all, hair to make a goat envious"—whatever that meant—"and slender fingers. I've always been partial to fingers. I think Timmy should compose an ode to your divine digits."

Kathy was trying to decide if her fingers were, indeed, divine when the third in her pantheon of local heroine role models entered the store.

"Stormy," she cried. "What a nice surprise."

"Hello, Kathy. How's the book biz?"

"Kind of boring at the moment. I'm thinking of becoming a private detective."

"Did she leave you alone again?"

"I don't mind. Mostly, anyway."

"That woman. I'll have to speak to her."

"Oh, don't do that, Stormy. It's kind of nice to have all this responsibility and be trusted."

"Trust and responsibility are one thing. Loneliness is quite another. Penelope should hire Timmy to keep you company."

"He's written another poem," Kathy said shyly.

"On the same topic?"

Kathy nodded, blushing slightly. If Timmy ever published his collected works, she planned to spend the rest of her life wearing a bag over her head.

Stormy took the single sheet of paper and read. "Hillocks?" Stormy arched an eyebrow.

"It's a small hill."

"I know that, but you're quite well-endowed."

"Well, a hill is smaller than a mountain. I think it's just poetic license."

"And free verse. Wait till he sees you in a Super Bra. I'll get you one. We're filming on Sunday."

"Sunday?"

"It's the only day we could rent the library. 'The nicest things happen in a library when you're wearing a Super Bra.' That's the theme. I came by to tell Penelope. She wasn't answering her phone last night. I suppose she was out looking for killers. And, I wanted to see how Mycroft is doing. All that excitement at the bank can't be good for his digestion."

"Mikey's fine, but Penelope's acting very much like Penelope."

"I wish she'd get a cell phone, or a beeper. It's very difficult chasing her through the desert all the time."

"You know how she feels about mechanical devices."

"It's maddening that she doesn't even have an answering machine. Everyone has an answering machine. I'm surprised she doesn't brew coffee over an open fire."

There were armed guards at all the ranches and stables now. It was Rent-a-Cop here and Rent-a-Cop there. Some were quite surly, as Penelope and Big Mike discovered, while others were more than willing to be helpful and pleasant, providing directions once they had ascertained through astute questioning and direct observation that the woman and her cat were probably not planning to abduct a championship horse in the middle of the day.

"As you can see," Penelope pointed out, "there is no hitch on the Jeep and I'm not likely to conjure up a portable horse trailer out of my purse."

"Well. . . ."

Penelope flashed the smile usually reserved for Andy when she was feeling particularly wicked.

"Okay, you can go on in."

Once admitted, Penelope told Big Mike, "While I admire the work ethic, it's been my experience that there are reasons certain individuals choose the careers they do."

Mycroft quite agreed. Not everyone could be a cat. The qualifications were most exacting and a great many past lives were required to achieve a degree of perfection.

They were working through Horace Melrose's self-defined enemies' list. Penelope had been surprised to find Mattie Bates on the list and was saving her for a grand finale.

Pat Hardesty guffawed and nearly tipped over the rocking chair he happened to be occupying at the time. The fact that the rocking chair was next to a corral didn't seem at all strange to him—or Penelope. Apparently, she had lived in Empty Creek too long with its many residents so well suited to the Rent-a-Cop profession.

"That little runt," Hardesty howled, rocking back precariously. "Who's Melrose think he is? Richard Nixon?" He knocked his cowboy hat askew on the forward motion, bumping his head against a corral rail in the process.

Similar responses were elicited at the Running T, the Howard Ranch, the Triple Bar, and the Over and Under Ranch. Penelope didn't know what that name meant and since she had a curiosity that equalled Big Mike's, she asked.

"Always bet the over and unders on football games," Mike Hovington told her. "It's more fun that way."

"Do you win often?"

"Nope, not at football games anyway, but it's more fun. What do you think about the Monsters' chances Friday night?"

The Gila Monsters were taking on their hated rivals, the Coyotes. "If Dirk Tindall's on . . ." Penelope didn't need to finish the sentence.

"Yeah, the kid's a piece of work, ain't he? And only a junior. Man oh man."

"What do you know about Jack Loomis?" Penelope asked.

That put a definite crimp in the conversation.

While Horace Melrose was universally despised by his colleagues and competitors in the Arabian horse world, Jack Loomis drew mixed reactions.

Pat Hardesty had once tried to hire Loomis away from Melrose. "But he was loyal. Had to respect that. I like loyalty in a man."

The Howards, however, had a different opinion. "Weasel eyes," Archie Howard said. "Never trust a man with weasel eyes."

Penelope thought of Mr. Richard Russell's pencil-thin mustache and Ms. Susan Vaughn's too-thin lips and agreed. Look at the ruckus she had caused. But since neither she nor Big Mike knew any weasels personally, they had to accept the Howards' assessment of Jack Loomis for what it might be worth.

In contrast, the Triple Bar folks admired Loomis and the ac-

complishments of his horses at the various shows. "Wish he'd
worked for us."

But now Mike Hovington shook his head at the mention of
Jack Loomis. "Never liked the man. There's trainers and then
there's trainers. He was one of the bad ones. Never saw that he
cared for horses much. Animals should be treated with respect.
Like that cat there. Never hurts to say, 'Howdy, Mr. Cat.
How's it hanging today?' You know?"

Penelope did know. She invariably greeted all creatures of
nature politely, even Clyde the rattlesnake who sometimes
slithered through the backyard patio of a summer evening to
see what she was reading, although her salutation was usually
made while hastily retreating into the house.

But she didn't know Jack Loomis. Who was he—a devoted
lover who liked to woo his girlfriend in haystacks, a flirt attracted to younger women, a loyal and trustworthy employee, a
good trainer, a bad trainer, a shiftless loner with a mean streak?

The public address system in her mind went off.

Will the real Jack Loomis please report to Accounting?

Mattie Bates's place was like any number of small ranches
around Empty Creek where people made a meager living from
boarding horses and teaching riding to weekend cowboys and
cowgirls. There was a row of covered pens where the horses
spent their days in good weather and a barn for inclement
weather. The horses were outside today. Penelope recognized
Lady Brenda standing placidly in the end pen.

Although Mattie's barn appeared run down—it really
needed a good coat of paint or two—it was clean inside and all
of the tack was properly stored on hooks. The stables were
mucked out every day and fresh hay spread on the floor.

"What are you doing all the way out here?" Mattie asked, brandishing a pitchfork, when Penelope and Big Mike jumped down from the Jeep.

Penelope thought she sounded rather cross and irritated. Perhaps things weren't working out with Red the Rat. "You made Horace Melrose's enemies' list."

"Good," Mattie said abruptly. "I must be doing something right."

"I thought we'd better talk about it."

Mattie leaned the pitchfork against the barn. "Well, you better come in the house and get it over with. I got work to do, but I guess there's time to sit a spell."

Mattie lived in a double-wide mobile home set apart from the pens and barn. Flower beds lined the stone walkway. Inside, Penelope was amazed—as always—to find how spacious a mobile home could be. Mattie's wasn't at all like Jack's little trailer. The living room was big and comfortably cluttered with books and magazines, mostly having to do with horses although there was a smattering of paperback novels, including most of Laney's smoldering romances. There was even a fireplace.

The dominant feature in the living room, apart from the normal furniture, was a gun rack on the wall with a glassed cabinet beneath. A Model 94 Winchester 30–30 hung above a double-barreled shotgun. Below, in the cabinet, there were boxes of ammunition and several handguns, all revolvers.

"Yep," Mattie said noticing Penelope's interest, "they're loaded. Don't do to run around looking for shells when you have a need."

Penelope, who kept her own AR–15 unloaded, could see the wisdom in that. She *did* keep a loaded magazine close at hand after all.

"Do you have a forty-four?"

"Yep, but it ain't been out of the holster in months, except for cleaning. I didn't shoot Jack Loomis with it if that's what you're thinking."

The possibility, however remote, *had* crossed Penelope's mind briefly. "I thought I should ask."

"That's the way you learn things, by asking. That's what I told Reggie. Ask away."

Penelope agreed and would have asked a question if Mattie hadn't continued on a monologue.

"Take the forty-four when I ride back into the hills—and the Winchester. Girl can't be too careful. Got a thirty-eight for my purse and a twenty-two for rats and snakes if they don't take the hint and get too worrisome."

When she was sure Mattie had run down, Penelope said, "You sold Beau to Melrose. Why? Surely, you knew his potential, even as a colt."

Mattie shrugged. "It was right after I run off that worthless third husband of mine. I didn't have the time or the inclination to do what was necessary to turn Beau into a champion. Besides, I needed the money. Wish now I'd starved before turning Beau over to Melrose and Loomis. Beau was such a sweet little guy. I hope he's okay and I hope you find him before . . . something bad happens to him . . . if it ain't already."

"We'll find him," Penelope promised.

"I hope so," Mattie said, "I surely hope so."

"When I bought Chardonnay, you made me promise to be good to her always. I thought you were never going to accept my character references. Why didn't you do that with Melrose?"

"I did," Mattie said. "He lied."

Big Mike loved a visit to The Tack Shack and not only because he adored Lora Lou Longstreet, the shop's owner whose mother appreciated alliteration, and the cat treats she kept on hand for his visits, but also because it was a veritable paradise of neat little hidey-holes from which to pounce on unsuspecting customers if the urge for pouncing should suddenly strike.

There were many rows of shelving laden with assorted wares of the canned variety and a section devoted to riding boots of all kinds. The changing room was covered by a brightly colored Navajo blanket that fell six inches short of the floor. From inside that vantage point Big Mike could lurk unseen and observe the parade of passing feet until a likely candidate for maiming appeared.

He also liked to perch on one or another of the saddles on display. He had favored a certain Australian saddle until Lora Lou sold it, practically right out from under him. After that particular catastrophe, he took a fancy to an English saddle for a time and then went back to the Australian version after Lora Lou reordered it.

A stack of saddle blankets was a fine place for sleeping.

The various bridles, riding crops, ropes, and harnesses hanging on the walls were always good for a passing whack or two. Like a boxer working on the speed bag, a cat had to keep his paws in shape.

But Big Mike's favorite spot was a top shelf in the boot department. From that vantage point, he could alternately sleep or observe, as the mood favored. So, after greeting Lora Lou with a good leg rub and having his chin scratched just right in return, and a quick hello to Leia, Lora Lou's shy Russian wolfhound who preferred the back office during working hours, Big Mike hied himself gracefully to that shelf and settled in.

As well as counting Lora Lou among her friends, Penelope liked visiting The Tack Shack for other reasons. The Tack Shack was a veritable kitchen cabinet of gossip. Lora Lou was one of Laney's prized informants on the desert telegraph, always providing a snippet or two of valuable information for instant transformation on Laney's own personal wire service.

"Hey, Lora Lou, how are you?" Penelope refused to call the very handsome woman of her own age L.L., as some of the men around town did. In fact, Penelope carried on a continuing campaign to refer to Lora Lou only by her given name because she thought it was so pretty.

"Fine, Penelope, I've been expecting you."

"Well, Mikey and I have been making the rounds, but we wanted to save the best for last. So, what have you heard?"

"Nothing."

"That's too bad," Penelope said attempting to hide her disappointment. She had been counting on Lora Lou.

"Wrong question," Lora Lou said with a smile. "Ask me what I've seen."

"All right. What have you seen?"

"A couple of days before the murder, Loomis was outside arguing with someone."

"Who?"

"I don't know that. A man, but I've never seen him before. I suppose he was from out of town." Lora Lou closed her eyes. "He was about six feet. Probably about forty. His hair was longish and blondish, kind of like Fabio, but not so pretty. He wore a cowboy hat, blue jeans, and a blue polo shirt."

"Polo shirt?"

"Yes," Lora Lou said opening her eyes and smiling again. "That didn't fit with the rest of the outfit. I didn't see his boots."

"Have you told the police?"

Lora Lou shook her head. "I figured you'd be around. Might not mean anything. They could have been arguing about the weather."

"Perhaps. What happened after?"

"The stranger stomped off mad. Jack came in and ordered some feed for delivery. He was still mad, too. Usually, he'd pass the time of day, but he didn't say much that time."

"I think we'd better get you together with the police artist," Penelope said. "Would you mind?"

"Not at all, but I didn't know we had a police artist."

"We do now. Dutch recruited David Macklin during the Western Days Celebration. He's the art student who does the sketches of snowbirds."

"Oh, sure. I've seen him around."

"Well, Dutch saw him work and hired him on the spot. He's just freelance, of course, but Dutch thought he could do the job. He's been wanting to try him out."

The final stop of the day was at the Empty Creek Police Department. It was time to find out what the detectives had learned and if *they* were forthcoming, share a little information of her own.

From Penelope's point of view, this visit was more satisfactory with Big Mike rummaging through the papers and the In and Out boxes to the consternation of Tweedledee and Tweedledum. But they were learning to tolerate Big Mike's foibles even if both detectives quickly rolled their chairs back to take themselves out of harm's way.

"We hear you been busy," Tweedledee said as the senior and therefore primary spokesman for the partnership. "Beating up on insurance investigators." He eyed Big Mike warily.

"It was her own fault."

"Wish I'd been there," Tweedledum said wistfully. "You oughta get a video camera. Record these moments for posterity. Then, when you have kids and they start fighting with the cat, you'll be ready."

"Who needs children when I have you?" Penelope asked sweetly. "What have you found out?"

"Aw, Penelope, we always go first. Whatever happened to ladies first?"

"Who says I'm a lady?" Penelope said, waiting for one of them to spring to her defense.

"Oh, all right. We'll go first. Again."

So much for gallantry.

"We've been out to maybe a third of the stables so far. No luck on the horse or the killer."

"Perhaps he's disguised."

"Of course, he's disguised. We don't know what he looks like."

"I meant Sir Beauregarde."

"How do you disguise a horse?"

"I don't know," Penelope admitted, "but I'll ask around."

"Okay, now it's your turn. Give."

Penelope smiled rather smugly. "Well, did you know that Maryanne Melrose is divorcing her husband and that she was having an affair with Jack Loomis?"

That got their attention. "She is?"

"She was?"

"She went to meet him that morning. They were going to make love in the hay, but she found his body instead. Very sad."

"In the hay?"

"Yes, and I believe that Jack Loomis might have had a weakness for younger women although I'm not sure of that, but I'll follow up on it."

"Everybody's got a weakness for young women. That's not news."

"Think what you like," Penelope said. She was ready for the *pièce de résistance*. "And Jack Loomis was seen arguing with a strange man outside The Tack Shack two days before he was killed." Penelope shut up and waited for the applause.

And waited.

"So what? Lots of people argue. Doesn't mean they're killers. If I was going to kill someone for arguing, my wife wouldn't have made it through the honeymoon."

"If you were my husband," Penelope said, "you wouldn't have survived the ceremony."

"See!" Tweedledee said triumphantly.

"She should've told us."

"You should've asked." Penelope sighed. What dolts. "Well, I think we need to get David Macklin together with Lora Lou Longstreet." God, I love that name.

While they might be dolts, Tweedledee and Tweedledum weren't completely stupid. They both knew how itchy Dutch was to try out his police artist. "Good idea," they chorused.

"Now, there's just one more thing."

"What's that?"

"Why didn't you take the handcuffs?"

"We did," Tweedledee said holding up a plastic evidence bag. The handcuffs inside looked suspiciously like something Laney might have ordered from an adult book store and marital aids shop run by behemoth twin brothers named Ralph and Russell. Of course, Laney would have purchased from the mail-order catalog she had urged Ralph and Russell to compile.

"Then, who do these belong to?" Penelope asked holding up her own shining set, wiped clean again after the previous evening's activities, "and how did they get in Jack Loomis's nightstand?"

CHAPTER
SEVEN

"Rabbits, rabbits, rabbits," Penelope said as quickly and as clearly as she could considering the fact she was still reluctantly fighting her way out of a deep sleep. Damn those college schedulers anyway.

Andy had been trying—unsuccessfully—to ease her transition to consciousness by wafting the aroma of freshly brewed coffee toward her. Now, he stopped waving his hand over the coffee mug and looked down upon his lady love with some considerable degree of puzzlement. "Did you say rabbits, rabbits, rabbits?"

Penelope opened one eye, briefly checked the state of the world, and quickly closed it again. "Yes."

"*Why* did you say rabbits, rabbits, rabbits?"

"Because. . . ." Penelope rolled over and pulled the pillow over her head.

Andy pulled the pillow away. "You have to get up. You'll be late for work."

Penelope groaned. "You're mean."

"I am not mean. I'm efficient."

"You're anal retentive."

"That's true, but I'm also efficient."

"Where's Mikey? I want Mikey."

"He's having breakfast, which is what you should be doing. I gave him some liver crunchies."

"I don't want liver crunchies. I want coffee."

"Here."

"Oh, all right," Penelope said opening both eyes and sitting up simultaneously. Plumping the pillows and squirming back against the headboard, she managed to remain upright, keep her eyes open, *and* reach for the coffee. She thought it quite a feat.

Andy agreed, particularly since the sheet dropped away and he was treated to a partial view of what he considered to be the most exquisite female body in the world. "Good morning," he said.

"You just said good morning to my breasts."

"Yes, I did, and now I'm going to give them a good-morning kiss."

"Mmm," Penelope murmured. What with hanging around with Mycroft all the time, she had developed quite a good purr herself. "That's nice. What a lovely way to wake up. If you have to wake up, that is."

"You said rabbits, rabbits, rabbits."

"I did? You must have been dreaming."

Andy sat up abruptly. "I distinctly heard you say rabbits, rabbits, rabbits."

"You're beginning to sound like Elmer Fudd. Is that wascawly wabbit getting you down?"

"Penelope!"

"Oh, all right. It's southern folklore. If you say rabbits, rabbits, rabbits when you wake up on the first day of the month, you'll have good luck all month long."

"But it's not the first of the month."

"Doesn't hurt to say it anyway. I'm beginning to think I could use some luck on this case." Penelope sipped at her coffee and casually glanced at the clock radio with the well-used snooze button. "Good God!" she shouted, scaring the bejesus out of Andy in the process. "Look at the time! I'm going to be late. Why didn't you wake me up?"

Andy groaned. Life with Penelope Warren was always interesting in one way or another, but there were worthwhile compensations such as watching her walk toward the shower. "Cute butt," he called.

Penelope paused long enough to blow a kiss over her shoulder. Then she turned the shower water on.

Andy waited.

"God, I hate the morning!" Penelope screamed right on cue.

Samantha Dale was beginning to hate the morning as well. Standing at the window of the bank, she could see the two insurance examiners sitting in their parked rental car just down the street. They had been there since the bank opened.

Just sitting.

Samantha went back to her office and tried to concentrate on her preparations for the examiners who would arrive right after the conclusion of the horse show. First, Jack Loomis and Sir Beauregarde and then the bank examiners. It was too much. She went back to the window.

They were still there.

Sitting.

What *were* they doing?

When Penelope and Big Mike threw open the door of Mycroft & Company—only a little late—Laney was waiting impatiently with Alexander and Kelsey straining at their leashes. "I thought you'd never get here. I've been waiting for hours."

"Liar, liar, pants on fire."

"Ten minutes can seem like hours."

Mycroft hissed, not very menacingly, but just enough to issue a warning. Keep a civil tongue in your head, pup.

Alexander sat next to Big Mike and growled softly. Yeah.

Kelsey sat and looked perplexed.

Penelope, feeling sorry for the puppy, scooped her up and was instantly rewarded with a half dozen or so slobbery dog kisses. Penelope thanked her politely, put her on the floor, and reached for a tissue.

"Do you like it?" Laney threw off her windbreaker, revealing a pink angora sweater and a greatly enhanced bosom.

"My God, did you have an operation?"

"Of course not, silly, it's a Super Bra. Stormy gave it to me."

"You look like Lana Turner in search of a drugstore."

"It's driving Wally mad, and every other male within a hundred yards. I thought Red the Rat's eyes were going to fall out, but then Mattie dragged him away. I love it, but it's not for everyday wear. How do you like yours?"

"I didn't get one."

"You didn't? Is Stormy mad at you?"

Penelope shrugged. "I don't think so. I haven't seen her. But I wouldn't wear that thing anyway."

"Andy would find it sexy."

"Andy finds me sexy enough as it is, thank you very much."

"Honestly, Penelope, you're such a prude sometimes."

Alexander barked again. Penelope wondered if he agreed with Laney's assessment of her character. Or perhaps he hadn't quite forgiven her for dumping him in the puddle.

"Kelsey, play nicely with Alex and Mikey. She's such a cute little dog, but Alex hates her. I suppose he'll get over it but . . . if he doesn't . . . would you like a present?"

Penelope shook her head. "I'm a one-cat woman."

"I just thought it would be nice for Alex to have a little play-mate."

Penelope noticed that Alex was keeping Big Mike between himself and his little playmate who was now running about the store playfully and barking, Look how cute I am.

"They'll adjust. A puppy takes some getting used to after being number-one dog for so long."

"He's still number-one dog."

"Tell that to Kelsey."

"What do you think I've been doing? And speaking of which, what have you been doing? Have you made any progress?"

Penelope quickly summarized her results, leaving out any mention of the handcuffs. There was no use getting into *that* with Laney. It would be all over town by sunset.

"It sounds like a soap opera," Laney said. "Mysterious assignations, rumors of younger women, an enigmatic personality, a missing horse, insurance money, an argument with a stranger. I wonder what's next?"

So do I, Penelope thought, so do I.

———

They were on the move. At least, *he* was moving. Peeking through the curtains from her vantage point at the bank's expansive window, Samantha watched as Mr. Richard Raymond got out of the car and carefully locked the driver's side door. Was he leaving Ms. Susan Vaughn behind? Sam wondered. No, he was simply being gallant, like Big Jake, crossing to the passenger side and opening the door for Ms. Vaughn.

They stood there on the sidewalk after he locked the door. Their discussion appeared animated. What *were* they saying? After a few moments, Mr. Raymond touched Ms. Vaughn's arm in what appeared to be a tender, even intimate gesture. She nodded, took *his* arm, and together they marched down the street. There was no sign of a limp on Ms. Vaughn's part.

"I'll be out for a few minutes," Samantha announced to no one in particular and slipped through the door.

The insurance investigators seemed to be in no hurry to reach their destination, stopping frequently to gaze into one shop window or another.

Thus, Samantha ducked into doorways each time Mr. Raymond and Ms. Vaughn paused and was treated to a display of wedding cakes at the bakery, a funeral wreath with matching fax machines at ten and two o'clock and an inscription which read, JESUS FAXED AND HIS SERVANT ANSWERED, at the mortuary, and a very nice red satin negligee at Martha's Clothing for the Young at Heart.

Wondering if Big Jake would like to see her in such a thing—it was slit nearly to the hip and exposed a great deal of leg—and feeling very much like a private investigator on a tail (no wonder Penelope liked tracking down killers so much) Samantha paused only briefly at the music store and then moved on to the computer store. The display of various computer games available reminded her of the program for strip poker on her own home computer and set her to speculating on the best way to get Big Jake to play. Momentarily distracted while deciding the direct approach was probably best—How about a game of strip poker after dinner?—Samantha had to hurry to catch up and was nearly caught when Mr. Raymond turned and looked back, just avoiding his brief glance by leaping through the doors of the bar favored by aging and imitation Hell's Angels.

The sudden, albeit brief, appearance of an elegantly clad, blond businesswoman in their midst quite distracted the leather-jacketed bikers playing pool. A big hulk who probably dwarfed the Harley parked outside promptly scratched, knocking the eight ball into the side pocket when he had distinctly called the corner pocket. Samantha smiled sweetly and exited the premises before there could be recriminations over the errant shot. After all, they might have been playing for money.

Samantha emerged just in time to see the insurance investigators enter Mycroft & Company. My God, was Ms. Vaughn really going to sue?

When Kathy returned from class, it was obvious that Stormy had struck again. Penelope wondered if her sister was passing out the product to every woman in Empty Creek. If she kept on giving them away, there would be no one to entice with the television commercial. I swear, she thought, if Mrs. Burnham shows up wearing a Super Bra, I'm going to have Stormy committed.

"Do you really think Timmy needs added inspiration?"

"Isn't it terrific?" Kathy said, twirling about for Penelope to admire her enhanced figure.

"It's certainly uplifting. How was *Paradise Lost* today?" Penelope asked in her eagerness to change the subject.

"Long."

"Well, it is an epic."

"Satan and Eve are really the only interesting characters though. All those goody-goody angels are boring."

"Evil is always more interesting than good. That's one reason mysteries are so popular. It's difficult to make perfection interesting. Satan and Eve are like us. Torn with conflicting emotions. Their fall from grace is inevitable, but we want to experience it with them. It's cathartic."

"Oh, Penelope, I'm never going to catch up with you."

"Nonsense. Just spend another five or six years in college, study hard, and you'll know more than I ever did. Just remember that all tables have four legs; all sheep have four legs; therefore all tables are sheep."

"That makes sense."

"That's what I thought, so I dropped logic immediately. I suggest you do the same, particularly if it's an early morning class. Oh, God. . . . Quick, put up the closed sign."

"What?"

"Never mind. It's too late."

"What?" Kathy cried again. "I never know what's going on."

"Here comes Ms. Roller Coaster and the insurance industry's version of Ricky Ricardo."

Mr. Richard Raymond and Ms. Susan Vaughn were indeed marching imperiously to Mycroft & Company with Samantha Dale skulking along behind them, ducking into various doorways. Penelope wondered idly if she, too, was wearing a Super Bra. Probably not, she decided, bank presidents were much too conservative. But then she didn't know that Samantha was thinking about a game of strip poker with Big Jake either.

Mr. Raymond and Ms. Vaughn turned abruptly at the entrance to Mycroft & Company, impeded only briefly by Mr. Raymond's insistence that the door opened outward when, in fact, it was the opposite.

"Flash your cleavage at him," Penelope said. "Perhaps he'll swoon."

"I'm going in the back and get some work done."

"Traitor."

As Mr. Raymond finally managed ingress, Penelope smiled brightly and said, "Good morning. How is our patient today?"

Ms. Vaughn entered cautiously, looking about warily for her nemesis. Spying Big Mike on the hearth of the little fireplace, she halted abruptly, holding the door open for a hasty egress if necessary. "Much better," she said through her pinched, thin lips.

"Oh, come in. He won't hurt you. He was just trying to be friendly."

That did seem to be the case as Big Mike cocked one eye at Ms. Vaughn as if to say, Hi, Toots.

He didn't seem inclined to another tumultuous ride on her lap so Ms. Vaughn allowed the door to close reluctantly. "I came to apologize. I'm afraid I overreacted."

"No apology is necessary. I'm glad you're all right. Would you like to sit down?"

"No, thank you," Ms. Vaughn said quickly.

"I would also like to tender my apologies," Mr. Raymond said. "It seemed like a good idea at the time."

"That's the way with ideas," Penelope agreed, "but again, no apology is necessary. Right, Mikey?"

Apparently, Mikey held no hard feelings, for he had dozed off.

"With that out of the way," Mr. Raymond continued, "I thought, since we are, in a way, colleagues in this matter, that we should pool our information."

"Good idea," Penelope said. "I mean, it *is* a good idea, not like yesterday. What have you learned?"

Mr. Raymond and Ms. Vaughn looked sheepish. "Well," he said, "in a word, nothing. No one will talk to us."

Having a rather suspicious mind generally and, when it came to people who threatened lawsuits, specifically, Penelope was not surprised. She *had* thought the apologies somewhat of a ruse.

"Well," Penelope said, "I suppose we are colleagues in a way."

"Exactly," Mr. Raymond said. "We are both after the same thing. Justice."

Penelope thought they were a lot more interested in keeping their company from having to make a rather large payoff in the event Sir Beauregarde wasn't found, but she didn't voice that opinion. Instead, stalling for time, she said, "Well . . ."

Mr. Raymond and Ms. Vaughn waited expectantly, as did Samantha Dale who had crept into Mycroft & Company through the back door, and was now standing with Kathy behind the curtain that covered the doorway, eavesdropping shamelessly.

Big Mike turned over and stretched.

Ms. Vaughn took a quick step backward.

"Well . . ."

Ms. Vaughn Sneezed. Perhaps she *was* allergic to cats, after all.

———

"You have a very devious mind," Samantha said emerging from the workroom, "I like that in a woman."

"Never trust insurance investigators bearing olive branches," Penelope replied, "and what were you doing creeping after them like that?"

"I was curious, of course, but I think it was mean of you to send them off to Sedona like that."

Sedona was a two-hour drive north of Empty Creek and considered by New Age devotees to be one of the power centers of the world.

"Why? I could have sent them to someplace really awful like Bisbee or Yuma. At least, they'll get to see the Red Rock country and perhaps they'll have a vision at one of the vortexes. They might even find Sir Beauregarde. He *might* be there."

"And in the meantime . . ."

"We can get on with finding a murderer."

Penelope wondered how David Macklin could concentrate with such an audience peering eagerly over his shoulders as he worked. Besides Big Mike, who was taking an active interest in the proceedings even though he had not been a witness, Dutch, Tweedledee, and Tweedledum were all watching and listening as Lora Lou described the man who had argued with Loomis.

She figured it had to be all those sketches for tourists and snowbirds during the Western Days Celebration. It must have been a good training ground for working in the midst of many distractions.

Besides listening to Lora Lou's description and ignoring the helpful hints offered by the police officers, Dave was taking quite an interest in Lora Lou. In fact, he was hitting on her in a very nice manner.

Penelope was pleased. So much for Tweedledee's theory that everyone was interested in younger women. At twenty-two, he was some fifteen years Lora Lou's junior.

"I'd like to paint you," Dave said.

"All right," Lora Lou agreed. She stroked Mycroft's fur softly. He had taken up residence in her lap for an unobstructed view of the proceedings.

In contrast to running The Tack Shack in a very brisk and businesslike manner, Lora Lou was quite a free spirit. Penelope often thought that it would be easier to catch the wind than Lora Lou Longstreet. Thus, she wasn't at all surprised when Lora Lou agreed to pose without the slightest hesitation.

"How's that?"

"His eyebrows were a little bushier."

Dave quickly filled in the eyebrows. "Like that?"

"Perfect. Now put some little wrinkles around the eyes."

Dave complied. "Perhaps walking through a garden. Do you have a garden?"

"Yes."

"In the nude."

"If it's not too cold."

"Geez," Tweedledee complained.

Penelope shushed him. "Dave's working."

"We'll wait for a warm day."

"I can see that."

"The hat was a little lower on his forehead."

Slowly a portrait emerged. Dave sketched and erased and sketched again as Lora Lou went through the description.

When the sketch was complete, everyone looked at one another questioningly. Apparently Lora Lou was the only person in the room who had seen the man.

"Well," Dutch said, "after Dave makes copies, I'll distribute them to other agencies. See if we get a match."

"I want to see a copy of Lora Lou," Tweedledee whispered.

Penelope gave him a sharp elbow to the ribs.

"Whoosh," Tweedledee gasped.

"What's wrong with you?" Dutch asked.

"Must be something I ate, boss."

"I told you all those jelly donuts aren't good for you. I think I'm going to start a department fitness program."

"We traced those handcuffs you found," Tweedledee said after Dutch escorted Dave and Lora Lou out. It was his turn to be a little smug. Finally.

"How did you do that?" Penelope asked.

"There weren't any fingerprints on them."

"I know. I used a little of the powder at Jack's trailer to check. They'd been wiped clean."

"Didn't even have your prints on them," Tweedledee said, "after you handled them and all."

At the memory of the dangerous female criminal Penelope tried to stop the blush from galloping into her face, but she might as well have told Big Mike to jump through a hoop for all the good that did. "I thought I should return them in the same state I found them," Penelope said. It sounded lame even to her.

Tweedledee grinned.

Tweedledum smirked.

Big Mike, who had not been admitted to the bedroom until

after the seduction had been completed and, as a consequence, didn't have the foggiest of what was going on, yawned.

Dutch popped back into the office. He had taken his jacket off and was wearing the shoulder holster that carried his 9mm Beretta upside down. Penelope always thought that looked pretty cool. Tweedledee and Tweedledum carried theirs on their belts. Not nearly so cool.

"Did you tell her yet?" Dutch asked.

"Just getting to that, boss."

"So, how did you trace them?" Penelope asked trying unsuccessfully to act nonchalant.

"Called the handcuff people, of course."

"Of course." Why didn't I think of that?

"They've got a serial number on them."

"They do?" How did I miss that? It's all Andy's fault. I'll get him for this.

"Yep."

"So?"

"So, I called the handcuff people and had them trace the serial number." Tweedledee paused dramatically. He was going to make Penelope ask.

Penelope wanted to outwait him, but decided she would be here for a week or two if she tried. And Mikey would get pretty cranky if he had to wait that long for his lima beans. Sighing, she surrendered. "All right, who do they belong to?"

"Don't know."

Penelope forced herself to remain calm. She wanted to shriek, After all this, you don't know! Instead, she took a deep breath and asked rather calmly, "After all this, you don't know."

"They sell them in lots to law enforcement agencies all over the country," Dutch said. "We don't know the specific person who owns them, but we do know which agency bought that particular lot."

Now Dutch paused, waiting, smiling.

My God, do they all think they're auditioning for Hamlet? Penelope gritted her teeth. "Who . . . bought . . . that . . . particular . . . lot?"

"The Federal Bureau of Investigation," Dutch said.

"The Federal Bureau of Investigation," Penelope exclaimed.

"Yep," Dutch said. "We got a Special Agent from the FBI running around Empty Creek."

"Did you call them?"

"Of course, I called them," Dutch said.

"Well, what did they say?"

"Nothing."

"Nothing?"

"Lied and denied. Fellow I talked with seemed a little put out. Warned me not to even think of interfering with a continuing investigation."

"He's put out! What about us?"

"We're locals. Don't count for much with the Feds."

"Well, I think we should call in Alyce Smith. Get her to establish contact with J. Edgar Hoover. I'd bet he'd tell us."

"Bet he wouldn't, even if Alyce did have a number where he could be reached."

CHAPTER EIGHT

"There," Penelope said sitting back on her heels, "what do you think of that, Mikey?"

Big Mike evidently approved, for he reached out with one big paw and gave the bumper sticker a final endorsing pat.

JIMMY BUFFET FOR PRESIDENT
PARROT PARTY '96

After all, Jimmy was Big Mike's favorite singer. But then, as Penelope always explained to disbelievers, "Of course, he's going to like someone named after a cat food."

Penelope scratched Big Mike behind his ears. "We might even have to register you to vote this year."

It was not a bad idea, considering the average cat was a lot smarter than the average politician. And when it came to Big Mike, who was the smartest cat Penelope had ever met . . . well, there was just no contest. As a devoted Parrot Head, Mycroft might even make the perfect running mate for Jimmy and then run for President in his own right. He certainly couldn't do any more harm than some presidents and a lot less than most. Liver crunchies in every pot and a mouse in every garage. Mikeynomics. Cat paw diplomacy. Walk softly but carry a sharp claw. The summer White House at Empty Creek. Lima beans at state dinners.

"I like it, Mikey, but I don't want to be First Lady. You'll have to appoint me Secretary of State or perhaps Defense. I'll have to think about it."

With Big Mike's political future well in hand, Penelope went back into the house and the nagging legal tablet on the kitchen table. She could have fired up the computer but with so little to work with, it hardly seemed worth the effort to walk down the hall to the home office. So far, all she had was a brand new legal tablet and a few conflicting opinions about Jack Loomis.

Penelope sighed, picked up the ballpoint pen, and started two columns. One was headed, Jack Loomis; the other, Sir Beauregarde.

She started with Sir Beauregarde. That was easy. The horse was missing and unless Mr. Raymond and Ms. Vaughn somehow managed to find Sir Beauregarde in Sedona—which she doubted—Penelope didn't have the foggiest notion where he was or even if he was alive. She wrote "Missing" under his name and felt rather dumb for having done so. Of course, he was missing. Every plumber's apprentice in Empty Creek knew that. She added "Insurance?" and "Investigators." It made her feel a little better. At least, the column didn't look quite so barren. Turning to Loomis, she underlined his name and wrote:

Jack Loomis   Sir Beauregarde

Maryanne Melrose   Missing
Haystack tryst   Insurance?
Earring.   Investigators
Handcuffs/FBI
Young women?
Good trainer/bad trainer
Stranger/argument/sketch

All of which told her exactly nothing, something Big Mike had already ascertained after a brief glance at her efforts. As a result, he was stretched out on the windowsill, dozing peacefully, if a little precariously, on the narrow perch.

Penelope waited.

Plop.

Big Mike looked around sheepishly to see if anyone had witnessed his less than graceful descent.

"How many times do I have to tell you?" Penelope asked. "You're too big to sleep there." At least, she thought as an undaunted Mycroft leaped right back to the sill, some things remain constant in the world. She wondered if the Oval Office had bigger windowsills.

The sketchy list continued to nag at Penelope until midafternoon when pregame anticipation tried to take over. This was *the* big game for the league championship, a good seeding in the playoffs, momentum. Both teams were undefeated with rugged defenses and volatile offenses.

But, of course, the more Penelope tried to focus on the game, the more her list plagued her, like an irritating itch in a hard-to-reach place in the small of the back. An itch, however, could be easily subdued by backing up to a pointed surface like an open door and rubbing or rolling over in the dirt or going back home for the back scratcher Muffy had thoughtfully given her for Christmas. If all else failed, you could always howl at the moon. It might not be as good as a vigorous scratch, but it relieved tension and frustration.

"Owooo," Penelope cried. "Owooo!"

Startled, Kathy rushed from the back room, ready to administer whatever aid might be necessary. "What's wrong?"

Equally startled, Penelope looked at her quizzically. "Nothing. Why?"

"What was that noise?"

"Oh, that. I was howling at the moon."

"It's the middle of the afternoon."

"Well, the moon's up someplace."

"I'm afraid to ask."

"I was thinking about the game and that made me think about the murder and Sir Beauregarde, which made me think about an itch in my back, and howling at the moon seemed tidier than rolling around in the dirt. It's quite simple, really. You always make such a fuss over nothing. You'll be a great mother."

"You'll scare your children half to death if you insist on suddenly making odd noises for no reason at all."

"I told you. . . ."

"Or rolling about in the dirt. Why didn't you just ask me to scratch your back?"

"I didn't want to interrupt you."

"What do you call this?"

"Oh, never mind."

———

Penelope met Andy at the Double B for a quick dinner before the game. Because the bank was open late on Friday evenings, they were meeting Samantha and Big Jake at the game. But the Double B was filled with fans and excitement. Everyone was rooting for the Gila Monsters. It had been a long time since the team was this close to a championship season. For Penelope, it was almost as exciting as a San Diego State game. SDSU was her beloved undergraduate alma mater and she followed Aztec football fortunes avidly, keeping season tickets even when it was difficult to get to San Diego for a game. If the Gila Monsters won tonight and the Aztecs beat BYU in two weeks, all would be right in Penelope's world—except for a murderer and a missing horse.

"Grr," Penelope growled.

"Pardon me?" Andy replied.

"Grr," she repeated. "I'm getting my game face on."

"Oh."

Nearly everyone was at the game, except for Big Mike who didn't much care for football and all the hollering and carrying on that went with it. So he had elected to stay home and keep the bed warm. Horace Melrose was also among the absent as were Mr. Richard Raymond and Ms. Susan Vaughn. Feeling only slightly guilty, Penelope hoped they were having a spiritual experience in Sedona.

But Penelope ran into Mattie and Red at the concession stand. Red was still all slickered up. There was no doubt that Mattie was having a beneficial influence on Red. At this rate, some wag was going to have to come up with a new nickname for the old desert rat.

"Any progress?" Mattie asked.

"Not really," Penelope said noticing that Mattie was pretty slickered up herself, having had her hair done. "Jack Loomis seems to have invoked differing reactions from people."

"I meant about Beau."

Penelope shook her head. "Nothing at all there."

"Penelope will find him," Red said, "if anyone can."

"I sure hope so. I hate to think of poor Beau all alone in the world. I hope someone's taking good care of him."

Penelope watched them walk off, jabbering away like teenagers. At this rate, Mattie would be off prospecting with Red in no time at all or, more likely, they would have His and Hers pitchforks and Red would be mucking out pens.

Samantha and Big Jake climbed into the bleachers to sit beside Penelope and Andy. Jake politely offered everyone a little something for the chill, although spirits were prohibited at high school games. Still, it was only medicinal and winter nights in Arizona could be quite cold.

"We need a pact tonight," Samantha said. "No talking about the case. Let's just enjoy the game."

"I agree," Penelope said.

"Absolutely," Big Jake said. "What's the latest?"

"Well, we have a sketch of the man seen arguing with Jack Loomis. And there appears to be some FBI agent running loose in Empty Creek. I don't know what that's all about."

As the stands began to fill, Lora Lou passed by on Dave Macklin's arm. She smiled and winked at Penelope. Nora and Reggie were present, of course, and when Reggie went off to the student cheering section, Penelope beckoned for Nora to come and sit with them. Even Maryanne Melrose was there in the company of Abigail Wilson.

Stormy and Dutch arrived as the teams took the field for their pregame warm-ups. Stormy greeted everyone, winking at Nora. "Where's Laney and Wally?" she asked.

Penelope shrugged. "I thought they were coming, but you know Laney. She probably stopped to play ice cream cone or something."

"Brr, it's too cold for that."

As long as the subject had come up, Dutch offered everyone a little something for the chill.

Penelope asked the question with her eyes.

Dutch answered with a barely perceptible shake of his head. Damn. Nothing new.

Andy excused himself and headed for the field with a camera slung around his neck and carrying a big black bag. It was a working evening for him, helping out his sports editor by doubling as the photographer. Apparently, like everyone else on the field, Andy needed to warm up the camera for he stopped where the cheerleaders were limbering up and snapped several shots of the female members of the pep squad, including one gorgeous young lady with very long legs.

Watching Andy through her binoculars, Penelope muttered, "Better keep those pom poms where they belong."

Nora laughed. "It's not the pom poms you should worry about."

"It depends on your definition," Penelope responded. "I think Reggie is every bit just as pretty."

"And smart. Don't forget smart."

The hated Coyotes won the toss and took the ball, running the opening kickoff back to their own thirty-two. Two running plays took them to the forty-one. On third and one, Hank Dan-

ning, who had been infatuated with Penelope since the spring
of his sophomore year, stuffed the ball carrier at the line of
scrimmage.

"Way to go, Hank," Penelope yelled.

The punt rolled dead at the Monster nineteen-yard line.

Dirk Tindall trotted on the field.

No huddle.

The ball was snapped. Dirk dropped back, looked short,
threw long.

Touchdown!

The Monster fans went nuts.

Dirk trotted off the field.

Piece of cake.

Until the Coyotes ran the kickoff ninety-two yards for a
touchdown.

"Good Lord," Penelope said, "they think they're playing in
the Western Athletic Conference."

But the game settled down then as the teams exchanged a
series of punts. The Coyotes took a fourteen-seven lead in
the second quarter. Dirk brought the Monsters right back
passing for ten yards, seventeen yards, twenty-one yards.
Hank gained twelve on the fullback draw, taking the ball
down to the Coyote nineteen. Dirk hit the tight end on a
slant pattern who then carried two tacklers into the end zone
just inside the marker.

Andy got a great shot just before they clobbered him.

Concerned about Andy, Penelope missed the extra point
that tied the game. But her sweetie scrambled up. "I told him
to stay out of the way," she said to no one in particular.

————

At halftime, Penelope and Samantha offered to go for coffee. As they joined the line for the concession stand, Samantha said, "Isn't that Maryanne Melrose?"

Penelope turned. "Yes, I wonder where she's going."

Maryanne was walking briskly toward an exit, talking sharply on a cellular telephone. She left the stadium, still talking, and waving off the student who offered to stamp her hand for readmittance to the game.

For a moment, Penelope was tempted to follow, but she didn't want to miss the second half. How could anyone leave a tie game at half-time?

The Coyote fans went berserk when their team went ahead thirty-four to twenty-eight with less than a minute to go. The Monster fans groaned. There goes the league championship.

No time-outs remaining.

The miracle bag was probably empty.

Dirk Tindall trotted on the field after the kickoff bounced through the end zone for a touchback.

Eighty yards to go for the winning score.

A few disgruntled fans stood up and headed for the aisles.

A sideline pattern went for eighteen yards and the receiver stepped out of bounds stopping the clock.

That sent them back to their seats.

Fourteen yards and across midfield. Out of bounds again.

Incomplete.

Another incompletion.

Third and ten. Seventeen seconds to go.

Dirk hit a receiver on the fly. Out of bounds at the sixteen. Ten seconds on the clock.

Hut, hut, hut!

Dirk dropped back, looked left, looked right. Everyone was covered. Dirk scrambled, bounced off a tackle, nearly losing his jersey in the process, reversed his field, and took off heading for the corner.

The ten. The five.

Two defensive backs converged.

He'd never make it.

Dirk faked right, juked left, and then lowered his head and ran right over them.

"Monsters win!" the public address announcer screamed a bit prematurely. There was still the little matter of an extra point.

The Coyotes called their last time out to ice the kicker.

Penelope held her breath. Kickers made her nervous. Kickers made everyone nervous. She visualized the ball splitting the uprights.

The Gila Monster kicker nonchalantly measured his distance.

Dirk Tindall knelt for the snap.

The snap was good.

The placement was good.

Even the kick was good.

"The Monsters really win!"

A strange phenomenon swept through the adults in the stands as the student body stood and sang the mournful Gila Monster alma mater. It was as though they were all suddenly transported back to their own high school days. Forgotten were the anguished torments of growing up. Remembered were the pleasant moments after the big game when they dispersed with their dates to victory parties and dances. Many an eye filled with tears and brimmed over with the long-ago memories of their youth. The cheer that went up at the conclusion of the alma mater did nothing to dispel the mood.

When Andy climbed back into the stands, Penelope greeted him with a big kiss. "I missed you," she whispered falling into his hug.

Samantha's hand disappeared into Jake's big paw and she snuggled close to him.

Dutch put his arm around Stormy's shoulders.

Penelope told Andy to hug Nora so she wouldn't feel left out, which he did rather enthusiastically.

Even those whose high school days weren't all that far behind them felt it.

A trembling Dave Macklin, who had been working up his nerve all evening, suddenly kissed Lora Lou who kissed him right back with the major league, big-time assurance and affection of an older woman for the younger man who might become her lover.

"Did I ever tell you," Timmy whispered to Kathy, "that you have the cutest nose in the entire world?"

Nose?

Helmet dangling from his hand, sweaty grass-streaked jersey still pulled askew from that last grasping attempt at a tackle, Dirk Tindall accepted the congratulations of teammates, coaches, parents, classmates, and a certain long-legged cheerleader. As the crowd swirled and eddied about him, he turned back to look at the field and saw Regina Pryor for the first time, at least the first time he had really noticed her. He dropped his helmet, the only thing he had fumbled all season long.

Reggie smiled shyly. "Great game," she said.

"Thanks." He tried to smile, but his mouth was suddenly dry.

"Well, would you look at that," Penelope said. She turned to a beaming senior heartbreaker. "Now, we'll just have to find someone for you."

At the Double B after the game, there was no dissipation of sentiment. Samantha enticed Big Jake to the dance floor even though there wasn't a single Johnny Mathis song on the juke-box. Still, dancing to George Strait's "You Look So Good In Love" wasn't at all a hardship. Despite his protestations to the contrary, Big Jake shuffled rather gracefully around the floor. She rested her face against his shoulder and followed, growing more and more intoxicated by the scent of his cologne. If this relationship continued on its present course, Samantha decided she'd buy a gallon or two of the damned stuff. She didn't want him running out of cologne anytime soon. "I think," Samantha whispered, "we should go back to my place and play Dance Hall Girl and the Gunfighter."

Big Jake lurched.

Samantha closed her eyes. "I have a strip poker game on my computer," she murmured.

Jake gulped.

Samantha smiled. That got him.

Penelope watched from the table. "She does look so good in love. I'm happy for her."

"As do you, my dearest," Andy said, "as do you."

Penelope smiled. "What do you think? Would you like to dance . . . or go home?"

"Why don't we drive up to Crying Woman Mountain and look at the lights. We could hold hands and kiss and stuff."

"What a wonderful idea, but I think we should save the stuff for later."

It was a good idea, but unfortunately Andy was not the only male in Empty Creek to come up with it. When they glided into the view area, headlights politely turned off, they recognized the automobiles of a good number of their friends. At this rate, the high school kids would have to find a new place to park.

Andy took Penelope's hand. She leaned against his shoulder. Together, they looked out at the lights of Empty Creek far below. Together, they jumped when a horn blared.

"Sorry," someone muttered.

"Was that Red the Rat?" Andy asked.

"It sounded like him. He and Mattie are probably out of practice at this sort of thing."

"Well, we better keep our hand in."

"Good idea."

They practiced kissing for a while and then moved on to fondling and stroking. Penelope managed some work on her contented purr while Andy cultivated his heavy breathing.

Things were just starting to get interesting when a siren wailed and a police car raced past, heading down the hill, red lights flashing.

"That's Dutch," Penelope cried jumping up and looking back over the seat. "Where's he going in such a hurry?"

Their respective professions kicked in.

"I don't know," the newspaperman said, "but we better follow him."

"Hit it, sweetie," the amateur detective cried pulling her sweater down. "We can practice fooling around later."

———

This game of Dance Hall Girl and the Gunfighter wasn't going at all the way Samantha had planned it. While Big Jake was a more than competent dancer, he was a lousy poker player. After an hour, he was down to his size forty paisley boxer shorts while Samantha was still nearly fully clothed, having removed only her jewelry, shoes, and—blushing modestly—her sweater, crossing her arms instinctively to shield herself before dropping her arms to stare boldly into his eyes. After all, *that* was the point.

Now, Big Jake frowned at the screen, simultaneously sneaking another quick glance at Samantha's creamy white naked shoulders. He thought they were the prettiest shoulders he had ever seen. "Double or nothing?" he asked as he made the mistake of dropping his gaze even lower, quickly averting his eyes—again—but not before Samantha had seen that same wild look, as though he wanted to flee.

Samantha smiled wickedly. "Double or nothing," she agreed quickly, pressing a key and drawing to the inside straight despite her father's sage advice to the contrary. If Big Jake ran, he was damned well going to do it without his trousers.

The card flashed on the screen.

Samantha lost.

Finally, she thought. Samantha wet her lips nervously, stared directly into Big Jake's eyes, and reached demurely for the clasp of the lacy black bra that had been distracting him since winning his fourth hand way back when.

"Wait."

Samantha paused. He'd better not be thinking about my honor. That wasn't the way this dance hall girl played poker.

"Let me do it," Jake stammered.

"All right." That's better. Samantha closed her eyes and waited, trembling, breathing huskily, relishing the faintness that swept through her at his first hesitant fumbling touch at the offending clasp. And then the bra fell away and he was kissing her. Oh, yes, darling, that's just perfect, just the way I dreamed it would be.

And right then, the damned telephone rang.

Well, fudge. Let it ring.

Mmm. Nice. Mmm. Mmm. Very nice.

The answering machine picked up.

"Samantha, are you there? It's Penelope. Someone just took a shot at Mr. Raymond or maybe it was Ms. Vaughn. . . ."

CHAPTER
NINE

Big Mike was definitely disgruntled. It was one thing to stay home from a football game, keeping the bed warm and, incidentally, guarding hearth and home from burglars. He had done his job and quite well at that. Not one miscreant had dared attempt entry and there was a very nice warm spot on the bed that corresponded exactly to the circumference of a twenty-five-pound cat.

But it was quite another matter having to keep heart and soul together by subsisting only on liver crunchies when the tummy was primed for a generous helping of lima beans, particularly when the individual in charge of doling out the lima beans was late, late, late!

And to be left out of the excitement, totally forgotten, like some old shoe . . . well, that was a situation not to be tolerated.

Big Mike voiced his objections vehemently when Penelope and Andy finally rolled in well after midnight.

He meowed vociferously. Someone could have called.

He did his bear imitation, rearing high on his hind legs, and charged Andy, who hastily retreated behind the couch. What if there had been an accident?

The whir of the electric can opener mollified him somewhat and when the lima beans spilled into his bowl, Big Mike decided to accept everyone's apologies, at least while his mouth was full. There were no guarantees for later. Cats shouldn't have to worry about where their friends were and what they were doing.

Andy peeked around the corner. "Is it safe?"

"He's purring."

Mycroft was actually emitting soft growls as he tucked into his long-awaited repast.

"How can you purr and eat at the same time?"

"It's his eating purr as opposed to his after-dinner purr. It's his wild heritage," Penelope explained. "Right now, he thinks he's a lion having a nice zebra steak for dinner."

"Ugh."

"And he's letting his wife know that he appreciates her going out and bringing dinner back. He's also telling her to stay the hell away from his zebra, or in this case, his lima beans."

"I've never been partial to either lima beans or zebra."

"Kudu is very good. So is warthog. I don't know about wildebeest." Such exotic fare had occasionally turned up on the mixed grill lunch at Penelope's favorite restaurant in Dire Dawa, Ethiopia.

"Ugh, ugh, and ugh."

"I think I must have been a lioness in a previous life, but don't get the idea I'm going to drop a warthog under your nose every time you get hungry."

"I'd rather eat rattlesnake."

"Now, that's weird."

"So was tonight."

"What was so weird about kissing me? Have I lost my mysterious allure?"

"That's not what I meant and you know it."

Actually, Andy was more than a little disgruntled in his own right. Since the *News Journal* had been put to bed well before kickoff, the Monsters' triumph over the Coyotes would be old news by the time the next edition came out. He also thought that if shots *had* to be fired, then whoever was doing the shooting should have the decency to do so in a more timely manner, one that suited the *News Journal* deadlines—no later than mid-afternoon on the day before the paper was to come out.

Penelope knew the source of his ire and sympathized, realizing it must be difficult when you were always being scooped by daily newspapers and television and radio news through no fault of your own. Knowing that, Penelope decided to offer a little succor—it wouldn't hurt to play devoted lioness just this once—but was undecided whether to pour him a glass of wine or give him a big hug and a kiss. Wishing the whole time she had a handy warthog, Penelope did both.

That rekindled the passion interrupted by Dutch's siren and it was some considerable time before they were in a state to compare notes on the evening's concluding events. By then, however, they had fallen asleep in each other's arms on the couch and coherent speech was difficult when they finally awakened and stumbled off to bed.

Thus, it was late the next morning before Penelope finally said, "Whowadjudosucating?"

Andy, who had climbed out of bed somewhat earlier and was already on his second cup of coffee, translated this curious phrase as, "Who would do such a thing?" He was unsure, however, whether Penelope meant, "Who would make her get up so early on a Saturday morning?" or "Who would take a shot at Mr. Raymond or Ms. Vaughn?" Choosing the latter, Andy replied, "I don't know."

"Dumwoodardanbernsteinuarge."

Translation: "Some Woodward and Bernstein you are."

"Have some more coffee, my dearest."

"Dinku."

Shortly thereafter, Penelope forced her right eye open. It was followed somewhat reluctantly by her left one. "Well?" she asked.

"Even Woodward and Bernstein wouldn't know yet. It's been less than twelve hours. Perhaps Deep Throat will call."

"It must have been a warning," Penelope said, ignoring his sarcasm.

"Or he is a lousy shot."

"He didn't miss Jack Loomis."

"True, but he was a lot closer."

"If he wanted to kill them, why only one shot?"

"Conserving ammunition?"

"No, it was a warning shot. It had to be."

"But why a warning in the first place?"

"Why, indeed?"

Penelope waited impatiently for Dutch to return her call, filling the time alternately by standing on the sidewalk looking down Main Street at the Lazy Traveller Motel—its neon sign was just barely visible—and actually doing some work by ordering a slew of new novels. When the telephone rang, Penelope grabbed it. "Mycroft & Company."

"This case must really be disrupting your sleep patterns," Dutch said. "Out late, up early."

"It's not quite the way I would plan it. Any news?"

"Just as we thought last night. Too small for a forty-four. It was a thirty-thirty."

Penelope thought briefly of the rifle in Mattie's gun cabinet, but dismissed the suspicion immediately. Mattie and Red had been on Crying Woman Mountain when the incident went down. Still, it was curious that she had weapons of the caliber used in both crimes. . . .

"Did you ever get anything out of them last night?"

"Not much. The Vaughn woman was too upset. Raymond said he'd think about it and let us know."

"Who would want to chase them out of town?"

"Horace Melrose, *if* he's running an insurance scam. Samantha Dale, *if* she's worried about her bank's loan to Melrose. Jake Peterson, *if* he wants to protect his new girlfriend."

"Dutch! You don't really suspect Samantha or Jake?"

"Not really, but people do strange things. Unexpected things."

"But Sam and Jake? I can't believe *that*. Besides, they were at Samantha's last night when I called."

"Doesn't take long to fire a shot and drive home."

"You've been a cop too long."

"Probably," Dutch agreed. "Anyway, you want to take a crack at Raymond and Vaughn? You seem to have established a rapport with them."

Some rapport. Extreme trauma induced by cat and a wild-goose chase to Sedona. "Sure," Penelope said. "I'll let you know."

She hung up and stared at the telephone for a long time.

Samantha and Big Jake? Finally, Penelope looked up and said, "I'm going over to the Lazy Traveller."

"Okay," Kathy said.

The Lazy Traveller Motel offered the finest accommodations in Empty Creek. In fact, it offered the only real commercial accommodations in town, although the city council had been talking for years about trying to attract one of the big hotel chains to Empty Creek. But each time serious negotiations began, the local Not-In-My-Backyard folks—and there were a great many NIMBY's who liked Empty Creek just as it was, thank you very much—flooded the council chambers with vocal, placard-waving protesters, driving nervous hotel executives and attorneys to the safety of Scottsdale or Phoenix, and the business-oriented council members to the Double B for strong drink. And that was why the other cities had so many resort hotels and golf courses and why Empty Creek had the Lazy Traveller Motel.

Not that the Lazy Traveller was bad. It offered one hundred and twenty rooms at reasonable prices. It was built in a horseshoe around an olympic-size pool where many of Empty Creek's finest citizens liked to gather on a hot summer's evening for cool and refreshing drinks.

Both the coffee shop and the restaurant offered early-bird dining specials for snowbirds and the senior citizens who fled the Burning Cactus Golf and Condominium Club, Empty Creek's own retirement community, for an evening on the town.

The video game room was a popular hangout for the young people who thought books made fine doorstops. It was a place where they could wreak havoc on any number of alien invaders with their electronic weaponry.

Entertainment and dancing was offered on Friday and Saturday nights.

In short, the Lazy Traveller Motel was an excellent establishment, presenting a little something for every taste, including the occasional clandestine rendezvous in one of the rooms featuring water beds, lush lavender drapery, nonstop adult entertainment on the television sets, well-stocked honor bars, complimentary bathrobes, and assorted oils and lotions in the bathrooms.

Standing there at the edge of the pool in the bright and warm afternoon sunshine while Big Mike searched for a deck chair to his liking, the events of the night before seemed distant and surreal to Penelope.

Shots fired!

It wasn't a police call often heard in Empty Creek except for New Year's Eve when the town idiots ignored safety and blasted away indiscriminately at the Milky Way, conveniently forgetting the basic precept of gravity if, indeed, they had ever mastered it in the first place.

When that chilling message went out, every police officer on patrol, and some that weren't, responded instantaneously, ignoring for the moment citizen complaints about barking dogs, loud parties, aliens blocking television reception, and the ever-popular fight in a bar.

By the time Penelope and Andy arrived at the Lazy Traveller, Hieronymous Bosch could have set up his easel and found inspiration for a hundred bizarre depictions of the human condition.

The bedlam was bathed in the flashing red lights of a half-dozen police cars with more arriving at one- and two-minute intervals. Having just extinguished a victory bonfire in an oil drum, firefighters from trusty Fire Station Number One popped on by with hoses at the ready just in case.

Geezer World was represented by Cackling Ed who, when he was not guarding the august gates of the retirement community, spent a great deal of time trying to peer down the blouse of any woman younger than himself. Since Ed was older than dirt, that encompassed most of womankind. He had apparently fallen asleep at the dance and, awakening alone, somewhat disoriented, and hearing the continuous wail of sirens, thought that the Luftwaffe—or perhaps the Japanese, he was a little hazy on that point—were bombing Empty Creek and tried to herd the women and children to air raid shelters while singing "It's a Long Way to Tipperary" at the top of his lungs, feeling this rendition was necessary in order to keep up their spirits. Since the women and children in his befuddled state of mind consisted entirely of shotgun-wielding cops, hose-carrying firefighters, and curious guests, Ed was having a difficult time finding any cooperative women and children. Undaunted, Cackling Ed shouted, "Everyone get to Cannon Street Tube Station. You'll be safe there." Since Cannon Street was some six or seven thousand miles distant, anyone who cared probably *could* find safety there.

The management was out in force with the night clerk, the fry cook from the coffee shop, three bus boys, two waiters, a waitress, and the portly part-time motel detective who had also been awakened rather abruptly from a sound sleep in which he had been dreaming of a ham and cheese on rye with a big side order of German potato salad. Had it been a good American po-

tato salad, he might not have ended up in the pool crying for
someone to throw him a life preserver.

While Andy immediately started shooting pictures of the
chaotic scene, Penelope waded into the melee and grabbed
Dutch's elbow. "What's going on?" she cried.

"Shots fired. That's all I know."

"It's a long way to Tipperary . . ."

"Penelope, up here!"

The voice was faint but certainly familiar in the hubbub. Penelope looked up and found Laney and Wally standing at the
second-floor railing. "My God," she exclaimed, "what are you
doing here?"

"Celebrating our anniversary," Laney said, not at all bothered by the fact that she was wearing nothing but the bathrobe
with the Lazy Traveller logo embroidered on the breast
pocket.

"Who won the game?" Wally asked.

"Monsters in a thriller."

"All right!"

"Who won . . . whatever it was you were doing up there?"
Penelope asked nodding toward the purple glow flowing from
the open doorway.

"It's tied," Wally said. "We're going for best two out of
three."

"My money's on Laney."

"Mine, too," Wally said, crinkling his eyes laconically.

Penelope admired his ability to do that. Try as she might,
Penelope had never mastered the technique although she had
spent hours practicing in front of one mirror or another.

"What *is* going on down there?" Laney demanded.

"Not sure yet. Something about a shot."

"Who got shot?"

". . . it's a long way to go."

"I don't know," Penelope shouted cupping her hands for better transmission.

There was a loud splash from the pool.

"Gotta go," Penelope cried. "Have a nice evening."

"Help! I can't swim! Help!"

Good Lord, now what? Penelope ran to the pool.

"Hi, Penelope."

"Hi, Ed," she replied, instinctively pulling the collar of her windbreaker together, although she was taller and he would have had to find and climb a small stepladder to look down her blouse tonight.

"Remember Pearl Harbor," he said tossing a life preserver to the floundering motel detective.

"Remember the Maine," Penelope replied. "What happened?"

"Nazi sympathizer," Ed said pulling on the rope attached to the life preserver. For an old doofer, he was still pretty strong. "He was mumbling about German potato salad, so I shoved him in the pool."

"Why?" Penelope thought it was a reasonable question under the circumstances.

"So he couldn't light the way for the bombers."

"What bombers?"

"Didn't you hear the air raid sirens? The Luftwaffe is bombing London again."

"Ed, that war has been over for more than half a century now."

"I know that. I'm old, but I ain't stupid."

"But . . . oh, never mind." This was the kind of thing that

passed for logic in Empty Creek. "Keep the home fires burning," Penelope said turning to confront more immediate matters.

"It's a long way to Tipperary . . ."

An hysterical Ms. Susan Vaughn was prostrate on a reclining lounge chair, covered by a blanket. "I can't take it anymore," she cried.

At least, Penelope thought, Mycroft couldn't be blamed for this incident, although she took a quick look around just in case. No, he still appeared to be safe at home.

Mr. Richard Raymond paced back and forth beside Susan Vaughn, alternately wringing his hands and trying to stop the violent tic that made him look like a skinny Herbert Lom in the *Pink Panther* movies. "My God, I can't believe it. I just can't believe it."

Since he was otherwise unoccupied at the moment, Penelope took Mr. Raymond's arm and attempted to draw him aside for a quick chat.

Mr. Raymond tugged free. "I can't leave Susan." He knelt and took Ms. Vaughn's hand. "I'm here, darling," he said.

Darling? What happened to 'Ms. Vaughn'? "All right," Penelope said kneeling on the other side of the young woman. "What happened?"

"I can't stand it," Ms. Vaughn cried.

"Someone shot at us."

"It whizzed right past my ear."

Penelope had spent considerable time pulling targets for other shooters on Marine Corps rifle ranges and knew that when a bullet passed overhead, it cracked. But she had never experienced a bullet passing next to her ear. Perhaps those whizzed. She was willing to give Ms. Vaughn the benefit of the doubt.

"Did you see anyone?"

"It was too dark."

"I can't take anymore."

"Perhaps," Penelope said, "she should spend the night in the hospital. The doctors can give her something for her nerves."

"No, if I must die, then I will die at Richard's side."

"Oh, Susan."

"Oh, Richard."

Oh, Barf.

"Wanna snuggle?" Cackling Ed had crept up behind her.

Double barf.

The management of the Lazy Traveller Motel had placated the jittery and overwrought insurance investigators by moving them from the two adjoining rooms they had previously occupied to the Lilac Suite, which also doubled as the Presidential Suite and the Honeymoon Suite when necessary. Since no President had ever visited Empty Creek and very few newlyweds chose to spend their honeymoon at the Lazy Traveller, the suite was most often utilized in its present guise of accommodations for discriminating and consenting adults.

Dutch had further placated the agitated couple by stationing a police officer at their door, a post now occupied by Sheila Tyler who waved cheerfully at Penelope.

Big Mike had apparently found a lounge chair that satisfied his stringent requirements for sun bathing, so Penelope left him and went over to the three old-fashioned telephone booths against the wall next to the pool shop where a young lifeguard cheerfully dispensed towels to the guests and kept a watchful eye on a nubile young thing working on her tan, hoping that she would fall off the deck chair and into the pool, necessitating a rescue and mouth-to-mouth resuscitation. Since she was at least fifteen feet from the edge of the pool, it was probably a forlorn hope.

"Hi," Penelope said as she went to the middle telephone booth.

"Hi." The lifeguard leaned over the counter and watched as Penelope crouched in the telephone booth. "Whatcha doing?"

Penelope had assumed a quite credible sitting position, considering the narrow confines of the telephone booth. Any Marine Corps rifle instructor would be proud of the solid support she offered for the imaginary rifle she now aimed at the door of the room formerly belonging to Ms. Susan Vaughn. "Re-creating," she said.

"Last night, huh? That's where it happened?"

"That's what we think. The angle is right."

"You a cop?"

"No," Penelope said. She breathed in, expelled half, and squeezed the trigger. Bang, crack—or whiz. It had to be a warning shot, Penelope thought. There's no way I would miss at this range, even with a thirty–thirty. She got up and dusted herself off.

"Did you get him?" the lifeguard asked.

"Absolutely."

Big Mike was dozing happily so Penelope left him undisturbed, figuring that Ms. Vaughn was probably not in the right frame of mind for another visit with the big cat. And if he got lonely, he could always make friends with the object of the lifeguard's attentions.

Sheila Norton had a tray with a coffeepot, water pitcher, and appropriate glasses and cups beside her chair. "It's not even noon yet," Sheila said. "This must be important."

"I can get up if I have to," Penelope protested. "I just prefer not to," she added, echoing Melville's *Bartleby the Scrivener*. "Are they up?"

"They were," Sheila said. "They had breakfast delivered about an hour ago, but let me check." She took the empty water glass and placed it against the wall and her ear against the glass. "I don't know. It's pretty quiet in there. You should have been here earlier."

"You didn't!"

"I certainly did. How can I protect them if I don't know what's happening in there? What if some thug climbed in a back window?"

"Well, what did you hear?"

Sheila grinned. "The female watchee was quite enthusiastic about whatever the male watchee was doing."

"That's disgusting," Penelope said. "Let me listen." She took the glass from the pretty police officer and put it to the door. "Nothing. They're probably sleeping. That's what sensible people do at this hour."

She knocked on the door. No reply. She knocked a second time, louder.

"Who is it?" Mr. Raymond called.

"Penelope Warren."

"Stand in front of the peephole so I can see you."

Penelope complied, rolling her eyes at Sheila.

"Is the police officer still there?"

"Yes."

"I want to see her, too."

Penelope stepped aside and Sheila took her place, smiling at the tiny glass eye in the door.

"Okay." A chain rattled, a dead bolt thudded, the doorknob clattered, and the door finally opened.

"Good God!" Penelope exclaimed.

CHAPTER
TEN

"It is rather garish, isn't it?" Mr. Raymond said.

Garish was one word that came to Penelope's mind. Excessive, flamboyant, gaudy, ostentatious, tasteless, tawdry, and vulgar were a few others that popped in. Little wonder that presidents never came to Empty Creek nor blissfully wedded couples to the Honeymoon Suite.

Still . . .

Although she had never been in one—at least not during this lifetime—Penelope thought the Lilac Suite looked exactly the way a lush Victorian bordello might be appointed. Perhaps Laney knew what she was doing after all. Mikey would love it, but it would embarrass the libido right out of Andy.

Although there was evidence that the insurance investigators had enjoyed a quiet breakfast atop the water bed—the trays and coverings still rippled softly—there was no sign of Ms. Vaughn. Penelope ignored the purple garter belt draped over a lamp shade and examined an oil painting above the bed. A number of satyrs leered after Rubenesque young women in various states of undress.

Hmm.

She turned to find Mr. Raymond fumbling with the remote control for the television. He managed to switch it off, but not before Penelope caught a glimpse of something that looked suspiciously like *Debbie Does Dallas*, or even the entire Southwest if the number of intertwined bodies were taken as evidence. As the screen went black, the room was filled with the melody of the "Hawaiian Wedding Song."

"I haven't mastered everything yet," Mr. Raymond said apologetically. More fumbling managed to quiet the "Hawaiian Wedding Song." "There." He turned his attention to Penelope. "Coffee?"

"Please."

Penelope took a seat in an ornately covered armchair in what apparently served as a sitting room portion of the suite, crossed her legs, and arranged her purse primly in her lap.

After serving the coffee—dainty china—Mr. Raymond opened the thick lavender blinds.

"How was Sedona?" Penelope asked.

"Lovely, although unproductive. But, of course, you knew it would be."

Penelope nodded a little sheepishly. "Why did you go then?"

"I thought our absence for a while might give you and the local authorities a little room to work. Did it?"

Perhaps Mr. Raymond wasn't quite the dunce he sometimes appeared to be. "Some," Penelope admitted, "but what about last night?"

"Ah, yes, last night."

Ms. Susan Vaughn emerged from the bathroom, sedately and conservatively clothed, befitting a good insurance investigator. "Good morning," she said cheerfully and then, horrified, spied the garter belt decorating the lamp shade. "How are you, Penelope?" she asked, nonchalantly edging toward the bed. "Oh, quick look!" she cried pointing to the window.

Penelope rolled her eyes, but turned to the window anyway, while Susan whisked the offending garment beneath a pillow.

"What was it, Susan?"

Ms. Vaughn smiled brightly. "Oh, it's just such a lovely desert scene, Richard. I wanted to share. Like Sedona." She crossed the room and stood with him at the window looking out.

The fact that the desert had been there in its present form for quite a number of millennia and would probably remain so for the next few minutes didn't seem to bother Mr. Raymond in the least. If Ms. Vaughn had suddenly noticed the desert's beauty, that was quite all right with him.

"What about last night?" Penelope asked interrupting their viewing of the desert. "Who would want to scare you away from Empty Creek? Whoever took Sir Beauregarde should know that a big insurance company isn't going to just pack up and leave."

"I can't imagine," Mr. Raymond replied, turning reluctantly away from the window—and Ms. Vaughn. "It was just so unexpected."

"And close," Ms. Vaughn offered.

"Well, if you were killed, they'd just send another team of investigators."

Mr. Raymond nodded agreement. "It does defy reason. Perhaps, he or she or they are amateurs."

"Or . . ." Penelope paused. A very interesting possibility had suddenly occurred to her. "Or perhaps he, she, or they are afraid one of you might recognize them. Presumably, you've done this sort of thing before."

"I have," Mr. Raymond said, "many times. Unfortunately, horses are often the target of get-rich-quick schemes by unscrupulous owners and others. But Susan . . . well . . . this is her first time in the field. I've taken her under my wing in a manner of speaking. Showing her the ropes."

And a whole lot more, Penelope thought. "So we must presume you were the target."

"I would say so."

"Hmm." Penelope dug into her purse and removed the sketch. "Do you know this man? He was seen arguing with Jack Loomis a day or two before the murder."

Mr. Raymond took the sketch and examined it carefully. "My goodness."

Bingo!

"What is it, Richard, darling?"

"Something before you came to work for Amalgamated Equine Surety. Back in Arkansas." Mr. Raymond turned to Penelope, still examining the sketch. "I can't be entirely positive. It looks like him though. Yes, I would have to say this is Dr. Wendell P. Oliver."

"Would you excuse me, please," Susan said. She retreated hastily to the bathroom.

Raymond looked after her with concern. "Poor thing. This has been very unsettling for her."

"I can imagine." Penelope thought Susan looked a little pale. It was, no doubt, Post-Being-Shot-At Syndrome.

"Did the coroner's office fingerprint the corpse?"

"I'm sure they did," Penelope replied.

"Perhaps the police should send the prints to Arkansas. Would you ask them?"

"Yes, but why? And who is Dr. Wendell P. Oliver?"

"That's a long story."

Penelope used the same telephone booth to call Dutch and fill him in on the latest revelation from Mr. Raymond. He quickly agreed to send Jack Loomis's fingerprints to Arkansas. Penelope then heard a distinct hem on the other end of the line. "What is it, Dutch? Something new on the Loomis case or Beauregarde?"

"No," Dutch replied. "Nothing like that."

The haw, although unspoken, was loud and followed by another hem.

"What then?"

"It's this commercial thing," Dutch finally blurted. "I don't like the idea of Stormy running around half naked in front of a camera."

"Oh, Dutch, that's sweet of you to worry, but it's just a television commercial. It'll be less revealing than a bathing suit."

"That's true."

"And much better than when her agent forgot to tell her about the nudity clause in the contract."

"I guess."

"And besides, we'll all be there. You know how protective Mycroft is about Stormy. He'll keep her safe from the avarice of television."

"I suppose."

Penelope thought Dutch was sufficiently mollified, but he rang off after saying glumly, "See you tonight."

Tonight was Stormy's dinner party for the Super Bra commercial's director and her costar.

Penelope depressed the hook, dropped another two dimes, and called Laney. "How about a ride this afternoon?"

"Love to," Laney said immediately.

That was the good thing about having Laney as a best friend. You never had to convince her to do anything. She was always ready for a little adventure, even if it consisted only of a horseback ride into the desert.

Penelope hung up, awakened Mycroft, and waved goodbye to Sheila Tyler. Sheila cheerfully brandished her water glass in reply.

Mycroft watched from where his big body overflowed the top of a corral post as Penelope saddled an eager Chardonnay. When everything was ready, Penelope swung easily into the saddle and eased Chardonnay next to the corral.

Big Mike stretched one tentative paw and at the exact right moment stepped gracefully into the saddlebag, spent a moment arranging his back paws firmly, wiggling his butt a little, mewing softly as he propped his front paws on the edge of the saddlebag.

"Ready, Mikey?"

Giddy up.

Penelope had discovered that Mycroft liked riding on the day Chardonnay came to live with them. He had raised such a fuss when he was about to be left behind that Penelope decided to teach him a lesson, plopping him into the saddlebag, fully expecting him to leap out at the first movement.

Fat chance.

There was nothing for it, but to ride by Laney's to show off her equestrian cat. Alexander, of course, raised his own hulla-baloo, probably thinking that anything a cat could do, a dog could do better and so he wound up in the other saddlebag, looking quite satisfied with himself. It was almost as much fun as riding in the car with his face out the window.

And that was how Mikey and Alex wound up on the front page of the *Empty Creek News Journal*, proving that Empty Creek animals could be just as weird as the people.

Although empty once again, the recent storm had rearranged the bed of Empty Creek, depositing some considerable number of rocks and boulders, a testimony to the strength and fury of Mother Nature when aroused. The next storm would probably sweep the creek bed clean again, but Penelope decided to follow the dusty dirt road rather than her usual course along the creek.

From his perch behind her, Big Mike watched the passing scene with his usual avid interest. There were twittering birds to silence with a glare and scurrying lizards to freeze with a twitch of the nose. The fact that the birds and lizards ignored him didn't bother Big Mike one little bit. It was just practice anyway. His place in the great food chain of life in the desert was pretty much limited to herding the occasional mouse or lizard or baby bunny rabbit into the house as a present for Penelope, just to show her he could do it if he really wanted to, but he wasn't about to *eat* one of the little creatures. Good God, just think of the fat content and the cholesterol!

Penelope leaned forward and patted Chardonnay's neck. The golden horse hadn't been out for a good romp since before the storm and she answered Penelope's gesture with a bob of her head and a high-spirited skitter step. Chardonnay, for one, was ready to lay her ears back and run.

Around them, the placid desert teemed with activity as its inhabitants went about nature's business with diligent enthusiasm. But for the occasional opening in the form of a dirt driveway leading to human habitation, they might have been in the midst of the vast Superstition Mountain Wilderness Area. The desert had a propensity to swallow human endeavors whole. Oh, the people and homes were there, but you would never know it. That was what Penelope liked about the desert. The vast solitude was a reminder of one's insignificance in a greater splendor than man could ever achieve.

The splendor, however, was shattered by the persistent yipping of a certain Yorkshire terrier puppy and the irritated complaint of a certain redheaded author. "She won't stay in the saddlebag," Laney cried. "She insists on riding up front."

Kelsey was, indeed, up front, her paws perched on the horn of the western saddle. Alexander, who *was* in his saddlebag, was sulking again at the preferential treatment being accorded this upstart female.

Wally appeared to be asleep in a hammock, but he waggled his fingers in greeting. It was probably a wise move on his part not to get involved in the proceedings.

Penelope edged Chardonnay next to Juliette, Laney's own Arabian named for the first of her long-suffering and oft-ravished heroines, and while the two horses said their howdy-do's, scooped Alex from the saddlebag and deposited him up front. Restored to his rightful place, Alex rewarded Penelope with a few dog kisses and settled in.

Big Mike, who was unconcerned with such fawning political ploys and maneuverings about who was top dog, looked a little disgusted. Dogs were so insecure.

"Well, I'm glad that's settled," Laney said. "We're off, honey bunch sweetie."

"Have fun, dear heart," Wally said from beneath the big cowboy hat that covered his face. He waggled his fingers again in farewell. Somehow, he even managed to do that laconically. Penelope was impressed.

They rode quietly, climbing high into the hills above Empty Creek, following their familiar trails easily. Even Kelsey fell quiet. In point of fact, she looked rather terrified, although she wasn't about to admit it, and clung desperately to the saddle horn, even though Laney held her securely. Alex, an old hand at horseback riding, grinned quite malevolently at his nemesis. Big Mike, lulled by the soft swaying motion, curled up in his saddlebag for a little nap. Call me if anything exciting happens.

It wasn't until they reached their favorite clearing and Laney opened a chilled bottle of chardonnay—no relation to the horse of the same name—that either woman spoke.

"Cheers," Penelope said.

"Here's looking at you, kid," Laney replied in her best Humphrey Bogart imitation.

They clinked their plastic containers and sipped.

"God, we're lucky," Laney said.

Looking down at the desert and a distant Empty Creek, Penelope agreed, but the tranquil setting was not as restorative as she usually found it. From the vantage point high in the hills, it was impossible to tell that a cold-blooded murderer had struck only a few days ago. But Jack Loomis *had* been killed and Sir Beauregarde *had* disappeared and Doctor Wendell P. Oliver *had* moved to the top of the suspect list and *might* be down there right this instant.

Penelope sighed and asked, "Have you ever been in the Lilac Suite?"

"Oh, no. Wally's much too embarrassed for that. It's all I can do to get him to make reservations for the Waterfall Room."

"I can see how the Lilac Suite might be unsuitable for a cowboy."

"Yes, the Waterfall Room is much better. It's supposed to be a jungle setting. All zebra stripes and leopard spots with the sounds of murmuring waters and birdcalls. Lions growling. That sort of thing."

"And you play Jane to his Tarzan, I suppose."

"Puh-lee-zee," Laney protested, "nothing so mundane. I'm Leopard Woman and Wally is the Great White Hunter."

"They're called professional hunters now for political correctness."

"Whatever. Is it lovely?"

"Is what lovely?"

"The Lilac Suite, of course."

"In its own fashion. Mr. Raymond and Ms. Vaughn seem to like it. They probably don't get such accommodations in the normal course of their investigations."

"They probably don't get shot at either."

"It's most curious . . ." Penelope's voice trailed off.

Alex edged a little closer to Penelope. He was getting older by dog standards and his hearing might not be as good as when he was in his prime. Kelsey followed just to make sure she didn't miss anything. Big Mike, whose hearing wasn't at all impaired, stayed right where he was and continued his ablutions.

"What's curious?"

"Raymond recognized the sketch. It appears to be one Wendell P. Oliver, a vet specializing in horses. He was sent to jail in Arkansas some ten years ago."

"Are you going to say what I think you're going to say?"

Penelope nodded. "He killed horses for the insurance money."

Dinner was for ten, just about the limit considering that Stormy and Dutch's house had only one bathroom. In addition to Penelope and Andy and Laney and Wally, there were a director, a costar, and the costar's girlfriend. Always a matchmaker, Stormy had invited Nora Pryor to fill in the last spot.

Penelope was pleased to see that the commercial's director, an Englishman, had not succumbed to Hollywood fashions. Instead of a shirt open nearly to his waist and a heavy collection of gold chains hanging around his neck, Anthony Lyme-Regis wore a threadbare Harris Tweed and a checked dress shirt with an ascot billowing nattily about his throat. Instead of tight designer jeans and Gucci loafers, Lyme-Regis wore rumpled brown slacks and scuffed lace-up oxfords. Nothing in his ensemble matched. In short, he looked like an Englishman who had popped down to his local for a pint or two with his mates.

Stormy's costar, a Fabio-like Hunk, whose name Penelope missed, more than made up for Lyme-Regis, however. He was disgustingly resplendent in all of the Hollywood accoutrements. Indeed, the gold chains were the only thing of substance about him, Penelope discovered when the Hunk asked Laney if her novels were fiction or nonfiction.

Although it was a social occasion, Andy played reporter for a time, interviewing Lyme-Regis briefly for the story he would write and, incidentally, pissing the Hunk off when he failed to record any of the actor's comments which sent the Hunk off for a dose of adoration from his girlfriend whose thighs were just a little too plump for the tight leather miniskirt she wore.

Dutch renewed a sulk every time he looked at the Hunk who would be playing opposite his beloved Stormy. Penelope tried to bring him out of it by asking, "Have you heard anything from Arkansas yet?"

"I just sent the inquiry today."

"Well, aren't they open on the weekends? Eternal vigilance, all that sort of thing?"

"Have you ever been to Arkansas?" Dutch replied before going back to sulking.

Lyme-Regis, delighted to discover that Penelope owned a mystery bookstore, entered into a spirited discussion of the respective merits of Dashiell Hammett, Raymond Chandler, and Ross MacDonald and their influences on the hard-boiled school.

Penelope expounded right back, drawing Nora into the conversation who was then encouraged to explicate local history for Lyme-Regis.

Stormy, always the gracious hostess, moved easily among the groups whenever it appeared a conversation was about to lag, even managing to make the Hunk preen and puff his chest, which sent the girlfriend with the too-plump thighs over to sulk with Dutch.

What with all the sulking going on, however, Stormy's dinner party was pretty much a disaster until after the Hunk and his girlfriend left. Penelope figured they were probably staying in the Waterfall Room. She hoped the gurgling waters and the birdcalls kept them awake.

Over brandy—and a nice port for Lyme-Regis—the director

suddenly broke into a rendition of "Take It Off, You Zulu Warriors," which he explained was an old rugby drinking song.

Penelope had once seen England play France at Twickenham and had thoroughly enjoyed the French fans who ran across the field carrying a banner that said, "Remember Agincourt," so she quickly joined in, although she didn't know the words. It didn't really matter since the song seemed to consist entirely of bellowing, "Take It Off, You Zulu warriors." But she declined to follow Lyme-Regis's example, who was energetically disrobing as he sang.

Nora was aghast as she watched her cultured dinner companion bob and weave and undress while the others clapped in unison and bawled, "Take It Off . . ." Oh, what the hell. Her face a much darker shade of red than her strawberry blond hair, Nora joined the festivities. ". . . You Zulu Warriors!"

When Lyme-Regis was down to his underwear—to the complete astonishment of his audience, no one had expected him to get that far—Penelope stepped in with the San Diego State fight song and then the "Marine's Hymn."

Wally was a hit with a bawdy version of "She Wore a Yellow Ribbon."

Andy, having had a little too much brandy, fell asleep on the couch during charades.

Nora stopped blushing long enough to accept Lyme-Regis's offer of a nightcap and to say, "Well, this was certainly more stimulating than working on the second edition of my book."

And that was that.

Penelope was restless and bored, an intolerable situation after what had turned out to be such a spirited evening. She was ready to play through the night and wondered if her friends were equally afflicted. If she had but known. . . .

Samantha and Jake had skipped the poker preliminaries and proceeded directly to the main event while Johnny Mathis crooned softly in the background.

Mr. Raymond and Ms. Vaughn had adjourned to a couch, finding—once again—that the water bed made them quite seasick. After a brief respite to allow the dizziness to subside, Mr. Raymond renewed his lecture on the respective roles of underwriter and investigator.

Stormy was conducting a dress rehearsal for the impending Super Bra shoot. Her audience of one, while appreciative, was growing quite impatient to remove the object of the commercial.

Laney and Wally were busy plotting out what Amanda and Bret might do after he rescued her from the gallows. To their mutual delight, they found there were any number of possibilities, including one inventive scenario at the edge of a remote desert water hole.

A giggling and only slightly embarrassed Kathy displayed the bosom that was shortly to launch a thousand Faustian space ships in her deranged poet's sudden inspiration for a futuristic updating of *The Iliad*. So much for a brief flirtation with the cutest little nose.

Lora Lou Longstreet had not known quite how tiring it could be to pose for a painting nor how marvelous it could be when the artist laid down his brush and gently massaged stiff and aching muscles to tingling life again.

Nora and Tony closed the Double B in rapt conversation, straying only occasionally from the twin topics of local history and the nature of directing. No reference was made to Zulu warriors, although Nora found herself regretting that Penelope had halted the proceedings at the penultimate moment. . . .

Penelope growled softly.

Andy failed to stir. What an old poop. He had slept all the way home, awakened long enough to stumble into the house, and promptly fallen asleep on the couch.

Leopard Woman growled louder.

The Professional Hunter began snoring.

Leopard Woman raked her claws softly along the Professional Hunter's arm. That stopped the snoring, but still failed to awaken the Professional Hunter's sense of danger. Good Lord, he might sleep through an elephant stampede.

With a ferocious howl, Leopard Woman pounced.

That got him.

Although initially startled by the sudden entrance of another predator, Big Mike, who had always thought Penelope would make a pretty decent cat all things considered, approved of her direct approach.

CHAPTER
ELEVEN

Leopard Woman reluctantly dragged herself from her lair. She was pleasantly tired from the hard night's cavorting with the Professional Hunter who, once pounced upon, responded as any self-respecting Professional Hunter who was still drinking the client's whiskey, should. The P.H. even added a new variation or two for L.W.'s consideration, gaining her instant approval. The resulting caterwauls frightened a coyote who happened to be passing through the backyard at the time and sent Mycroft to scratching furiously at the bedroom door demanding to be let in. Someone needed protection and he was just the cat to provide it, although entry was denied for the longest time.

Now, as L.W. pointed herself toward the kitchen and the life-restoring properties of caffeine, she mumbled, "It's all your fault, Mikey."

Mikey, who hadn't been read his Miranda warning, took his Constitutional rights under the Fifth Amendment anyway and remained silent. He wasn't about to provide the slightest meow, even for Penelope, that could be used against him.

"If you hadn't knocked those other scripts to the floor, Stormy would have done *Warrior Women on Mars* or *Slaves of the Exosphere* and we wouldn't have to go watch her film a Super Bra commercial."

In reality, it was Penelope who had recommended *Vanessa Diamond, P.I.*, a minor point of fact now completely forgotten. Such were the vagaries of Penelope's sometimes selective memory, but Andy had already stumbled off home so Penelope couldn't blame him.

After several cups of coffee, however, and a brisk walk down to the barn to feed Chardonnay, Penelope had mellowed enough to think that watching the Super Bra filming might be fun.

It was and, then again, it wasn't.

Penelope and Big Mike barged through the library door and interrupted Take Four.

"Cut," Anthony Lyme-Regis said. It came out as kind of a croak.

"You're late," Stormy said, "and you interrupted a perfectly good take."

"Well, I'm sorry," Penelope replied with a little testiness of her own. "Aren't you supposed to have a red light on or something?"

"Good morning, dear lady," Lyme-Regis said. "Pay Stormy no mind. She's having a few creative differences at the moment. Ten-minute break, everybody."

"Good morning," Penelope said. "I'm sorry to be late, but I didn't sleep well last night."

"I can well imagine," Lyme-Regis replied. "I have the most horrendous headache. It's the port, don't you know. It's always the port."

Penelope thought there was little visible evidence of a hangover. The director was turned out just as he had been the previous evening, although his wardrobe was completely altered—different tweed jacket, a tattersall shirt, paisley ascot, tan slacks—all perfectly rumpled. She believed there must be special tailors for Englishmen only.

"Hi, Penelope," Nora said. "Tony's letting me be the Script Person." She held an elaborately bound folder in her hand although as far as Penelope could tell it contained only a single page. "He missed his cue again, Tony."

"It's a motivational problem," the Hunk said. "What is my motivation?"

"You turn the corner and see this lovely, exquisite vision," Lyme-Regis replied. "Slowly, you lower the book, staring at the most beautiful creature you have ever seen."

"Yes, yes, I know all that, but what is my motivation?"

"Just remember, the nicest things happen in a library." Lyme-Regis gulped several aspirin tablets.

"Oh."

Penelope turned away to hide her smile. It seemed that Stormy wasn't the only one having a few creative differences.

For a closed set—Dutch had insisted upon having as few human beings of the male persuasion present as possible—the Empty Creek Public Library teemed with people. In addition to the camera crew, makeup, lighting technicians, grips, and best boys—whatever they were—Stormy seemed to have invited a great many of the female populace in and around Empty Creek.

Leigh Kent, always the perpetual favorite in any Sexy Librarian Pageant that might be held, waved cheerfully from her desk. Kathy hovered near Stormy as her makeup was freshened. Samantha Dale watched with interest as lighting was adjusted.

"Any news yet?" Penelope asked.

"It's still Arkansas," Dutch replied.

"Whatever that means."

"It means that they're all out having chitlins for Sunday brunch," Dutch said uncharitably.

"Boy, one little underwear commercial really sets you off. I think Stormy looks beautiful."

Stormy *was* stunning. She wore an elegant velvet evening skirt and heels. She appeared for all the world like a woman who, getting ready for a formal night on the town, had suddenly had an irresistible urge to rush down to the old public library to check on some nagging quotation or another. She just forgot to put her blouse on before dashing off. Of course, the Super Bra did enhance her bosom considerably.

"Overexposed," Dutch insisted.

"You can't see a thing."

"Ha!" Dutch stalked off.

Stormy came over to apologize. "Nothing's gone right today. He has one simple line and he's fluffed it every time," she said shaking her head. "And Dutch is in a tizzy. Does this look so bad?"

"Of course not, Sis, you look terrific. It's just what I'd wear to the library."

"See!" Stormy shouted at Dutch.

He put his hands over his ears and closed his eyes.

"Men! I don't know why I invited him. Where's Andy?"
"He was too embarrassed to come and watch."

"Ready on the set."
"Everybody quiet."
"Camera."
"Speed."
The slate was inserted in front of the camera. Take Five was written in chalk. The clapper clapped.
"Action."
The Hunk tripped. "Sorry, Anthony."

Take Six. The Hunk garbled his line.
Take Seven. A helicopter flew over the library.
Takes Eight, Nine, and Ten. More ambient noise.
Take Eleven. Stormy burst out laughing. "He looks like the book's going to bite him."
"Lose the book."
"Really, Anthony, we must talk. Why are we in a library rather than a park or a gas station?"
"It's because you're a stupid ignorant twit and you don't want to be."
"Oh."
Take Twelve. Slate. Clap.
The Hunk stopped.
Stormy stopped.
"Do you come here a lot?"
Lyme-Regis rolled his eyes again. How difficult was it to memorize five words—five-simple-easy-little-words like "Do-you-come-here-often?"
"Of course, the nicest things happen in a library."

Stormy giggled.

Mycroft poked a furry little face from beneath Stormy's gown.

"Cut."

"Now where did you come from?" Penelope asked.

Who, me?

"Lose the cat, please."

With a certain cat now banished from the immediate vicinity of the set, Penelope and Big Mike joined Samantha at a large coffeepot set up next to a table laden with a variety of pastries and donuts. "And how is Empty Creek's favorite bank president today?" Penelope asked, eyeing a cheese Danish.

"Just fine," Samantha replied, "although it's certainly been an interesting weekend."

"Until now."

"Yes," Samantha said staring at the object of Penelope's scrutiny. "It's not quite what I expected."

"That's a very polite way of putting it."

"We could share it," Penelope said. "That way each of us would gain only five pounds instead of one of us gaining ten pounds."

"An excellent idea."

With cups of coffee in one hand and their shared Danish booty in the other, the two women left Big Mike crouched beneath the pastry table contemplating his revenge on the surly Best Boy who had said, "Lose the cat," and retreated to a library table next to the beginning of the fiction section.

"Have you discovered anything more about the shot?" Samantha asked.

"Not much. I talked with them again yesterday, but I can't

imagine who might want them out of town. Except you, of course."

"Yes, I wish they *would* go away, but you know I was at home."

"Too bad. In some of the best mystery novels, the client is the perpetrator of the evil deed. What *were* you doing when I called? You sounded like you had just finished running the Empty Creek Marathon."

Samantha smiled enigmatically. "If you must know, I was teaching Jake how to play poker."

"The musical chairs version, I suppose."

"Something like that."

Penelope put that comment aside for further investigation at a later date. The conservative bank president might have hidden depths worthy of exploration. "We may have identified the mysterious stranger who argued with Loomis outside The Tack Shack. Raymond said he was a vet convicted of murdering thoroughbred horses in Arkansas. We're waiting to hear."

Samantha shuddered. "How could anyone kill a horse?"

The afternoon dragged on. William Goldman was right. Moviemaking, even a commercial, *was* boring. There was endless preparation for each shot—lighting had to be adjusted, everyone looked through the viewfinder to frame the shot, makeup was touched up, Lyme-Regis huddled with Stormy and the Hunk after each flub, tempers were held in check by a single frayed strand of a none-too-strong string, precariously close to snapping.

"Is this as dull as I think it is?" Nora asked, trying hard to stifle a yawn.

"More so," Penelope answered. "I'm glad the artistic muse peed in Stormy's gene pool and not mine."

"That's certainly graphic."

"But apt."

Nora yawned again. "Excuse me."

"Out late?"

"Tony and I stayed at the Double B talking forever. Reggie grounded me."

"That's a switch."

"Well, Dirk did bring her home exactly on time."

"So, young love strikes."

"He's asked her to the President's Ball."

"She certainly stood out from the rest of the girls. How is it working out with Mattie?"

"It's been terrific. Reggie's learned a lot. I think she has a real chance to win. It's been pretty exciting, although Mattie sometimes seems . . ."

"Script Person!" Lyme-Regis shouted.

"Have to run," Nora said. "Isn't he adorable?"

Detectives Larry Burke and Willie Stoner stood at the library door with their noses pressed against the glass like two little boys at the window of a candy store.

Penelope saw them and since they were between takes at the time, waved for them to come in. They motioned for her to come out. Because she was dying to know what they were doing, chalking up the overtime on a Sunday, Penelope complied.

"Phew," Penelope said. They smelled like horses and horse by-products. "Where have you been?"

"Where ain't we been?" Tweedledee said disgustedly.

"That horse is gone," Tweedledum said, "if he was ever here, which I'm beginning to think he wasn't."

"Tell Dutch to come out, would you?"

"Why don't you just come in?"

"Dutch said he'd make us crossing guards if we went in there."

Oh, bother. Since Stormy would shortly be seen on national television in all her feminine glory—if the commercial from hell was ever completed—Penelope couldn't see why Dutch was making such a fuss. Men. Shaking her head, she turned and yelled through the door. "Dutch!"

"You almost done in there, Boss?" Tweedledee asked when Dutch joined the little group on the library steps.

"We'll never be done. Whatcha got?"

"We been to every stable, barn, ranch in the county. We looked at every horse there is. That horse is gone."

"Then, start in on the next county. I want that horse found."

"Aw, boss, even them insurance investigators say the horse is probably dead."

"Where did you see them?" Penelope asked.

"They've been out looking, too. Peggy was showing them around. They're pretty nice."

How curious, Penelope thought. I would think they'd be trying to prove malfeasance on the part of Horace Melrose, rather than attempting to find Sir Beauregarde. But either way, Amalgamated Equine Surety would not have to pay off on the policy. At least, they weren't sitting around the Lilac Room getting into mischief.

Take Twenty-Three.

Dutch took matters in his own hands, pushed the Hunk out

of the way, grabbed a book from a shelf, took a deep breath, and walked slowly around the corner of the bookshelf.

"Wait," the cameraman hollered.

Dutch ignored him.

"Camera," Lyme-Regis cried.

"We got speed," the cameraman said. "We're rolling."

"Action!"

Finally.

Dutch turned the corner around the bookshelves, stopped. He was perfectly transfixed, captivated by the lovely woman before him. Penelope imagined it was the same look that had been on his face the first time he saw Stormy, although she couldn't be sure since she had been incarcerated in the holding tank of the Empty Creek Police Department at the time.

"Do you come here often?" he said with perfect timing.

"Of course," Stormy replied meeting his eyes with a mesmerized gaze of her own. "The nicest things happen in a library."

"Cut. That's a take," the director said, "let's play it back."

"What about me?" the Hunk asked plaintively. "I'm ready now."

"Oh, sod off."

Everyone gathered around the monitor and watched anxiously as the scene began. They held their collective breath as Stormy and Dutch appeared on the screen. They mouthed the lines as they were spoken. They waited for a book to fall, an airplane to land just behind Stormy, Big Mike to rub against Dutch's leg, spontaneous combustion, an Act of God.

Nothing but perfection.

"That's definitely a wrap!"

Stormy took Dutch's hand and they bowed to thunderous applause.

"I'm calling my agent," the Hunk said.

"I'm going home," Penelope said.

Penelope dropped a few peppermint candies for Chardonnay in her pocket, filled a Baggie with carrots and lettuce for the bunny rabbits and, accompanied by Big Mike, made the short trek down the path to the barn.

The bunnies were there, waiting patiently, anticipating their store-bought goodies.

But Chardonnay wasn't.

In a trance, Penelope emptied the Baggie for the grateful rabbits and, then, ignoring the evidence, crossed the creek bed, calling plaintively, "Char, Chardonnay!" Standing at the edge of what now seemed a hostile and impenetrable desert, she listened desperately for an answering whinny. "Chardonnay!"

Biting her lip, Penelope returned to Chardonnay's pen and stood for a long time staring at the neatly latched gate. Even if Chardonnay had somehow managed to open the gate, she hadn't stopped to refasten it.

Chardonnay was gone.

Except for Andy and Stormy, no one in the room had ever seen Penelope cry before. But, even now, they saw only the residue of her emotions, reddened eyes that glistened until they filled to overflowing and a tear or two slowly coursed down her cheeks to be dabbed away with a tissue.

Only Mycroft knew the depths of Penelope's anguish. He had stayed close to her all the way back to the house, followed her into the bedroom, and paused only momentarily when she threw herself on the bed and cried uncontrollably, great sobs shaking her chest.

Hopping easily on the bed, Mikey silently edged close to her, crept forward, and nestled close against her, as he always did on those rare occasions when she was sick or troubled and needed the comforting companionship of a close friend, and waited, a reassuring paw snaking out to touch her arm. It was the consolation that only an understanding and sensitive cat could offer. Even in sickness or distress, Penelope could protest and argue with a human companion, but there could be no denial of Big Mike's love and concern. Not now, not ever.

Even as she tried to pull herself together and only cried all the harder, Penelope felt and appreciated Big Mike's presence, but she could not stop the racking sobs. The sense of loss and violation was too great. She had not lost a piece of property like the time her radio had been stolen from the Jeep; she had lost a trusted friend.

"Oh, Mikey, Chardonnay's gone." Penelope turned on her side and Big Mike crawled forward, allowing her to embrace him tightly. He nuzzled her neck with his cold nose as if to say, Don't worry. We'll find her.

They stayed like that for what seemed like a long time, but was no more than ten minutes. As her sobs subsided, Big Mike purred, one more way of letting her know that he cared and understood.

"Thanks, Mikey. Now, let's get to work."

Together, they went to the telephone and called Dutch.

While they waited for the police response, Penelope and Big Mike sat quietly on the couch. Mikey, still dismayed by Penelope's sudden emotional collapse, climbed into her lap. But as she stroked his fur gently and listened to his comforting purr, her grief at Chardonnay's disappearance turned to anger. By the time she heard Andy's key turn in the lock, she had worked up a pretty damned good mad.

"Hi, how was the commercial?"

"Somebody stole Chardonnay," Penelope wailed. Her anger slunk off again as she recounted what had happened. Penelope hated crying, but she couldn't help it, and made the shoulder of Andy's shirt wet as he patted her back gently, helplessly.

Tweedledee and Tweedledum arrived first. They were followed almost immediately by Dutch and Stormy.

Not far from the gate of Chardonnay's pen, they found a crumpled cellophane wrapper from a peppermint candy. It could not have been one Penelope dropped. She was always careful to place the wrappers in a pocket and dispose of them later back at the house.

But that was the sum total of the evidence they found.

"Who knew your horse liked peppermint candies?" Stoner asked. Both Stoner and Burke had been so solicitous of her loss that Penelope couldn't bear to think of them as Tweedledum and Tweedledee, at least for the moment.

Penelope shrugged. "All of my friends. Anyone who read Andy's story about the equestrian cat and dog."

It turned into a brainstorming session.

"All right," Dutch said. "Let's look at the facts of the case. We have one dead trainer, two missing horses, an apparent warning shot fired at one or another of two insurance investigators, and an undercover FBI agent running around for reasons as yet undetermined. What does it mean?"

"It means we don't know from shinola," Burke said.

"All right," Dutch repeated. "How is it all connected?"

"Beats me." This offering was from Stoner.

So much for charity. Penelope decided to go back to referring to the detectives as Tweedledee and Tweedledum.

"So, what are we going to do?"

"Wait and see."

Some strategy that was.

Andy insisted—something he rarely did—that Penelope and Big Mike spend the night at his place. "If we stay here, you're just going to brood. You need a change, if only for one night."

Looking down at Chardonnay's empty pen, Penelope frowned and nodded. The sight was just too painful.

Damn it.

Someone was going to pay for this.

But who?

CHAPTER
TWELVE

Monday morning.
"Fore!"

Despite the warm and calming presence of both Andy and Big Mike flanking her, Penelope awakened early to the golfer's warning cry of an errant shot, disoriented, and with her great loss burning a hole in the pit of her belly.

Monday morning.

Kathy had that damned early class in Milton. It was time to get up, go to work, open Mycroft & Company, cheerily sell books to her customers, replenish stock, perhaps change the display in the window, and find a killer—*and* whoever took Chardonnay.

Penelope carefully and slowly eased herself from bed, disturbing Big Mike, but he made no protest, only yawned, stretched, and followed her to the kitchen of Andy's town house, past the picture window that overlooked the fourteenth fairway.

That was the reason they rarely spent nights at Andy's.

There were just too many people out early, pursuing their passion of hitting little white—and occasionally lime and fluorescent orange—balls into various hard-to-find places.

Penelope had barely poured the first cup of coffee when Andy padded into the kitchen and embraced her from behind. "I'm worried about you. You're up far too early for the woman I love and cherish."

Penelope smiled ruefully at his reflection in the window. "Thank you. That makes me feel a little better."

"Only a little?"

"A lot, actually," Penelope said, discovering that she could pour coffee even while totally encumbered by his clasp.

"Good." He squeezed harder.

Penelope closed her eyes and relaxed in his arms. "Don't you want your coffee?"

"Later," he said, slipping the robe from her shoulders.

"Someone will see."

"I don't care." He kissed each of her shoulders.

"What if a golf ball comes flying through the window?"

"Unplayable lie. Free drop, no closer to the hole."

"How do you know that? You don't play golf, even though you live on the course."

"I will someday. You will, too. We'll have our own golf cart."

"I'll give you an hour to stop that," Penelope murmured.

"What?"

"That thing you're doing with your fingers."

"This?"

"Yes, that. Fifty-nine minutes to go and then I'm calling Nine-One-One."

"Then I'd better hurry."

Once more, a morning wasn't starting out the way Penelope

had planned, but this was a much nicer way to get the heart started than caffeine, although when Andy eased her to the floor, the cold linoleum against her back nearly gave her palpitations. All in all, it was almost enough to make her forget Chardonnay.

Almost.

"Fore!"

A long time later, Penelope said, "I have to go to work."

"Put a sign in the window. 'Gone Fishing.' "

"I can't. I'm being held prisoner by a dirty young man."

"We'll do it later then."

"Okay."

"We're taking the day off and spending it together. No arguments."

"I love it when you act macho, but I have to fight crime." Penelope frowned and bit her lip as memories of recent pleasure disappeared. "You know, I should be feeding Chardonnay right now."

"I'll help you find her. I never get to see you in action."

"I'd like that," Penelope said. "I just don't feel like being alone today." She kissed him on the lips.

"What's that for?"

"Just for being such a good guy."

"Aw, shucks, ma'am."

"And, as a reward, we can play dangerous female criminal tonight."

"But you turned the handcuffs in."

Penelope flashed her ever so wicked smile. "We'll improvise."

———

Penelope tossed Andy the keys to the Jeep. "You drive."

"Where are we going?"

"The bookstore first. Kathy will be there by now and wondering where I am. Then, we'll call Dutch and see if we've heard anything from Arkansas." Penelope smiled again. "And then, we'll improvise."

As they drove into town, Penelope glanced at Andy out of the corner of her eye, feeling all warm and fuzzy. He certainly knew how to make a girl feel better. Big Mike had been largely ignored during the morning's activities but had apparently forgiven everyone concerned because he was now standing with his back paws on Penelope's legs and his front paws on the dashboard as he watched the passing scene. Every so often, however, he glanced back at Penelope as if to say, Cool.

Both Penelope and Andy felt more than a little guilty as Kathy rushed to greet them, a bag of peppermint candies in her hand. "I was worried," she cried. "I've been calling and calling."

"I'm sorry," Penelope said. "I should have called you. I was distracted. Someone stole Chardonnay last night."

"Oh, Penelope, that's awful. I'm so sorry." Now, Kathy stared guiltily at the peppermints. "I thought it would be nice to have a bowl of candies for the customers."

Penelope nodded. "It's all right. We're going to get Char back," she said with a determination she didn't really feel. "The peppermints will be a nice touch. And, we're going fishing."

"Fishing?"

"That's a euphemism for taking the day off. With pay. Make up a sign while I call Dutch."

"But there's so much to do."

"You work too hard. I'm sure your brain's perfectly addled from all that *Paradise Lost*. Mine always was. And just wait until you get to *Areopagitica*."

"I've read that," Andy said. " '. . . who kills a Man kills a reasonable creature, God's image; but he who destroys a good Book, kills reason itself, kills the Image of God, as it were in the eye.' "

"Very good, Andy," Penelope said. "*Areopagitica* is a wonderful document, but dense, don't you think?"

Kathy looked from Penelope to Andy with some considerable degree of amazement. Conversations were often difficult to follow in the confines of Mycroft & Company, but the swift leaps from Chardonnay to fishing to *Paradise Lost* to Milton's impassioned defense of free speech sent Kathy scurrying to the back room for sign materials. If this was the way *her* day would go, fishing was an excellent idea.

"Not at all," Andy replied. "It expresses the very tenets of a free press most eloquently."

"Nearly impenetrable."

"Penelope!"

"I'm teasing, sweetie. It is most eloquent."

"Whew. That's a relief."

"In fact, perhaps we could have a few people over for a discussion of *Areopagitica* tonight."

"It's not *that* eloquent."

"Damn," Penelope said replacing the telephone. "Still no word from Arkansas. I guess we'll have to make it up as we go."

"How about starting with an early lunch at the Duck Pond?"

"We have Mycroft with us."

Everyone at the Duck Pond—it was the best Mexican restaurant for miles around and took its name from, quite naturally, the duck pond adjoining its patio—liked Big Mike, but he had been permanently banished from its dining room after an unfortunate incident involving a belligerent duck and the mayor's rather stout wife. Penelope still thought it was the duck's fault entirely and would not have been at all dismayed if duck tacos suddenly appeared on the menu.

As they crossed the street to the Double B, Penelope said, "I should have thought of this earlier and brought a picture of Chardonnay."

"No problem. I'll have camera print a batch of the one in the paper."

"Would you? I'll pay."

"Nonsense. It will be the *News Journal*'s contribution to the fight against crime. I'll even print it on the front page until we get Chardonnay back."

Andy went to the pay telephone in the back as Big Mike hopped on his stool next to a clean-shaven Red the Rat.

"What's all this, Red?" Penelope asked fingering a stack of videotapes on the bar.

"Aw, Mattie likes Robert Redford. All we do is sit around and watch old Robert Redford films."

"All?"

"Well, maybe not all. . . ."

Penelope read through the titles. *Butch Cassidy and the Sundance Kid, All the President's Men, The Electric Horseman, Three Days of the Condor, Rio Grande, Barefoot in the Park.*

Penelope backtracked. "Wait a minute. He wasn't in *Rio Grande*. That's John Wayne."

Red grinned. "Yeah, that was for me. I put my foot down.

Told her right out that we was gonna fit a little of The Duke into the program."

"That's a lot of movies."

"Ain't so bad. Spread 'em out over the weekend, and you can smooch through the boring parts."

"Even *Rio Grande?*"

"Well, no, Penelope," Red said. The exasperation in his voice was evident. " 'Course not The Duke. John Wayne ain't never boring."

Penelope refrained from bringing up some of The Duke's clunkers. Instead, she said, "Someone stole Chardonnay yesterday. Keep an eye out for her, would you, Red?"

"Aw, Penelope, I'm real sorry. I know how close you are to that horse. Same as me and Daisy."

"Thanks, Red."

"Horse thieves oughta be hung," Red declared vehemently. "Like the old days. That'd teach 'em."

"What next?" Andy asked after lunch. "The photographs won't be ready until late this afternoon."

Fishing seemed like an excellent idea, simply because Penelope was stumped and her capacity for ad-libbing strained. As always, she turned to Big Mike for inspiration, but he was curled up on his bar stool next to Red, sound asleep. While a nap might be a good idea, Penelope didn't find it at all inspirational.

"I'm thinking," Penelope stalled. "I'm thinking."

Her attention was drawn to the stack of videotapes on the bar. That was a better idea than fishing, particularly since Penelope didn't have the foggiest notion of how to go about mounting a fishing expedition. Rent a good movie, make some popcorn. . . .

Wait just a damned minute!

What had her horoscope said this morning? Follow your instincts.

"Let's get out of here," she said.

"Where are we going?"

"I'll tell you later."

"I never know what's going on. Sometimes I think I should find a normal woman."

"Oh, yeah, like who?"

"Well, like . . . like . . . well . . . someone."

"Sweetie, I'm as normal as they come in Empty Creek. And interesting besides."

"That's true."

Penelope went to the bar and stroked Big Mike gently. She had long ago learned to awaken him slowly with no sudden moves. "Wakey, wakey, Mikey."

"Damned shame about your horse," Red said.

"We'll find her."

"Hanging's too good. Oughta horsewhip 'em, and *then* hang 'em."

"Give Mattie our best when you see her."

"I'll do it. She's over to Carefree this afternoon, giving some lessons at the riding club. Say, how many movies did this Robert Redford make, anyway?"

"Quite a lot, but he's taken up directing now. See you later, Red."

"Okey dokey."

"Are you going to tell me what's going on?" Andy asked when they were settled in the Jeep.

"I'm following my instincts."

"And I'm supposed to find that reassuring?"

"We're going out to Mattie's," Penelope whispered conspiratorially, although there was no one within a hundred yards of the Jeep.

"Why?"

"Didn't you see those movies?"

"What movies?"

"Really, some investigative reporter you are. Mattie and Red watched *The Electric Horseman.*"

"So?"

"Don't you see? Robert Redford steals a very famous horse and rides off into the wilderness to set it free."

"Some wilderness if Jane Fonda can find him."

"Whatever. It could be that Mattie did the same thing, taking Beau to set him free."

"Why did she kill Loomis then? Matilda Bates is not a killer. And what about Chardonnay?"

"I don't know, but I find the coincidence of that particular movie showing up right now rather disturbing. Mattie told me she hated the training methods Loomis used. And, she does have a forty-four revolver. Poor Red. What if Mattie *is* the murderer? It'll kill Red, too."

It was eerily quiet at Mattie's small ranch with the silence broken only by the buzz of disturbed flies and the occasional snorted greeting of one horse or another, each lazing their day away in the warm sun.

Feeling guilty the entire time about her suspicions of Mattie, Penelope led Andy and Big Mike past each of the pens where they stopped to examine each horse carefully, whether or not it resembled Beau or Char in the slightest. Some skittered away; others looked on curiously; still others trotted right up to the fence to say hello and seek a midafternoon handout.

No Beauregarde.

No Chardonnay.

As they entered the barn through the open door, Andy said, "With all the horse stealing going on, Mattie really ought to lock up when she leaves."

"Why bother if she's the one doing the stealing?" Penelope asked, immediately regretting the statement.

"All the more reason."

Each of the stalls in the barn was empty.

"Well, some instincts you have."

"See if I ever give you an exclusive," Penelope said, mentally adding shame to her guilt as she silently apologized to Mattie. For good measure, she also tossed in a good measure of stupid, realizing that if Mattie had taken Beau and Chardonnay, she wouldn't be dumb enough to keep them in her own backyard anyway. Someone was going to have to speak to those astrologers who provided the daily horoscopes. Penelope's had also advised her to watch for an unexpected check. Yeah, right.

The silence was suddenly broken.

"Hi, what are you doing out here?"

In addition to scaring the hell out of Penelope, her first thought when she came back to earth was, Busted! But then she turned and found only a smiling Abigail Wilson, not Mattie Bates's accusing eyes.

"Jesus, you frightened me!"

"Sorry," Abigail said. "I thought you'd hear me coming."

"Next time, whistle."

"Hi, I'm Andy."

"The newspaper editor. I'm Abby Wilson."

Andy looked pleased at the instant recognition. "That's me."

Penelope, whose heart was still beating a little too rapidly, didn't look quite so pleased. Abby was pretty cute and Penelope wondered if she might fit Andy's concept of normal. "What are *you* doing out here?" Penelope demanded. "I didn't see your car."

"It's on the other side of the house and I guess I'm looking for Mattie, just like you. I wanted to see if she'd give me a job."

"You have a job."

"Yeah, but Horace keeps asking me out. I'm afraid if I don't accept soon, he'll fire me."

"Well, Mattie's not here."

"I know," Abby replied. "I guess I should have called first."

They stopped for a frozen yogurt on their way back into town—cones for Penelope and Andy and a small container for Big Mike who always had trouble finishing his. While Andy was at the counter, Penelope used the pay phone to call Dutch again.

"You better come on over, Penelope."

"You heard from Arkansas."

"Yes."

There was a pause. Penelope heard voices in the background. She waited. Nothing. Dutch had spent too much time with Stormy and developed her taste for the dramatic pause.

"Well?" she finally demanded.

"Jack Loomis was really Jim Loper. . . ."

"You're kidding, right?" Penelope interrupted. "Loper?"

"Do you want to hear this or not?"

"Sorry."

"Anyway, Loper was a drifter it appears with a record as a petty thief with the odd burglary and gas station heist thrown in. And . . ."

Penelope didn't try to wait him out this time. "And . . ."

"It seems that he was involved with one Dr. Wendell P. Oliver who was convicted of killing horses, but Loper took off with his girlfriend before they could pick him up. She was a quote, exotic dancer when she wasn't hookin,' ya' know, unquote. Nobody down there has seen them since."

Bingo!

"What about Oliver?"

"Nothing on him yet. We're bringing Maryanne Melrose in for questioning."

"You think she's the missing girlfriend?"

"Could be," Dutch drawled. "Could be."

"We're on the way as soon as Mikey finishes his yogurt."

"Yogurt?"

"He likes vanilla. Do you want one?"

"Just get over here."

Maryanne Melrose sat in the interrogation room looking like anything but the missing girlfriend of a small-time hoodlum. Dressed casually, but elegantly, in white blouse and beige slacks, Maryanne looked exactly like a rich matron about to divorce her husband and take him for everything she could.

The room was spartan. A wooden table was bolted to the floor as were the chairs in the room. Otherwise, there were no furnishings whatsoever. The walls were drab and peeling paint.

Looking at her from behind the two-way glass, Penelope tried to imagine a younger Maryanne Melrose bumping and grinding her way in some seedy topless bar while rednecks and farm boys gawked, or taking her tricks to some tawdry motel on the outskirts of town. It was too big a leap for Penelope. Probably, she was just who she said she was, but taken in by a scheming Jack Loomis—or Jim Loper. Penelope hoped that was the case. She rather liked Maryanne Melrose. It wasn't her fault Horace turned out to be such a jerk.

Tweedledee and Tweedledum were apparently out, presumably in the next county now, showing Sir Beauregarde's picture around, although Penelope didn't think Dutch really believed that would accomplish anything. As a result, Dutch and Sheila Tyler conducted the interview.

"Am I under arrest?" Maryanne asked when Dutch and Sheila entered the room.

"Of course not, Mrs. Melrose," Dutch said. "As my officers told you, some information has come to light and we think you may be able to help us."

"May I have a glass of water?"

"Certainly. I'll get it."

Maryanne and Sheila did not speak while Dutch was out of the room. When he returned, he poured a glass of water from a pitcher.

"Thank you."

"You're welcome."

Maryanne sipped delicately from the glass, placed it carefully on the table, folded her hands, and said, "Now, what is this all about?"

"We are in possession of information that indicates Jack Loomis was not who he was pretending to be."

"I don't know what you mean."

"His fingerprints were sent to Arkansas and he was positively identified as a small-time crook named Jim Loper."

If Maryanne Melrose was acting, Penelope thought she was very good at it. Her face registered shock and disbelief as she looked back and forth at the two officers. "But . . ."

"It's true, Mrs. Melrose. What can you tell us about the man you knew as Jack Loomis . . . or Jim Loper?"

If Maryanne caught the barb, she ignored it.

"Nothing . . . I mean . . . Are you sure?"

"There is no doubt."

"But . . . ." Tears welled into her eyes. She reached into her purse for tissues. "He lied to me. . . ."

"Possibly," Dutch said.

Maryanne didn't let that one pass. "You think I knew him as Jim Loper," she said angrily. "That's absurd."

"Tell us what you do know then."

"I met *Jack Loomis*," she said, spitting the name out, "when he came to work for my husband. Oh, it's no secret that Horace and I had problems, nor is it a secret that I'm divorcing him. Jack and I were going to get married. That's no secret now either. But to say he was someone else . . . I can't believe that. We didn't hide things from each other."

"When did you marry Horace Melrose?"

Maryanne turned to Sheila Tyler after dabbing at her eyes. The tissue came away with black streaks of mascara. "Eight years ago."

"And what did you do before that?"

"I was a waitress," Maryanne said. She named a fashionable and expensive Phoenix restaurant. "Is there a law against that?"

"Is that where you met your husband?"

"Yes."

Penelope and Andy watched as Dutch and Sheila went on to elicit the information that Maryanne had been born in New Mexico, she was an only child, her parents had been killed in a head-on collision with a pickup truck driven by a drunk driver when she was nineteen, she didn't like school, but she liked waitressing because the tips were good. When she met Horace Melrose, she moved into the upper strata of *his* world, which she took to very nicely.

Apropos of absolutely nothing at all as she watched, Penelope thought Dutch made a much better police officer than a poster boy for Super Bra.

"Where did you meet Loper?"

"I told you. I met *Jack Loomis* when he came to work for my husband."

"When was that?"

Maryanne sighed. "Two years ago. I told you that also."

"The Arabian show world overlaps a lot. You *never* saw Loper . . ."

"Loomis. . . ."

". . . at shows, auctions, other stables?"

"I *didn't* say that. Of course, I saw him around, but I didn't *know* him. And then . . . I was vulnerable. I fell in love."

"With Loper?"

"With Loomis. I knew Jack Loomis. I never heard of Jim Loper until today."

After Maryanne was allowed to leave, Dutch said, "Check that restaurant." Then, he pointed to the water glass she had used. "Lift the prints."

Penelope grinned. "That's the oldest trick in the book."

Dutch grinned right back. "Yeah, but it works every time."

That evening Penelope opened a letter from her mother and found a check for one hundred dollars. A note said, "Just thinking of you. Go out and buy yourself something nice."

"Now that," Penelope told Mycroft, "is just too uncanny."

CHAPTER THIRTEEN

Although Penelope loved Empty Creek dearly, there were those times when she felt the little city in the desert was the full-blown creation of Rod Serling, an episodic *Twilight Zone* soap opera in living, breathing color, as well as an out-of-the-way footnote in *The Hitchhiker's Guide to the Galaxy*. This feeling was reinforced when the respective attorneys for Horace and Maryanne Melrose had a high noon confrontation outside their offices, negotiating the interests of their clients with fisticuffs. Fisticuffs! Right there on the main drag in full view of God and a half-dozen biker types egging them on. So much for the dignified practice of law. The scene was all the more remarkable for the absence of the primary combatants in the divorce. In the end, the two spluttering, overweight lawyers—one with a bloodied nose—had to be restrained and separated by Empty Creek's finest.

Surely, Penelope thought, as she hurried down the sidewalk to see what the commotion was all about, Douglas Adams would end his Empty Creek footnote in the *Guide* with a stern warning *not* to converse with the inhabitants *or* drink the water.

She arrived in time to hear Horace Melrose's advocate shout, "I should just let him kill her. See what you get then."

Maryanne Melrose's counselor, who was sitting on his backside blocking traffic and holding a handkerchief to his nose, shouted right back, although his message was somewhat garbled in its delivery. Still, it sounded very much like, "We'll seeb whob kills whob."

Enraged, Horace's representative charged his counterpart. Unfortunately, he slipped on the curb and plopped on *his* ample backside. Thus, when the constabulary arrived in the personages of Sam Connors and Peggy Norton, they found two lawyers sitting in the street kicking ineffectually at each other, very much like two little boys in a mud puddle—sans the mud puddle, of course, since it hadn't rained of late.

Predictably, Penelope asked, "What's going on?"

"Something about a lime green Corvette," a burly biker with a pool cue in his hand replied.

"All this over a car!"

The biker looked at Penelope with disbelief. "Corvette's a very serious thing, man," he said dreamily, ignoring Penelope's obvious gender.

"But lime green? Really!"

"You could always have it painted."

"Owb, dat hurbs." This utterance came from the attorney who was being dragged from kicking range by a disgusted Sam Connors.

Peggy Norton, legs parted, hands on hips, ordered the other assailant, "Up against the wall. Assume the position." There was really no necessity for this action except that Peggy liked to say the words, just like the real cops on television and in the movies. She also liked to shout, "Freeze, Police!" although she rarely had an opportunity to use this second policewoman's delight. On the one occasion Peggy did have, during an abortive attempt to rob the Empty Creek National Bank, her voice was drowned out by a dozen other cops shouting the same thing.

For her part, Penelope thought Peggy took a perverse delight in searching overweight lawyers for contraband, which she was doing rather enthusiastically—and somewhat rudely—while her suspect shouted, "I'm an officer of the court."

"You're under arrest for kicking in public," Peggy said as she cuffed a now red-faced lawyer. She winked at Penelope who winked right back.

"There's no law against that."

"How about disturbing the peace, then?" Peggy threw in a few other allegations, as well, for good measure. She had reached lewd and lascivious conduct when Penelope decided to return to Mycroft & Company, determined to forget everything connected with the case and get some work done for a change, hoping that a change in attitude would bring divine inspiration and, incidentally, Big Mike's return, not realizing, as Douglas Adams might say, that a whole bunch of other stuff was about to happen.

Evidently, her stalwart feline companion felt the same way about the case as Penelope, for Big Mike had taken an evening stroll and hadn't returned. This was not all that unusual. He occasionally disappeared for a day or two. Penelope always believed that he was off on a refresher course in cat conduct or simply flexing his muscles, ensuring that the other critters in his domain remembered who was boss.

Normally, Penelope would not be particularly worried about Mycroft's well-being. A cat who had grown up in Ethiopia on a campus roamed at night by hyenas, jackals, and packs of wild dogs, could take care of himself, thank you very much. After that, living in the desert was a walk in the park and Big Mike feared nothing up to and including mountain lions. But with Chardonnay's disappearance, she couldn't help but be a little concerned. It would be unbearable to lose both of her friends.

Penelope also worried about another telephone call from Josephine Brooks announcing that Murphy Brown had once again escaped and, as a result, found herself preggers, all because Big Mike had invited the sleek calico out for a midnight dalliance and had his way with her. If that was, indeed, the case, Penelope would point out to Josephine for about the umpteenth time that, "One cat does not a tango make," and ultimately wind up standing in front of the supermarket with Jo, a smug Big Mike pointing out likely cat-loving candidates, and a basket full of cute, cuddly little kittens to give away (all of their friends already possessed the fruits of the Mycroft and Murphy love union).

And, if the truth were known, Penelope thought that it was more than a little inconsiderate of Big Mike to take off in this hour of her need, especially when she was still worried sick over Chardonnay. Penelope reminded herself once again that "A cat's gotta do what a cat's gotta do." But right now . . . "Please," she whispered, "take care of yourself, Mikey."

"What was that all about?" Kathy asked.

"A dispute over a point of law."

"In the street? It looked like a fight to me."

"The law has no boundaries, apparently, or restraints. Let that be a lesson to you. Any calls?"

"Yes. Stormy said she's taking you to lunch. She's worried about you. We all are."

So much for getting any work done, Penelope thought, with Stormy on a Florence Nightingale mission. "There's nothing wrong with me that a good confession and my cat and my horse wouldn't cure," she said. "Josephine Brooks didn't call by any chance?"

Kathy shook her head. "Just Stormy. She should be here any minute."

"Good God!"

"What?" Kathy cried.

"That lawyer. I must be losing it." Penelope grabbed the phone and pushed the automatic dial number for the police department. She had to talk to only three people to get through to Dutch himself.

"We still haven't heard anything new from Arkansas," he said when he came on the line.

"That's not it," Penelope said, "although I don't know why they can't work a little faster down there."

"Up there," Dutch said. "Arkansas is up there from Arizona."

"Whatever. Listen, Sam and Peggy are bringing two lawyers in for disturbing the peace. They're the ones doing the divorce work for the Melroses and they were fighting and one of them said, let me see if I can remember it exactly, he said, 'I should have just let him kill her.' What kind of lawyer goes around making threats for his client?"

"All of them."

"Not like that. Dutch, Horace is threatening to kill his wife!"

"He's made those threats before, but I can't do anything.

Sheila's already been out there to talk with Maryanne. She refuses to file a complaint. Says she doesn't want Horace in jail. She wants him to see her take everything he's got."

Hanging up, Penelope shook her head. "It's definitely the water," she said, a theme she reiterated when Stormy arrived a few minutes later.

"Well, forget the water. A nice glass of wine will calm you down. Now open your present." Stormy handed over a gaily wrapped package.

"What's this for?" Penelope asked, tearing into the wrapper. She dearly loved unexpected presents. "An early Christmas present?"

"Just a feel-good present from your baby sister."

"Oh, Stormy, you shouldn't have." Penelope held up an emerald green Super Bra. The nicest things happen in a mystery bookstore.

"I'm glad you like it. You thought I forgot about you, but I waited until I could get one that matched your eyes."

"No, I mean, you shouldn't have. I'm not going to wear this thing."

"Of course you are," Stormy said, not in the least daunted by Penelope's reluctance.

Penelope shook her head, giving up rather easily for her. "Oh, what the hell, thank you. I suppose Andy will like it."

"I can guarantee it from personal experience."

"So can I," Kathy said.

"You're both sex-crazed."

"It's so much better than exercise. I'm thinking of doing a video on the physical benefits of a good romp in the hay. Laney has offered to help."

"I'll bet she has," Penelope said remembering the last person who had looked forward to a tryst in a haystack and how that had turned out. The Surgeon General should issue a warning. Romping in the wrong haystack was definitely a detriment to health and long life.

Stormy was right. A glass of wine definitely helped. So did the sisterly chat over cheeseburgers and steak fries—a little extracurricular exercise would work off the calories, if not the fat content.

"It's been too long," Penelope said, licking ketchup from her fingers.

"I know," Stormy said. "We never seem to have time to get together like this and talk. We should plan a nice shopping trip or something. A day away from everyone and everything. Just for the two of us."

"As soon as this is over," Penelope said. "I promise."

"You always say that, but something always comes up."

"I mean it this time. Dutch and Andy can have a stag party or something."

"It's a deal, but no more talking about the case. Between you and Dutch . . . I saw Andy putting up posters with Char's picture and offering a reward for her safe return."

"He is?"

"You didn't know?"

"I knew he was making prints. A reward? How much am I giving?"

"It doesn't say, but no questions will be asked."

They were interrupted by some of that other stuff beginning to happen.

The aftermath of the un-lawyerly battle was a second knock-down, drag-out fight between Mattie Bates and Red the Rat in the Double B. Red, rather naively suggesting that men had rights, too, ran right smack into a feminist buzz saw, expertly wielded by an increasingly enraged champion of women's rights who finally stomped out of the bar shouting, "I never want to see you again."

"By God," a chastened Red said, "that woman's got spirit."

After Mattie slammed the door resoundingly—all present judged it a perfect ten in free-style door slamming—Penelope picked up her water glass and examined it closely, swirling it around until the water spilled over the rim and splashed on the table. Tentatively, she licked her finger and then wet it in the glass, tasting it gingerly. It just *had* to be something in the water, although Red never touched the stuff, always proclaiming repugnantly, "Fish pee in it."

"What *are* you doing, Sis?"

"Looking for mysterious bacteria."

"Oh." Stormy looked for a moment as though she might be considering having her sister committed for the duration, but then her purse began talking like a deranged smoke alarm.

"Good God!" Penelope exclaimed. "What's that?"

"My new beeper. Dutch gave it to me." Stormy went into her purse and pulled the offending instrument out and examined its message. She smiled and said, "Isn't that sweet. Dutch says he loves me."

"How do you know?"

"Right there," Stormy said, pointing to the display window. "Five-Five-Five. That's our code for 'I love you whole bunches.' Six-Six-Six means 'I can't be without you another minute' and Seven-Seven-Seven means . . ."

"Never mind," Penelope interrupted. "I don't want to know. What's the Nine-One-One for?"

"Oh, that's an emergency," Stormy said. "I think it's for you. We better go."

Penelope regretted the glass of wine at the Double B, although it had had its intended effect. She was really quite mellow and relaxed, albeit now incapable of solving even the simplest of calculus problems in her head, not that she ever could.

Stormy drove with the reckless abandon she always used, even before becoming the beloved intended of the police chief. Hanging on to the armrest, Penelope thought, as she invariably did when her sister was at the wheel, that Stormy would have made an excellent ambulance driver if she hadn't turned to acting. If her film career ever went sour—unlikely if the Super Bra commercials were a hit—she could probably find work as a stunt driver.

"Dutch probably got the results from Arkansas," Stormy said, blithely honking the horn at a motorist with the mistaken notion that a green light meant he had the right of way.

"Shouldn't you get a siren or something?" Penelope asked, closing her eyes and bracing for the impending crash. When nothing happened she opened her eyes in time to see a rude hand gesture from an angry driver. "Or at least put your flashers on."

"Oh, we're almost there." Stormy hit the accelerator for the straightaway, braked slightly as she approached the entrance to the department's public parking, and executed a pretty neat four-wheel drift, managing to avoid a parked black and white at the same time.

"Well, here we are," Stormy announced glancing at her watch. "Less than four minutes."

Despite the way Stormy drove and the ominous nature of the

Nine-One-One signal on her beeper, it was anything but an emergency if you took into account—and Penelope did—the long and leisurely greeting exchanged between Dutch and Stormy. One would think they had been parted for years rather than the few short hours since Stormy had kissed him goodbye that very morning.

After a final peck, Dutch sat down behind his desk. Stormy promptly sat in his lap. Penelope rolled her eyes, wondering what Andy's editorial staff would think if she sat in the managing editor's lap while he was trying to get the paper out. Actually, Penelope conceded, it wasn't such a bad idea.

"Well?"

"Dr. Wendell P. Oliver is dead," Dutch said.

"You're kidding!"

Dutch shook his head. "Shanked in the prison yard by some cowboy who loved horses. That good old boy didn't even try to hide it. Just walked up and stuck it to him. Probably thought it was justifiable homicide."

"I'm inclined to agree, but who was arguing with Loomis, then? This doesn't make any sense at all. Could it be a twin brother?"

"Nope, I asked. Oliver had a younger brother, but not a twin. The brother doesn't have a criminal record and no one down there knows where he is."

"Up there."

"Whatever." Dutch grinned.

"It has to be the brother," Penelope said.

"Why? You and Stormy don't look anything alike."

"But you can tell we're sisters," Penelope said. "She's prettier, but I'm smarter."

"You are not!" Stormy said.

"Ow! Don't jump around like that. You're heavy."

"Heavy!"

"Ow, ow, ow!"

"That'll teach you."

Water, water, water.

"I'm going to talk to Raymond again," Penelope said. "There's something funny going on. Did you hear anything about Maryanne?"

"Not yet."

"Damn. They're slow down there."

"Up there."

"Right. But what takes them so long on a simple inquiry?"

"Some bureaucrat probably figured there wasn't much of a hurry since Oliver was dead."

"We'll all be dead of natural causes by the time they feel any sense of urgency."

Richard Raymond was not at the Lilac Suite. Nor was Susan Vaughn.

"He went to the home office for a couple of days," Ms. Vaughn said when they finally tracked her down at Mom's Do-Nuts where she was sitting with her police escort. "I'm covering things here until he gets back."

When Stormy dropped her off at Mycroft & Company, Penelope called the main office of Amalgamated Equine Surety in Phoenix and asked for Mr. Richard Raymond. She listened to music while the call was transferred.

"Mr. Raymond's office."

"This is Penelope Warren. Is Richard available?"

"No, I'm sorry. Mr. Raymond is in Empty Creek."

"Was he in earlier today?"

"No. I don't expect to see him until next week at the earliest."

"He hasn't been there at all?"

"As I said, he's in Empty Creek."

Penelope hung up and stared at the telephone. Where was Richard Raymond and why was Susan Vaughn lying about his whereabouts?

No Big Mike.

No Chardonnay.

No Andy.

Guppies, Penelope thought as she wandered the house listlessly and feeling a little sorry for herself. I should get a big bowl of guppies. At least, they wouldn't take off and leave me alone, but living in a bowl filled with Empty Creek water would probably turn the little fish into some sort of weird mutants. Oh well, there were always the bunny rabbits to feed.

But even feeding the rabbits was unsatisfactory without the presence of Big Mike and Chardonnay. The usually playful bunnies seemed to sense a changed mood. They ate quietly and with determination, omitting their usual antics, and then hopped off to hide in the desert scrub.

Penelope trudged back to the house, even wishing Josephine Brooks would call. At least, she'd know what Mycroft had been doing. She looked hopefully at the telephone, but it refused to ring. Finally, as a last resort, Penelope turned to her new Super Bra. Might as well see what effect it has on Andy.

Penelope went to the bedroom, shedding upper garments along the way. Well, I'll be damned, she thought as she posed before the mirror, turning this way and that, Stormy was right. The green complemented her eyes very nicely.

She found her favorite green sweater and pulled it over her head, smoothing it over her creatively enhanced bosom. She smiled then for the first time since coming home. *I could be the sweater girl for the state booksellers' association newsletter.*

Feeling better, Penelope went back to the living room, took the first book from a stack of mystery novels awaiting her attention, and started to read, discovering to her delight that she had to hold the book a little farther away in order to see the print. *Now, maybe Red the Rat will suggest I register deadly weapons.*

Poor Red. Penelope hoped Mattie and Red would make up. Despite *The Electric Horseman* and her earlier suspicions, she really liked Mattie and thought she and the old desert rat made a good pairing. It was about time Red got caught although he had to get rid of the silly notion that men had rights.

Penelope was still reading when Andy pulled into the driveway and parked. She ran to the door and opened it, waiting for his reaction.

"Hi," he said, giving her a quick peck on the cheek.

"Hi, yourself," Penelope replied, waiting.

"How was your day?"

"Okay. I hear I'm offering a reward for Chardonnay's return."

"I just finished distributing the posters. That's why I'm late. But I'm offering the reward. I thought it might help."

"You're sweet to do that. Thank you. Would you like a glass of wine?"

"Yes, please," Andy said following her into the kitchen. "Anything new on the case?"

Penelope poured the wine, handed over his glass, and told

him about Oliver, ending with the declaration that "Someone's out there impersonating a dead man. That's not very nice."

Andy smiled. "But the nicest things happen in the kitchen," he said.

Finally.

And, of course, the damned telephone picked that exact moment to ring. Sighing, Penelope went to answer it. "Hello, Josephine."

"It's Dutch."

"Oh, I was expecting to be told that Mikey's going to be a father again."

"We just heard from Arkansas on Pammie Pom Pom."

"Who?"

"Otherwise known as Maryanne Melrose."

CHAPTER
FOURTEEN

I t was time to make something happen, one way or another.
Sitting in her favorite chair in the flower garden behind
the house, Penelope had a sweeping view of the desert on the
far side of the dry Empty Creek bed and the hills beyond. It
wasn't really a flower garden at all, simply an extension of the
desert flora bordered by rocks. Still, Penelope liked to refer to
her little cactus patch as a garden. Her favorite was the small
barrel cactus; she figured that under desperate circumstances
she could always cut one open for its life-sustaining moisture.
It would certainly be better than drinking from Empty Creek's
municipal water supply.

Normally, Penelope enjoyed sitting outside sipping her coffee even if it was too early in the morning to be up and about.
But Andy had left early and Penelope had been unable to fall
asleep again after he left. For a time, she thought she might be
coming down with something, although she could usually be
the centerfold for any magazine specializing in good health. Finally, she realized she missed Big Mike's furry presence.

There was nothing for it but to rise early and confront the day and its problems.

Confrontation! Penelope snapped her fingers.

Yes, she thought, that was one way to make something happen. There were at least two people ripe for plucking confrontational-wise.

And just then Big Mike came home, walking up the path from the stables where Chardonnay should have been, meowing like crazy in his haste to tell Penelope of his adventures. Meow this, meow that, and then meow, meow, meow!

Thank God. Penelope rushed to greet him with a big hug. That was one animal down with one to go.

Rowr!

"That's nice, Mikey, but you're a mess. And just wait until you hear what *I* have to tell *you*."

If Big Mike took offense at Penelope's assessment of his condition, he didn't show it. As the big cat rubbed against her legs, purring like a 747 revving its engines for takeoff, Penelope checked him over for wounds, but apart from some tangled fur and a few burrs, Big Mike seemed just fine. And, Josephine Brooks still had not called. Perhaps they would yet be spared the supermarket excursion. Unless . . . Murphy Brown might have sneaked out and back again before Josephine realized it. Murphy *was* rather wanton when it came to midnight assignations with Big Mike.

"Well, did you, Mikey?"

Big Mike refused to tell. There were just some things a gentleman did not talk about. After all, this wasn't some sweaty locker room filled with men boasting of their conquests. Mikey, in fact, disliked locker rooms. There was always too much water sloshing around for any self-respecting cat. He did, however, demand breakfast and the several other meals he had missed.

"First," Penelope insisted, "you're going to get a good brushing."

Mycroft tolerated the attention with good humor, still talking nonstop. Penelope surmised that he had had a pretty good time out there in the nocturnal desert. She gave him another quick hug. "It's good to have you home."

When Penelope was satisfied that all the snaggles and burrs were gone, she opened a can of lima beans, which Mycroft ate with gusto and appreciative growls—the cook should always be praised lavishly—before turning to the liver crunchies in the next bowl over, but he finally ran down, plumb tuckered out, and fell asleep with his paws curled around the bowl just in case there was a liver crunchie bandit lurking in the kitchen.

"Well, then," Penelope said, "you're just going to have to wait. I'm not repeating the story all day long."

As pleased as she was that Big Mike had returned, she wasn't about to admit it to him for a second time. There was no use feeding his ego as well as his stomach. But feeling considerable relief, she went to the telephone and called Samantha Dale.

Then, it was confrontation time. There were two somebodies that better have some answers.

Penelope found Susan Vaughn playing gin rummy with Peggy Norton in the Lilac Suite.

"Where's Raymond?" Penelope demanded without preamble.

"I told you. He's at the main office in Phoenix."

"He isn't there. He hasn't been there."

"But . . . but . . . are you sure?"

"I called yesterday afternoon. His secretary hasn't seen him and says he's in Empty Creek."

"But . . . he told me . . . oh, God . . . what if something's happened to him? I told him he should stay here where we were protected." Susan began sniffling. "I'm calling the police."

"I am the police," Peggy reminded her gently. "I'll take care of it."

So much for that confrontation. Penelope actually felt sorry for Susan Vaughn and believed Big Mike would, too—if she hadn't made him wait in the Jeep. Mikey was quite proficient at comforting young ladies in distress.

The object of her second confrontation was nowhere to be found. He didn't answer Penelope's insistent ringing of the doorbell and he wasn't presiding over the day's activities at the HMM Arabian Ranch. Penelope wondered if he might be out looking for his wife. Perhaps Maryanne Melrose had some secret hideaway she went to when she was troubled, like Penelope always saddled Chardonnay and rode off into the peaceful hills behind Empty Creek.

Penelope and Big Mike found Abigail Wilson in the ring putting a horse through its paces. The young stallion was good, but he was no Sir Beauregarde to Penelope's eyes.

"Know where your boss is?" Penelope called out.

"Haven't seen him," Abigail shouted. "Just let me finish here and I'll be with you."

Penelope watched for a moment and then turned away, wandering over to the barn. Perhaps revisiting the murder scene might provoke a thought.

In the barn, Big Mike went directly to the spot where Maryanne discovered the body. Penelope watched as he sniffed at the fresh hay on the floor. Although there were no visible signs of foul play remaining, Mycroft could probably still smell the residue of blood.

Beauregarde's name remained posted above his stall and the door was open, as though awaiting his imminent return. Penelope peeked in, wishing she could force the walls to talk. Everything was clean, but its emptiness stared back at Penelope, a palpable force accusing her of . . . of what . . . failure, ineptitude, negligence, inadequacy? All those and more.

Damn it! So far, making something happen wasn't going at all well.

"I miss him," Abigail said. She stood next to Penelope and looked at the stall. "I'm keeping everything ready for when he comes home."

"I'm glad to see you're optimistic."

Abigail nodded. "I've put Max on the hot walker to cool down. He hates it, but it'll give us a chance to talk."

"Do you know where Horace went?"

"No. He's been berserk since Maryanne left. He just wants the Corvette back though."

"Figures."

"Do you have any idea where Maryanne might have gone?"

"We never talked much. Oh, she was polite enough but I think she always looked on me as a rival."

"For Horace?"

"Who else?"

"Jack Loomis, or rather Jim Loper. You knew they were longtime lovers."

"I do now."

"Well, when Horace returns don't tell him I was here. I want to surprise him."

Samantha cleared the screen on her computer when Penelope entered the office. It was apparently a casual day at the bank, for Samantha was wearing blue slacks and a white silk blouse with a red, white, and blue scarf. Penelope thought Sam looked her usual elegant self as they shook hands.

"I'll have to start dressing better if I'm going to be around you all the time," Penelope said.

"Don't be silly," Sam said as she went back behind the desk. "I'd wear jeans every day if I could. Sit down and tell me all about it. Pammie Pom Pom? My God, I still can't believe it."

"Her professional name."

"What kind of professional name is that?"

"She was a hooker and an exotic dancer."

"Whatever that means. The dancing part, I mean. I know what a hooker does."

"She danced topless with a cheerleader routine. Apparently, she was a great favorite with the vice squad officers down there."

"Up there."

"Don't you start in on my knowledge of geography, Samantha Dale. It's in the South. It ought to be down there."

"Only if you're in the North."

"Oh, never mind. The point is, what does it all mean?"

"I haven't the foggiest."

"Neither do I."

"Why did she take off unless she was involved in the murder somehow?"

"That doesn't make any sense. She was in love with him. If

Maryanne were going to kill someone, you'd think she'd bump off old Horace. That's what I'd do."

"Was she involved in Beauregarde's disappearance then?"

"Possible, but again why run? That's tantamount to an admission of guilt."

"She was embarrassed by her past?"

"Still, tough it out, get her divorce, and whatever she could from Horace. She had reformed, lived a very respectable life. Why be embarrassed by her past when some substantial sums of money might be involved? Horace isn't exactly poor."

"Not if Beauregarde is found and fulfills his potential," Sam said. "Let's look at it logically. We are two very bright and intelligent women."

"I think we should look at it illogically for a change," Penelope replied. "The other way doesn't make any sense at all."

"All right, illogically then. You start."

"No, you begin."

"It was your idea. You go first."

Penelope thought for a moment. "Space aliens," she said.

"Third-world terrorists."

"Very good. The Empty Creek Militia."

"I didn't know we had one."

"We don't, but if we did they'd be at the top of my list."

"I can't imagine Big Jake running through the desert playing defender of the Republic. Too much huffing and puffing."

"Andy's idea of roughing it is walking barefoot across the living-room rug. How is Jake? I thought he'd be here."

"Very sweet. He's off on some horse show business. I'll fill him in later."

"Have you tried his name on yet?"

Samantha blushed. "Yeah, I guess I'm in trouble."

"Good for you. When's the wedding?"

"He hasn't asked me yet."

"He will." She paused to let Samantha's blush subside. That took awhile and then Penelope asked, "How about the Vicenzo Family?"

"Dickie Vicenzo?"

"Well, he owns a restaurant. Mobsters always own restaurants to launder their ill-gotten gains."

"Dickie's president of Rotary and he's on the school board."

"Did Vito Corleone ever serve on the school board? I've forgotten."

"I don't think so."

"Probably a bad idea then. Dickie's off the hook. How about this? What if Beauregarde isn't involved at all?"

"That *really* doesn't make any sense. Perhaps we should go back to logic."

"Oh, all right." Penelope sighed. "These are the facts as we know them. Jack Loomis who was really Jim Loper is dead. Two horses are missing, as is Maryanne Melrose who is really Pammie Pom Pom nee Emma Snyder."

"Emma is her real name?"

"Didn't I tell you?"

"If my parents had named me Emma, I'd be a Pammie Pom Pom, too."

"Anyway, everyone seems to be someone else. The one link we had to Loomis-Loper is dead and someone who looks like him had an argument with the murder victim. Oh, yes, and Richard Raymond has gone missing, too."

"Maybe he won't come back."

"One can always hope, although Ms. Vaughn is rather upset."

"I do know one thing," Samantha said solemnly.

"What's that?"

"If Maryanne Melrose or Emma or Pammie Pom Pom or whatever she might be calling herself now is involved in Beauregarde's theft and death, the bank's in trouble. I'm in trouble. The insurance company will surely interpret Maryanne as being an agent of the owner."

"And they'll refuse to pay."

"Exactly. I'll have to explain to my board of directors why I authorized the loan. I don't look forward to that."

"Don't worry. Dutch has a bulletin out on her. Horace filed a stolen car report. It seems that Maryanne-Emma-Pammie Pom Pom took off in his Corvette. It shouldn't be hard to find a woman driving an ugly lime green Corvette."

Penelope drove back to the Melrose ranch. This time Horace answered the door after the first ring. And he looked surprised. Good old Abigail.

"I've told everything to the police," Horace Melrose complained. "Can't you see I'm upset?"

"I'm upset," Penelope said. "We're all upset."

"You didn't just find out your wife was a whore."

Despite what Abigail had said earlier, Penelope wondered if it was the knowledge of his wife's unsavory past that bothered him the most or the fact that she had taken off in his Corvette. She decided to side with Abigail's assessment. "Let's talk about Loper then."

"That bastard." Horace started to close the door.

Penelope blocked it with her foot. It was time for the high hard one. Penelope wound up and delivered it right at his head. "You threatened to kill Maryanne. Did you?"

"This interview is over, finished, terminated, kaput. Get out."

Penelope bristled. "Look, you stupid jerk, I'm trying to help you. This interview is over when I say it's finished terminated, kaput. Now, sit down and talk to me or I'll have Big Mike shred your trousers and a few other things as well."

Mycroft, unaccustomed to such vehemence from his friend, raised his fur, hissed menacingly, and glared at the only possible threat in the immediate area. Good old Mikey. Right on cue as always.

"All right, you might as well come in. I've got to talk to someone. Everyone else thinks I'm a crook and a murderer." Horace Melrose backed all the way to a chair in the living room and sat. "Would you like to have dinner with me?" he asked of Penelope although he was keeping a wary eye on Mycroft as he spoke.

Penelope shook her head in disbelief. Horse manure must contain some mysterious property that addled the brain with too much exposure. Coupled with the local water, Horace Melrose was around the bend. It was no wonder that Maryanne wanted out and Abigail was looking for another job.

"No, I will not have dinner with you. I assume the invitation was extended to me and not Mycroft."

"Nice kitty," Melrose said.

"He is not a nice kitty," Penelope lied. "He is mean and vicious and hates obnoxious, obstinate, and licentious men. Now, tell me what you know of your wife's past—and Loper's."

Apparently, finding an ugly sports car was more difficult than Penelope imagined. By the time she closed Mycroft & Company for the day, there was still no word. "Everyone's looking," was all Dutch would say.

Penelope went home dejected, feeling very much a failure. Maybe it was time to give up, leave the matter to the police who theoretically knew what they were doing. Even Tweedledee and Tweedledum had their moments.

Her efforts to make something happen, to generate even the slightest lead to savor and worry over and pursue, had come to naught. Again. There must be something that could be done.

But what?

Horace Melrose denied all knowledge of the previous lives of his wife and Jack Loomis.

No one knew where Richard Raymond had gone.

Maryanne Melrose couldn't be found.

Sir Beauregarde might be in somebody's glue pot right this very moment.

Chardonnay was still missing, despite the reward posters placed in strategic locations all over town. Friends had called off and on to offer condolences and to say they'd keep an eye open for the missing filly but . . . Not one lead.

Oh, fiddle fie!

"Three dirty words," Penelope said.

That didn't help much.

Damn it, I want Chardonnay back!

Penelope pressed the horn and listened to the blare for a moment. The noise raised her spirits a little more, although Mikey was perturbed. He was still trying to catch up on a few lost winks. And when she started trying to pick out the "Marine's Hymn" on the Jeep's horn, he curled up into a tight ball on the seat. Despite her mood, Penelope laughed when she glanced down at him. She swore he was trying to plug his ears with his paws.

"All right, Mikey, I'll be good."

He seemed to appreciate the sudden silence.

Over dinner, Penelope made a complete report to Andy. But talking it out with him didn't help any more than it had with Samantha. Perhaps space aliens *were* the perpetrators.

The telephone rang. Penelope answered it. "Hello." There was a loud crackling on the line. "Hello," she shouted, always firmly believing that twentieth-century devices could be defeated by turning up the volume. It didn't work this time, however, and whoever was calling hung up abruptly.

Penelope waited for the caller to try again, figuring it was a bad connection. Speaking of aliens, the noise on the line sounded like something from outer space, from somewhere beyond Venus perhaps. But the telephone didn't ring. Penelope shrugged and went back to the table.

"Ray guns," she said.

"Pardon me? Did you say ray guns?"

"Zap."

"Zap?"

"Or perhaps zzzst."

"I never know what's going on."

"I just told you. If space aliens killed Jack Loomis they would use a ray gun, not a forty-four-caliber revolver. Ray guns go zap, or maybe zzzst. I'm not quite sure."

"I'm calling the doctor."

"Call a space doctor. Then he can test sensory reactions on the beautiful earth female."

Which is how Andy came to be wrapped in aluminum foil—

it was the best they could do for a space suit on such short notice—performing a variety of experiments, crinkling and crackling the whole time, finally announcing that the sensory reactions of the beautiful earth female were perfectly normal.

"What a good use for aluminum foil," Penelope said. "We must remember to tell Laney."

The telephone rang.

And rang.

And rang, finally penetrating both Penelope and Andy's comatose condition at approximately the same time. What a hell of a time to try the call again. They bumped heads as they reached for the offending instrument.

"Ow," Penelope said, but she won the unwanted race to the telephone. "Josephine?" she answered.

Andy groaned and fell back.

Big Mike didn't even stir.

"Why do you always call me Josephine?" Dutch asked. "Everyone else in the world answers the telephone by saying hello. You say Josephine with a question mark."

"What time is it?" Penelope mumbled.

"Midnight."

The fact that Dutch was calling at the witching hour penetrated Penelope's groggy brain faster than it might otherwise have done. "Is everyone okay?" Penelope asked immediately worried that someone in the family might have had an accident. Or worse.

Dutch understood. "Everyone's fine, but we found Maryanne Melrose."

"Where?"

"Apache Junction. The Lost Dutchman State Park. I'm heading out there now. I thought you'd want to come along."

"Why don't you just have her brought in?"

"She's dead, Penelope. Shot to death."

CHAPTER
FIFTEEN

Normal people were on their way to work when Penelope, Andy, and Dutch drove back into Empty Creek considerably slower than when they had left some seven hours earlier. Commuters were heading off to Phoenix, Scottsdale, Tempe, and a dozen or more lesser communities where they would spend their days in pursuit of business and commerce, making telephone calls, attending meetings, serving customers, solving problems, making sales calls and visits, building homes, adjudicating civil and criminal cases, pouring cement, repairing roads, creating new government regulations—a million mundane occupations, like selling books, that kept society and the economy humming along, less than perfectly perhaps, but humming nonetheless.

After the last few hours, Penelope longed to erase the visions from her mind, wake up normally in her bed, kiss Andy, pet Mycroft, and beedle off to work like all the other little industrious ants.

But it was too late for that now. Far too late.

They had sped along narrow desert roads. Dutch kept his red lights flashing the entire trip, but disturbed the moonlit night with his sirens only when approaching an intersection. They made the trip to Apache Junction and the Lost Dutchman State Park in practically no time at all.

In the front seat beside Dutch, Penelope wished the journey would last forever. So long as she didn't see Maryanne's body, the woman would still be alive.

But the glare of the floodlights illuminating the scene had immediately dispelled hope. There was no mistake. Maryanne Melrose was, indeed, dead with the forbidding Superstition Mountains in the background, an ominous monument to her memory.

Standing beyond the crime scene tape with Andy, Penelope forced herself to watch as law enforcement officers went about their grim business. Her eyes kept returning to Maryanne Melrose's body sprawled beside the Corvette and she was thankful when a blanket was finally placed over the murdered woman.

Behind her, other officers interviewed an elderly couple outside their RV. "We just wanted to do a little hiking," the man said plaintively. His wife had brewed a big pot of coffee for the men and women who had swarmed to the park at the edge of the vast wilderness area. As she poured refills for the interrogating officers, she shook her head and said, "Didn't hear a thing until the shot. Knew right off it was something bad."

Dutch left a group of three men and a woman and wiped at his eyes as he approached Penelope and Andy. "Shot right through the heart," he said. "Just like Loper."

"Anything?" Penelope asked hopefully.

"Damned little."

"What the hell was she doing out here?" Andy asked.

The sun was setting the sky on fire when they left, no closer to answering that question or any others.

Dutch pulled into the parking lot of the *Empty Creek News Journal* and got out to open the back door of the black and white for Andy.

"Thanks, Dutch." He turned to Penelope. "I'll see you later, hon. After I've written the story."

She nodded and blew him a halfhearted kiss.

As Dutch pulled out again, Penelope turned and asked, "How do you stand it?"

"It's a job."

Penelope nodded again and was silent until they reached her home. "I'll be there in an hour," she said.

"No hurry," Dutch said. "I want him thinking for a while."

"He didn't do it, Dutch."

"Probably not, but he's going to sweat it out anyway, right along with Abigail Wilson."

Big Mike galloped from the bedroom to the front door and was all set to give Penelope a big homecoming welcome before remembering he'd been miffed at being left behind when everyone else went off to Apache Junction.

"Oh, Mikey. I'm sorry."

While he rebuked her with big brooding eyes for a while, his curiosity quickly got the better of him. "Meow?" he asked.

Penelope told him everything between showering, dressing, brewing coffee, and finally sitting down at the kitchen table with a reporter's notebook she had borrowed from Andy.

"There's something missing, Mikey."

Big Mike stretched out a paw, as though pointing to the list of items Penelope had taken down as Maryanne Melrose's possessions were catalogued by two federal agents. Since the murder had been committed on federal property, it was their case although Dutch had been quick to demand their cooperation in a continuing investigation originating in Empty Creek.

Big Mike's paw rested on the notebook just between where Penelope had scrawled "wallet" and "makeup bag." The wallet had contained the usual residue of life—fifty-seven dollars in currency, another three dollars and fifty-seven cents crammed into the change pocket, credit cards, driver's license, an appointment card for the dentist.

The rest of her purse contained nothing out of the ordinary. Her two suitcases, hastily packed, were crammed with clothes and little else—no mementoes, no photographic record of her life, no address book.

"If we were going to run away and start an entirely new life, Mikey, would I bring the address book?" Penelope decided she would, but then she couldn't imagine taking off and severing every relationship entirely.

Penelope went to the telephone. "Let's see what Laney would do." But when she lifted the receiver the line was dead. Penelope sighed and set about to find which extension Mycroft had knocked off the hook. It was a way he expressed annoyance.

Wait just a damned minute!

"That's it, Mikey. The telephone. She had a portable phone at the football game. It wasn't there!"

Big Mike grinned up at her from the kitchen table. Pretty neat, huh?

———

Penelope left Big Mike at the holding tank. The cops who booked suspects there liked Big Mike and always treated him like one of their own so, rather than bore him to tears with interrogations, Penelope dropped him off where something interesting was always going on. He could always supervise the taking of fingerprints or something.

Penelope, Tweedledee, and Tweedledum took chairs in Dutch's office.

The estranged husband was always the prime suspect in a wife's murder, especially when he had been heard making frequent and extremely vocal threats against, even if he had an ironclad alibi, which Horace Melrose did.

Penelope told them about Maryanne Melrose's portable phone.

"Harvey," Dutch hollered, "get in here!"

"Yeah, boss, hi, Penelope."

"How's Alyce?" Penelope asked.

"Living with the stars," Harvey Curtis said with a broad smile. His fiancée was Alyce Smith, Empty Creek's resident astrologer and psychic. "Wanted me to tell you that she thinks Chardonnay is fine. One of her feelings."

Penelope hoped Alyce was correct. She usually was. "Does she know where Char is?"

"She's working on it."

"Can you work on this?" Dutch said. "I mean if you're through passing the time of day. Get the telephone company to fax a printout of Maryanne's telephone bill."

"Police emergency," Harvey said. "You bet."

"Okay, you know the drill. Let's do it."

Dutch took the first turn at Horace Melrose and then sent

the second team to hammer away while he went to the other interrogation room and tried to shake Abigail Wilson's story.

Sitting behind the two-way glass, Penelope switched her attention from one room to another, feeling as though she were watching a high stakes tennis match.

"Did your wife have a portable telephone?"

"Yeah, I kept calling her," Horace told Tweedledee and Tweedledum, "but she didn't answer. The recording kept saying she had traveled beyond the service area."

Maryanne has certainly traveled beyond the service area now, Penelope thought sadly as she went back to eavesdropping on Dutch and Abigail.

"What were you doing?" Dutch asked for about the tenth time.

"We worked late on the books," Abigail replied.

"What time did you finish?"

"About eleven."

"Was anyone else there?"

"No."

It was just barely possible if—*if* Horace and Abigail were coconspirators in the murder of Maryanne Melrose—for them to drive to Apache Junction, meet Maryanne at the park, shoot her, and get back in time for Horace to answer the door when Tweedledee and Tweedledum came to inform him of his wife's death.

If. . . .

"What happened next?"

Abigail blushed for about the tenth time. "He tried to seduce me."

"Was this a normal occurrence on the part of your employer?"

"He is a very horny guy, and persistent."

Penelope left the enclosure and quickly called Samantha Dale. "When you dated Horace that one time, was he aggressive?" she asked. "I mean, did he try to kiss you or anything?"

"He was not a perfect gentleman," Samantha said. "I shooed him off with a can of Raid. The house smelled like bug killer for days."

"Thanks."

"Do you think he did it?"

"You know?"

"It's all over town. Mrs. Burnham told me."

"That figures," Penelope said. "No, I don't think he did it, but it is possible. There was a retired couple at the park. They were awakened by a gunshot and a car driving off at about eleven last night. The man went outside, took one look at the Corvette, and went back to his RV and called it in. At eleven P.M. Horace was trying to work his magic personality on Abigail Wilson. At least, that's what she says. According to Horace, they worked late on the books. He offered her a nightcap and then she went home about midnight. That's the only discrepancy in their stories."

Penelope returned to her spot in time for the shift change.

"Isn't it true," Dutch said pointing a finger and drawing himself up to his full height to tower over Horace Melrose, "that you were romantically involved with Abigail Wilson?"

"No."

"Isn't it true that, instead of working on the books and having a nightcap, you drove to Apache Junction and shot your wife because you feared what would happen during the divorce proceedings?"

"No," Horace yelped. "I didn't. Ask Abigail. We had a drink and then she went home and I went to bed."

"That's not what she says."

"That can't be," Horace cried. "Why would she lie?"

Dutch shrugged. "Someone is."

"All right, all right," Horace said. "So I tried to make out a little, but she wasn't having any of it. After that, she went home and I went to bed. That's all true. I swear it."

"So you lied about the drink. What else did you lie about?"

"Nothing! I swear it. Ask Abigail. She'll tell you."

Dutch shrugged again and turned to leave. "I will," he said.

"Wait a minute! Why don't you believe her? She's one of your own. She wouldn't lie."

"What did you say?"

"She's a cop, for Christ's sake. At least, I think she is."

For all his faults, Penelope thought, Horace Melrose certainly has a flair for stopping the show abruptly. She turned to look at Abigail Wilson with new interest.

"What makes you think that?" Dutch asked quietly. The dramatic finger pointing had apparently ended for the moment.

"The handcuffs. They looked like the real things."

"Where did you find them?"

"I was in her place right after the murder and when she went to the bathroom I was looking at her books. They were right there on the shelf with a gun. I guess she figured no one would ever look behind a bunch of romance novels."

"What did you do then?"

"Well, I couldn't very well take the gun, but I took the handcuffs and put them in Jack's trailer. I knew it was a good move when I found Penelope Warren snooping around the trailer."

"Why?"

"I don't know. Take a little heat off me, I guess. It seemed like a good idea at the time. I thought maybe you or them insurance investigators planted Abigail on me."

"Why would we do that?"

"You know, because of the horse."

"But the horse wasn't missing when she came to work for you. Did you know Beauregarde was going to be stolen? Is that why you were worried about an undercover officer."

"No! Yes! No! You're twisting everything around. I didn't do anything."

"We'll see. Did you ever think Abigail might use handcuffs for something else?"

"Like what?"

"A sex toy perhaps."

"Jeez, what are you?" Horace asked indignantly. "Some sort of pervert?"

Even under the circumstances, Penelope had to laugh. Her future brother-in-law was so straight and conservative that he thought skinny-dipping with Stormy in the privacy of their secluded swimming pool was the height of depravity.

She was still chuckling when Dutch left Horace and entered the cubicle. "Ah, Empty Creek's famous pervert."

"Don't start, Penelope."

"Wait until I tell Stormy her fiancé has fantasies about— Good Golly—sex toys!"

"I warned you."

"Oh, don't worry. Your secret is safe with me. I won't tell a soul."

"Very funny."

"That's your problem, Dutch. You have no sense of humor."

"She look like an FBI agent to you?"

"No," Penelope said, "but you don't look like a pervert either."

"I'm going in there and wring her neck until she tells us the truth."

"Don't forget your rubber hose."

Abigail Wilson stonewalled, right up to the point when Dutch threatened to call the United States Attorney General.

That got to her.

"I have to make a phone call," Abigail said. "Alone."

"Let her use your phone, Peggy. Don't listen, but keep an eye on her."

"You got it, Guv."

Penelope knew Peggy was a big fan of English cop shows where everyone went around saying Guv a lot.

Dutch frowned and drummed his fingers on the table while he waited.

Penelope tapped "Shave and a Haircut, Two Bits" on the glass.

Dutch stuck his tongue out at her.

Peggy and Abigail returned after less than five minutes.

"All right," the young woman said, "I'm Special Agent Abigail Wilson of the Federal Bureau of Investigation."

At least, Penelope thought, she hadn't changed her name like nearly everyone else in the case so far.

"Okay," Dutch said, "let's talk in my office."

"Let Horace go. He didn't do it. He really was with me last night."

"He could have hired someone to make the hit."

"No, he's a weak little dweeb." Abigail turned toward the

mirror. "And you might as well bring Penelope. I know she's back there."

"All right," Dutch said. "Give."

Abigail shrugged. "My boss is a little angry at me, but he said cooperate."

"So cooperate."

"I'm trying. Where do you want me to start?"

"Why are you in Empty Creek? That would be a good beginning."

"We have informants," Abigail replied, petting Mycroft who had taken up residence on her lap after being released from the cat slammer. "We received a tip that something would be going down at the Scottsdale show, that a lot of horses were in danger."

"The question remains the same. Why come to Empty Creek?"

"Your show is earlier than Scottsdale. It seemed natural to infiltrate here first. Just in case."

"Why is the FBI involved? Horsenapping isn't a federal offense."

"No, but criminal intent to defraud a bank is. We only focused on the horses where they were used as collateral for bank loans. Beauregarde was one of them. The only one in Empty Creek as it turned out."

"Did you suspect Loomis? Is that why you wanted to be an apprentice with him?"

Penelope thought Abigail paled at Jack's name. Not much, but just enough to be visible.

"No," Abigail said after a pause. "I was just as surprised to find out about his background as you were. I couldn't believe it. And then . . . to hear about Maryanne and Jack . . . well . . . people surprise you, even when you think you know them.''

Penelope wondered how well Abigail had known Jack and made a mental note to ask her later. For the moment, she contented herself with another question. "Were you working with Richard Raymond and Susan Vaughn?"

"I was a lone wolf," Abigail said shaking her head and smiling ruefully. "And not a very good one, I'm afraid. I could have stopped Maryanne from leaving, but I didn't. I thought she was just fed up with Horace."

"Raymond's disappeared now," Penelope said. "I'd like to know what's happened to him."

Abigail started to say something but she was interrupted.

"Got it, boss." Harvey Curtis waved a sheaf of papers. "I made copies."

"Let's see," Dutch said.

"Lot of incoming calls," Tweedledee said.

"No way to check those," Harvey replied. "They're just listed as incoming."

Incoming, Penelope thought, a term for hostile artillery or mortar fire. One of Maryanne's incoming calls might have been just as deadly as any artillery round.

"What about the calls she made?" Dutch asked.

"I haven't had time to check them all yet, but three of the most frequently called numbers are in Apache Junction."

"Who do they belong to?"

"That's the thing. They're not residence or business numbers. They're pay phones. Two gas stations and a Circle K."

Penelope was still going on adrenaline when she pointed the Jeep toward Mycroft & Company, but the long night and ensuing day was catching up to her. She wasn't always at her best going on what she figured was two hours sleep at most. The thought of a nap was growing more and more attractive but . . .

The weak little dweeb was waiting at the bookstore, pacing anxiously, wringing his hands. Kathy flung a hasty Thank-God-You're-Here-Look in Penelope's direction and fled to the back room.

"You have to help me," Horace said without preamble. "I'm innocent."

"You've been released. There are no charges pending."

"Yeah, but no one's going to believe me until the killer is found and Beauregarde is back in his stall."

Penelope actually found herself feeling a little sorry for Horace Melrose. He had just lost his wife and no matter how bad the marriage had gotten, there would be good memories to look back on. And, he'd had the good grace not to ask when he could get his Corvette back.

"Let's get one thing straight. I am not a snoop."

"What?"

"You called me a snoop."

"Ah, Christ, I can't do anything right." Horace started crying. Great big tears rolled down his cheeks. His body shook with heavy sobs.

So much for her feeble attempt at levity. Penelope really felt sorry for him now—and herself as she went about the business of consoling him.

Patting his shoulder, she guided him to the big chair in front of the fireplace. "There, there," she said. It was what her mother always counseled in moments of childhood distress. It never worked for Muffy either, but Penelope went on saying it anyway until Horace finally stopped weeping.

"I can't take much more of this," Horace said wiping tears away.

"We'll get to the bottom of it. That's a promise."

"On top of everything else, I'm being blackmailed."

He was doing it again with another show-stopping grabber.

"Blackmailed," Penelope said, "as in *blackmailed?*"

Penelope and Big Mike went home. Big Mike, with his full night's sleep, was ready for dinner. Penelope was ready for a glass of wine and bed, but she was still stunned by what Horace Melrose had told her.

And then, just as Penelope was thinking nothing else could possibly happen that day, Dutch called.

"Have you gone over the calls Maryanne Melrose made real carefully?" he asked.

"I haven't had the chance yet." Penelope muffled a yawn with her hand.

"Take a look at the last call she made."

Penelope did and found herself staring at her own home telephone number.

Good God!

The hang up!

CHAPTER
SIXTEEN

Penelope foolishly set the alarm, something she never did, but how could she lie abed in the morning wasting time? In fact, she set two alarms—one was the clock radio, tuned to a station that played a variety of soothing Easy Listening music. The second was the piercing Klaxon guaranteed to awaken every household within a two-mile radius, or was it circumference? Penelope was too groggy to figure it out—or care.

By the time she snapped off the lamp and crawled gratefully into bed, both Andy and Big Mike were already snoring gently. She plumped her pillow, gave Andy a good-night peck on the cheek and Big Mike a pat on the butt, and said, "Sleep well, sweeties." Then she lay back, closed her eyes, sighed deeply, and promptly fell wide awake!

That wasn't playing fair.

Penelope relaxed and waited. That didn't work worth a damn. She clenched her eyes, thinking perhaps force would do it. Nope. So much for the If It Doesn't Fit, Get a Bigger Hammer theory. Penelope counted about a million sheep. She got up and went to the kitchen and drank a glass of warm milk. Feeling triumphantly drowsy, she went back to bed all set to put her mind on snooze control. Except . . . some mischievous little gremlin whispered a single word in her ear.

Blackmail.

Instantly vigilant and alert, Penelope would have throttled the little demon if only she knew where to find him. Then, the imp in charge of keeping Penelope Warren awake added a postscript.

Maryanne Melrose.

Why did Maryanne call me? Why didn't she call back?

Blackmail?

The anonymous caller told Horace to share the insurance payoff or else, as well as all the other stuff blackmailers doted on in mystery novels—don't go to the police, you'll be told what to do next, that kind of thing. Penelope wasn't sure Horace had been able to provide the details exactly. After all, he was distraught and his bowl of cherries had pretty much turned to gruel of late.

But that meant Sir Beauregarde was dead or soon would be. Didn't it? Amalgamated Equine Surety wouldn't pay off on the policy unless they had the corpus delicti. Would they? Even then the money would go to Empty Creek National Bank. Wouldn't it? Unless, of course, Horace continued to make the loan payments. Could he?

She went back to counting sheep. It was better than debating questions she couldn't answer in the middle of the night. Resolved: Questions are better with answers.

The sheep kept changing into horses. They weren't even Arabians, for God's sake. They were little miniature horses and after about every third or fourth made the leap, Andy, dressed all in tinfoil, pushed his way into line and did a Fosbury Flop over the hurdle. It was kind of cute, but not very conducive to sleep.

Resolved: Sleep deprivation is no fun.

Neither is murder and horse theft.

The clock radio kicked in. Penelope slept away, missing the six A.M. national news (bad, as usual), the weather report (good, as usual), and a medley of Harry Connick songs (good or bad, depending upon taste), and the six-thirty update of local news (not as bad as the national scene, but almost).

At six fifty-nine, the backup alarm sounded with a vengeance.

On a U.S. *Man of War* the sound would have sent the ship's crew scurrying to their battle stations. It had somewhat the same effect in Penelope's bed.

Shocked into wakefulness by the alarm sounding General Quarters, Big Mike, who had been sleeping upside down with paws going every which way, leaped straight into the air and came down sprawled on Andy's bare legs. Eyes wide and searching, ears swiveling to find the threat, and ready to repel boarders, Big Mike unfortunately forgot to retract his claws on landing.

This simple lapse in memory interrupted a rather tender moment in a dream featuring a certain newspaper editor and Daryl Hannah, eliciting a loud screech from Andy who bolted upright without bidding poor Daryl even a cursory farewell. "Ow, damn, ow!" Andy cried, attempting to dislodge Mycroft at the same time who was having no part of it and dug in even deeper.

Eventually, the two males in the bed sorted things out—one of them managed to turn the offending noise off—and sur-

veyed the damage, while Penelope kept right on cranking off
the Zs.

When finally coerced from bed, Penelope repaired the injury to
a fragile feline psyche with a generous portion of lima beans
and ministered to the puncture wounds suffered by Andy during the rush to battle stations with a gooey antibacterial balm.
The former was appropriately appreciative while the latter continued to grumble all through breakfast.

"I wasn't doing a thing," Andy whined. He was smart
enough not to mention Daryl Hannah this time.

"At least the gods weren't having a cosmic chuckle at your
expense," Penelope countered. "I didn't get a wink." This
wasn't exactly true. She had managed a solid nine hours after
finally falling asleep to a parade of hot fudge sundaes.

Andy, who believed the gods were, indeed, laughing
uproariously at his goop-streaked legs, said, "Ha!"

Penelope determined she would not set the alarm ever
again. It was a most unnatural way to greet the day.

At least, it got Penelope and Big Mike into town in plenty of
time to open Mycroft & Company, although she drove right
past the bookstore to the Lazy Traveller Motel where she
found the elusive Richard Raymond and an effervescent Susan
Vaughn in the coffee shop.

"Richard was in the office the whole time, doing research,"
Susan said when Penelope joined them without waiting for an
invitation. "He told everyone to say he wasn't there. Wasn't
that clever of him?"

"Depends on what he found."

"What can I getcha?" a matronly waitress asked.

"Hot fudge sundae, please."

"Don't serve hot fudge sundaes till after lunch."

"You serve breakfast all day long, don't you?"

" 'Course we do. Breakfast is the most important meal of the day. You want breakfast?"

"I want a hot fudge sundae," Penelope replied beginning to feel like Jack Nicholson in *Five Easy Pieces*. "If you serve breakfast all day, you should do the same for hot fudge sundaes."

"I'll see what I can do," the waitress said.

"Thank you." Penelope turned to Raymond. "Well, what *did* you find out?"

Mr. Richard Raymond looked quite pleased with himself. He cleared his throat. "As one of the largest equine insurance companies, we have extensive computer files, as you can probably imagine."

Penelope couldn't, but nodded anyway.

"I've searched out every form of insurance scam used, those involved, methods of putting the horse down, that sort of thing. I'm still analyzing the data, of course, but I should have something soon."

"I'll be helping him," Susan said. "We have quite a lot of information to go through."

Penelope looked for her sundae. It didn't seem to be forthcoming, so she went for a piece of Susan's dry rye toast. "How can Horace Melrose be blackmailed, if he's innocent in the theft of his own horse?" she asked.

Both Richard and Susan looked a little perplexed at the abrupt change in topic.

"He's being blackmailed?"

"He received an anonymous telephone call saying that he had to share the insurance payoff. Further details to follow."

"If he's, indeed, being blackmailed, that would suggest a certain amount of culpability. It should be impossible to blackmail an innocent man."

"That's what I thought at first, but then another possibility occurred to me."

"What's that?" Susan asked.

"That someone is trying to frame him and get the insurance money."

Richard shook his head. "That's impossible, I'm afraid. I mean, someone could be attempting the frame, but there's no way I'm signing off on this case until I'm absolutely convinced that all parties and agents involved lack any culpability whatsoever. Right now, that hardly seems likely. Ergo: there will be no money." He slapped the table for emphasis, making the dishes rattle. "You can take that to the bank *or* the blackmailer."

"Ditto," Susan said.

"I will," Penelope said, "right after I savor this wondrous delicacy." The hot fudge sundae had miraculously arrived.

"I had to make it myself," the waitress said.

"The heavens will reward you, dear lady," Penelope said plucking the cherry from the chocolate-colored mountain. "By the way, where's your police escort?"

"Oh, now that I'm back, I'll handle that," Raymond said, putting a protective arm around Ms. Vaughn's shoulders.

"Isn't he sweet?" Susan said as she snuggled beneath his arm.

Puh-lee-ze, it's too early for that sort of thing, Penelope

thought as she dug into her delicacy, completely ignoring the fact that it was also too early for a hot fudge sundae.

The morning dragged on interminably. Penelope put herself on autopilot, serving customers mechanically, making recommendations, ringing up sales, and passing the time of day without remembering a word she'd said five minutes later. She even managed to carry on an intelligent discussion with Kathy on the heroic stature of Satan in *Paradise Lost*, all the while wondering why Maryanne Melrose had called her and who was attempting to blackmail Horace Melrose and how. The why was easy. Money. Everything else remained unfathomable.

By lunchtime, Penelope had decided George Orwell was right. All questions are created equal, but some questions are more equal than others. "I'm going to lunch," she finally said.

Crossing the street to the Double B with Big Mike in her arms, Penelope asked, "How do you blackmail an innocent man, Mikey?"

"That woman's talking to her cat, Mommy," a little girl said. "Why is she talking to her cat?"

"She's probably been out in the sun too long," the mother said looking nervously over her shoulder as she pulled her daughter out of harm's way.

Penelope, unaware of this brief exchange although it had taken place practically right under her nose, lowered Mycroft to the sidewalk before answering her own question, since no feline wisdom seemed forthcoming on the matter.

"The answer is, although I hate to admit it, Richard Raymond is right. You can't blackmail an innocent man. Therefore, Horace Melrose is guilty of something." She pushed through the doors of the Double B. "But what?"

"Talking to yourself is a bad sign," Red the Newly Fastidious Rat said.

"What?"

"Never mind. You alone today, Penelope?"

"Except for this black cloud over my head."

"Eat with me, then. I need your advice."

"I'll try to help."

"Mattie hates me. Won't talk to me. Never wants to see me again. I don't know what to do. That woman's driving me crazy."

"Flowers," Penelope said. "Take her flowers."

"That's it? Just take her flowers?"

"Works with me all the time. I'm a sucker for a nice bouquet. Sometimes I pick a fight with Andy just so he'll bring me flowers."

"Really?"

"No, but it makes a nice story. And it does work."

"I'll do 'er, then," Red declared.

Penelope wished she could solve all problems so quickly and efficiently.

"What are you doing down there, Penelope?"

"Hot fudge sundae," the proprietress of Mycroft & Company said from her position on the floor with knees flexed and hands clasped behind her neck.

"It looks suspiciously like exercise," Samantha said.

"She had breakfast," Kathy explained, "and then a hot fudge sundae and then lunch and now I have to hold her ankles while she does sit-ups."

"How many have you done so far?"

"One." Penelope grinned up at Samantha. "I'm resting."

"I'll just browse until you're finished."

"Oh, it can wait," Penelope said scrambling to her feet. "I'll work the rest of the fudge off later," she added, not realizing the prophetic nature of her statement.

Penelope had barely finished bringing Samantha up-to-date when Nora and Reggie entered the store.

After a chorus of greetings all around, Nora said, "Reggie needs a genre novel for her writing class. Then we're going out to Mattie's for her riding lesson."

"I thought mystery would be best," Reggie said. "I don't like science fiction much. We're supposed to show how the best genre novels compare with the classics."

"What would you recommend, Penelope?"

"Raymond Chandler, perhaps. You're a big fan, Samantha, what would you suggest."

"I've always liked Travis McGee and Lew Archer."

"Either John D. MacDonald or Ross MacDonald would be good."

Reggie, like any good bibliophile, couldn't make up her mind, so she took one of each. As Penelope rang up the sale, Reggie reached into the new bowl and pulled out a peppermint. "May I have some extras, Penelope?"

"Of course, Reggie."

"Thanks. Mattie likes to give them to the horses."

"What?" Penelope exclaimed. "Wait just another damned minute!"

"Is this too many?" Reggie asked holding out her cupped hands.

"No," Penelope replied. "Which horses does she give them to?"

"That's kind of funny. I've never seen her give one to any of the horses, but she says they like them. Mine doesn't."

But mine does, Penelope thought. She turned to Nora. "I think you should cancel Reggie's lesson for today."

"Why?"

"Mattie has Chardonnay and I'm pretty sure she has Beauregarde as well."

"You got all that from peppermint candies? There are probably lots of horses who like peppermint candies."

"Maybe, but how many have been stolen? Besides, she likes Robert Redford and he was in *The Electric Horseman* and he stole old what's his name and set him free."

"My God, if that's true, then Mattie is the killer."

"No," Reggie said, "not Mattie. I don't believe it."

"I don't either, Reggie. Mattie's not a killer although she talks a pretty good game."

"What are we going to do?" Samantha asked.

"I'm going out there, of course," Penelope said. Again, she thought. She won't fool me this time.

"Shouldn't we tell the police?"

"In good time," Penelope replied, "all in good time." Penelope wasn't about to instigate a raid on Mattie's place without having her facts in order this time.

"What's the plan?" Samantha asked.

"You're not going."

"Well, you're not going out there alone," Samantha said. "I'm going with you."

"So am I," Nora said.

"Me, too," Reggie chimed in.

"You are not, young lady, you're grounded."

"Aw, Mom, what for? I didn't do anything."

"For . . . for . . . not telling us about the peppermints sooner."

"That's no reason."

"Well, then, how about what you and Dirk were doing when you were supposed to be studying."

"You were spying on us!"

"I prefer to think of it as monitoring the social activities of my daughter."

"It's definitely spying," Penelope said.

"See!" Reggie said triumphantly.

"What were they doing?" Penelope continued.

"The K. word."

"Oh, no, not . . . gasp . . . kissing."

"It was no worse than what you were doing with Tony."

"You were spying on me? Reggie!"

"I prefer to think of it as monitoring the social activities of my mother. I certainly hope you were using Saran Wrap or something."

"Reggie!"

"It may be time for a mother-daughter talk," Penelope suggested.

"I agree," Samantha said, "but perhaps it should wait until later. Right now, we need a plan."

"We just go out there and confront her," Penelope said. "Peppermint candies and *The Electric Horsemen* aren't exactly the kind of evidence that you can take to a judge for a search warrant."

Besides, three fairly young and fairly strong women should be a match for a middle-aged woman, even if she did possess a formidable arsenal. Shouldn't they?

"Watch the store, Kathy."

"I never get to have any fun."

After dispatching Reggie back home to read her new purchases—"Yes," Nora relented, "Dirk can come over, but you have to keep both feet on the floor"—the three women and Big Mike piled into Penelope's Jeep.

"Are you sure this is wise?" Samantha asked. "What if Mattie *is* the murderer."

"Nope, I'm not at all sure," Penelope replied cheerfully, "but it's better than spinning my wheels, which I've been doing a lot of lately. Besides, can you imagine Mattie Bates going around killing people for a horse?"

"Not really."

"Mattie has been terrific with Reggie," Nora said. "I can't believe she would hurt anything or anybody."

"There, you see."

Samantha persisted. "But if Mattie does have Sir Beauregarde and Chardonnay, and if she is not the murderer, then none of this makes any sense. Why were Jack and Maryanne killed if not because of the horse?"

"There you go being logical again."

"This is all too confusing," Nora said.

"What if Mattie doesn't have Beau and Chardonnay?" Samantha asked. "And what about Arkansas and Jim Loper and Pammie Pom Pom and all that?"

"Then it will be time to heed the words of the Master," Penelope said. " 'When you have eliminated the impossible, whatever remains, *however improbable*, must be the truth.' "

Mycroft looked benignly upon Penelope's purloined pronouncement from his comfortable position on Samantha's lap, as though both he and his namesake—the elder brother of Sherlock Holmes—approved of Sherlock's insight.

"And," Penelope added, "someone will be in a world of hurt."

"Well, she's here today," Penelope said as they passed Mattie's old pickup truck. She pulled to a stop beside the barn, figuring that an industrious woman like Mattie would still be working while there was daylight left.

"There she is," Nora said, waving. "Hi, Mattie."

Mattie didn't return the greeting. She waited silently by the corral.

Penelope had an ominous thought as she approached Mattie. What if she *was* the killer? Oh, well, it was too late for that.

"Hello, Mattie," she said, "we came for Chardonnay and Beauregarde."

"Heard you was out here once," Mattie said. "Figured you'd be back."

"Where are they, Mattie?"

"You can't have them," Mattie replied, punctuating her statement by pulling the biggest damned gun Penelope had ever seen outside the artillery range at Camp Pendleton.

Oops.

A very definite oops.

Perhaps *we* should have brought flowers, Penelope thought.

CHAPTER
SEVENTEEN

Dumb move, Penelope, really dumb move. She didn't think Mattie would hurt anyone present, certainly not Big Mike, but there *was* a crazed look in Mattie's eyes. Mycroft seemed to agree. Penelope noticed he was wisely staying out of the line of fire. In fact, he appeared to have joined forces with Mattie, rubbing against her legs and working himself up to a good purr, but perhaps he was distracting her so that Penelope could pounce, like a cat on a mouse. At least, Penelope looked upon it as a distraction as Mattie reached down and scratched the back of Big Mike's neck. Not an instinctive mouser, Penelope flexed her knees slightly, tensed, ready to leap, and . . . missed her chance when Mattie straightened abruptly.

"Now what am I going to do with you three?" she asked.

Penelope assumed it was a rhetorical question and didn't bother to reply.

Nora made no such assumption. "Reggie will be out here for her lesson soon. You don't want to hurt her."

"I don't think so. You wouldn't allow Reggie to come out and confront a crazy old woman."

"That's right," Samantha said, "but we did tell her to call the police if we weren't back in thirty minutes."

"That I believe," Mattie said, "so we'd best hurry things along here. Nora, there's some rope over there in the barn. You go fetch it. Don't be messing around none. I like Reggie and I wouldn't want to hurt her mama none."

"Reggie's mama appreciates that, too, Mattie."

"Then get the rope, girl."

"Yes, ma'am."

"Why, Mattie?" Penelope asked. "Why did you take Beau?"

" 'Cause they was being mean to him. Oh, Loomis wasn't any worse than any other trainer. It's just the way things are when you want a national champion worse than anything else in the world. Beau deserved better."

"Did you kill Loomis?"

"I'm not a killer, Penelope. He was already dead when I got there. Gave me a shock, you can bet. When I saw that, I just got Beau in the trailer and skedaddled right quick."

Nora returned with coils of rope trailing from her hands.

Mattie nodded. "Let's go on over to the hot walker now. You first, Penelope."

Penelope led the way to the walker. "But why take Chardonnay?" she asked over her shoulder.

"Beau needed a nice girlfriend after being cooped up so unnatural for most of his life. Horses got feelings, too, just like people. Something that no good desert rat don't understand. They've gotten to be real friendly. Too bad Chardonnay wasn't in season. I'd like to see the colt they'd produce."

"I'll bet that colt would be something," Penelope agreed.

"They been real nice and affectionate to each other. The way men and women should be, but that old fool just don't understand nothing," Mattie said. "He don't know nothing about women or horses either. Woman likes to be serviced real tender like. You know that. All of you do. Bet Andy and Jake know how to please a woman."

Penelope and Samantha exchanged a quick glance. It wasn't so long ago that they had joked about being serviced, but now it seemed like a hundred years.

"Anyways," Mattie said, "that's why I borrowed Chardonnay for a bit. Wanted Beau to have a proper lady friend. Wasn't gonna keep her though. Know how much you like that horse, Penelope. Damned old fool."

"You don't have to do this," Penelope said.

"Get on over there to the hot walker, Penelope, you get now."

Penelope got.

"Okay, Nora, you tie Penelope to that first arm there."

A hot walker was a merry-go-round for horses, only they didn't get to ride. Four metal arms protruded from a revolving center. The horse to be exercised was fastened to one of the arms by its bridle and when the machine was turned on, the arms moved and the horse was led in a wide circular path.

"Not too tight," Mattie called out. "I don't want to cut the circulation off, but tight enough so she can't get loose."

Nora did as ordered.

"Now you, Samantha."

When Penelope and Samantha stood, wrists tied together and their arms raised above their heads and attached to their respective anchor points, Mattie put the gun away and repeated the process for Nora.

"What are you going to do?" Penelope asked.

"Take Beauregarde and set 'em free."

"Just like *The Electric Horseman*."

Mattie nodded. "Gave me the idea. That Robert Redford. He's a good one, ain't he?"

"What about Red?"

"That's over. He don't care nothing about me. You can take the rat out of the desert but you can't take the rat outta the man. Something like that anyway."

"He's in love with you. He won't like it when you're in jail."

"Won't matter none to him. I'll bring Chardonnay back when Beau is running free. Figure they'll want to say good-bye."

"Where are they?"

Mattie laughed. "Right out there about two hundred yards or so. Desert sure does make a good hiding place."

"Don't do it, Mattie. We can work things out."

"We'll stand up for you," Samantha said.

"Reggie will miss you," Nora chimed in.

"She's gonna be a real good rider. Tell her to keep working while I'm gone."

"I will."

"Might as well get a little exercise while you're waiting to be rescued," Mattie said turning on the hot walker. "Waste not, want not, I always say."

Penelope wasn't planning on waiting for help to arrive, but bided her time since there didn't seem to be a whole lot she could do at the moment as the walker herky-jerked into motion. After one complete revolution around the well-worn path, Penelope watched Mattie disappear into the desert and the gathering dusk.

"I'm going to have to dress differently," Samantha said, "if I'm going to spend much more time around you, Penelope Warren." She kicked off her high heels and then had to hurry to catch up with the walker tugging at her arms.

"Well, you wanted to work off that hot fudge sundae," Nora said.

"What now?" Samantha asked.

Penelope looked back over her shoulder at her two companions. "Let's stay in step, at least," she replied. Once a Marine, always a Marine.

"What are we going to do?"

"I'm thinking," Penelope said.

"You do that, Butch, that's what you're good at," Samantha said paraphrasing one of her favorite lines from *Butch Cassidy and the Sundance Kid.*

"Stop," Penelope said. "I've had enough Robert Redford for one day." But she went right on thinking as she looked up at the rope knotted around her wrists. If . . .

Pull-ups had not been one of her best things in the Marine Corps. But if . . . While contemplating the possibilities, Penelope had slowed. The walker pulled at the rope and urged her along.

If I grab the slack in the rope and pull myself up, I can reach the knot with my teeth and . . .

The walker creaked and groaned as Penelope pulled herself off the ground and reached for the knot. There . . . almost . . . yes . . . Penelope dangled from the walker arm pulling at the knots with her teeth while her audience cheered her on.

"You can do it, Penelope, hang on."

"Go for it. You've almost got it. Do it, Penelope."

Sweat burst out on her forehead. Her arms ached. Her muscles trembled and quivered. Almost. . . .

"You did it!" Samantha cried. "Way to go, Penelope!"

Penelope fell to the ground and then had to scramble out of the way so Samantha and Nora did not trip over her. She gathered her breath and got slowly to her feet. *Damn, one lousy pull-up and I almost didn't make it.*

"Where are you going? What about us?"

"I'll be right back." Penelope ran to the mobile home and burst through the door. *Mattie really ought to lock up when she leaves,* Penelope thought. She surveyed the armament in the gun cabinet. She would have preferred a rifle, but Mattie had taken that. It didn't really matter since she had no intention of shooting Mattie in any case. Still, it would be nice to chat about the situation on equal terms. *My gun's bigger than your gun.* Penelope took the double-barreled shotgun, broke it open, found it loaded, and stuffed some extra shells into her pocket.

A pickup truck drove by and stopped at the barn.

Now who was that?

Penelope sneaked quietly out of the house, just in case.

"What are you ladies doing?" Red asked holding a big bouquet of flowers. He pushed his hat back on his head and scratched. He looked just a little perplexed at the sight of two women tied to a hot walker.

"Exercising," Samantha replied.

"Oh."

"Would you turn this machine off, please?" Nora asked.

"Sure, Where's Mattie?"

"She's taking Beauregarde to set him free."

"Beauregarde? How did she get Beauregarde?"

"It's a long story, Red. Will you please turn this thing off."

"Oh, yeah, Samantha."

Just then Penelope, having identified the old desert rat, raced past with the shotgun. "Untie them, Red," she cried.

"Where you going, Penelope?"

"After Mattie!"

"I'm coming with you." Red broke into a trot.

"What about us?" a bank president and a local historian demanded in unison.

At the edge of the desert, Penelope skidded to a halt. Big Mike had decided to rejoin the fray and slid right into her. "Mattie," she shouted. "I'm coming after you."

"Don't you do it," Mattie shouted right back.

"Me, too," Red hollered.

"Red?"

"I brought you flowers."

"You did?"

"I want to marry you," Red bellowed, still brandishing the bouquet.

Penelope waited. A little matchmaking might be in order.

"You do?"

" 'Course, I do, woman!"

"Say it, then."

"Say what?"

"You know what."

"Go on, Red, say it," Penelope urged.

"Tell her, Red," Samantha said. "Then stop this thing and untie us."

"Well?" Mattie yelled. "This is your last chance."

"Go on, damn it," Nora cried. "I'm getting tired."

"Well . . . I love you." It came out as a muffled croak.

"I can't hear you."

Penelope thought Mattie sounded just like a drill instructor at Parris Island.

"I love you," Red roared.

The heavens heard that one.

How about that? The bouquet was mightier than the gun.

Mattie sat on the couch clutching her flowers. Red was beside her hanging onto her free hand, as though she might suddenly jump up and disappear into the desert night once more.

Samantha and Nora were in the kitchen making coffee.

Penelope was thinking—again. It was one thing to have Beauregarde and Chardonnay safe and sound, but the big question still remained—if Mattie didn't kill Jack and Maryanne, who did?

"What's gonna happen to Mattie?" Red asked. His philosophy of punishment for horse thieves had altered drastically when he discovered it was his beloved doing all the thieving.

"I don't know," Penelope replied. "I suppose it depends on Horace Melrose. How far he wants to press the charges."

"We'll all be character witnesses," Samantha said bringing a tray of cups and saucers. "It's not as though Mattie wanted to hurt Beauregarde."

"That's right," Nora said as she started pouring coffee all around. "She was just doing what she thought was best for his welfare."

"Well, we better call the police," Mattie said. "I'm ready to surrender."

"Aw, honey bunch."

"Will you wait for me, Red?"

" 'Course, I will."

"Nobody's calling the police," Penelope said. "Yet."

"Why not? They should know we have Beauregarde back."

"Oh, we'll let Dutch know, all right, but we can't return Beauregarde, or Chardonnay, for that matter. We have to keep them hidden. We have a killer to catch and Beauregarde is still mixed up in this somehow."

When Dutch arrived, he was more than a little irritated with Penelope. "I've told you before," Dutch said, "always call for backup first, not after."

Penelope didn't remember Dutch ever telling her that before, but she didn't contradict him. "I brought my backup with me," she said.

"They were pretty damned good, too," Mattie said, "but I got the drop on 'em."

"You hush," Dutch said. "I still haven't figured out what to do with you."

"You can't do anything, don't you see?" Penelope said. "Everything is to go on just like nothing happened. You can put Mattie in jail later."

"Aw, honey bunch," Red wailed.

"Can we have conjugal visits?" Mattie asked.

Dutch groaned. Everyone in Empty Creek *was* crazy.

"We keep Beau and Char right here. Mattie kept them hidden pretty well. You could have someone guard them while we trap the killer."

"How are *we* going to do that?" Dutch asked.

"Beats me," Penelope admitted.

Everyone in the room looked at Dutch expectantly.

"Penelope's right," Samantha said.

Nora nodded.

"What's a con-ju-gal visit?" Red asked.

In the end, of course, Dutch agreed. There *was* a murderer to find. Everyone was sworn to secrecy, including Reggie who had her grounding lifted as a condition of silence. "Little blackmailer," Nora said after getting off the phone.

"Yes, that's probably the next order of business," Penelope said.

"The next order of business," Dutch said turning to Mattie, "is to find out what our little horse thief saw the night she took Beauregarde."

Other than the Bulwer-Lyttonesque observation that it was "a dark and stormy night"—and Penelope's giggle to which Mattie replied, "Well, Snoopy is right. It *was* dark and stormy, and it *was* night"—Mattie saw very little that they didn't already know.

Still, Dutch took her through every step she had made that fateful evening and night.

"I knew the place pretty well so I didn't need to case it. Isn't that what they say in the underworld, Sheriff?"

Penelope suppressed her mirth this time, but vowed to get Mattie reading some modern mystery novels.

"Chief," Dutch said. "I'm not a sheriff."

"Usta have a sheriff, though," Red said. Now that he was committed, Red was determined to defend his lady whenever he deemed it necessary.

"Never mind. Go on."

"I took the back road in. Everything was dark and stormy, like I said, and when I got to the barn, there was just the one light on. Didn't need but one light to see that Jack Loomis wouldn't be training any more horses. Gave me a start, I can tell you. Still, I checked for a pulse. Couldn't very well leave him there if he was still breathing. He was warm, but dead."

"Did you ever think you might have surprised the killer?" Penelope asked. "That he might still be there?"

"The thought did occur to me, but everything was quiet . . . except for the storm, of course. Did I tell you it was a dark and stormy night?" Mattie smiled with a great deal of satisfaction at that one.

"I believe you did mention it. . . ."

"Can we just get on with it?"

"Don't rush me, Sheriff. I'm getting there as fast as I can."

"What time was it? Do you know?"

"Pretty near midnight straight up."

"That pinpoints the time of death, at least."

Dutch took her through the story a second time, but her tale remained essentially the same.

And that was that.

The case of the disappearing horses had been solved.

Now what? Penelope asked herself, thinking it was a pretty damned good question and wishing she had an answer.

"Where have you been?" Andy cried when Penelope and Big Mike finally got home. "I've been calling all over town looking for you."

"I'm sorry," Penelope said, "but I've been out with the girls." It was only a little bit of a lie. Penelope felt guilty about keeping the secret from Andy, but he was a newspaperman with a deadline looming. She hoped when all the *Sturm und Drang* was done, she would be able to give Andy an exclusive. It was the least she could do. But that was later. He deserved a little treat now for his obvious concern.

"Next time, call me, please."

"I will," Penelope promised. She grabbed his ears, pulled him close, and gave him a great big smackeroo, much to the disgust of Mycroft who was waiting impatiently for his dinner.

"Wow," Andy said when he was allowed to come up for air. "You should be late more often."

Samantha was experiencing much the same problem with Jake Peterson, and alleviating her guilt in a similar, although not quite so bold, fashion. She desperately wanted to signal him that everything was going to work out for the horse show, particularly when he announced, "There were another two cancellations today and then when I couldn't reach you . . . well, I just started to worry."

"I *am* sorry," Samantha said. She patted his hand and then kissed his cheek.

"What happened to your stockings?"

"Oh, I was out looking at some property," Samantha lied, "and I took my shoes off. Let me fix you a drink and then I'll take a quick shower. And then . . ."

Big Jake smiled broadly.

"I was thinking of dinner," Samantha said.

"No then?" he asked sorrowfully.

"We'll do *then* after dinner. You'll need your strength."

"Promise?"

"Of course, silly."

Since Tony Lyme-Regis was in Los Angeles and Reggie was already in on the secret, poor Nora had no one to feel guilty for or with. But just as she was feeling pretty left out in the let's make up department, Tony called and they giggled a lot as they planned his weekend visit. Nora knew exactly what a conjugal visit entailed.

As did Red the Rat, now having had the meaning of the word explained in a variety of different contexts.

Penelope wondered what Chardonnay and Beauregarde were finding to talk about. They *did* make a handsome couple. It was just too bad that neither of them spoke English. After all, Beauregarde knew who killed Jack Loomis and had probably shared the information with Chardonnay by now. What else did horses have to talk about?

That was another pretty damned good question.

Not wanting another bout of insomnia—however brief—Penelope tried to empty her mind of thoughts, but it didn't work. Like a fledgling journalism student studying for a first examination, the questions flashed through her mind.

Who? Why?

Why? Who?

Just before Penelope finally slipped away into the blessed land of dreamless sleep, it occurred to her that it was high time that somebody started eliminating the impossible.

CHAPTER EIGHTEEN

Although it had been less than sixty hours since Dutch had called to tell her of Maryanne Melrose's death at the hands of a person or persons unknown, Penelope felt as though it had been much longer—an interminable stretch of time punctuated by increasing confusion and frustration. Even the successful recovery of Chardonnay and Beauregarde did little to sustain her spirits. There was still a killer skulking around town and she was damned if she could figure out what to do next.

Apparently, two of the other coconspirators in the great Empty Creek cover-up were not equally downcast, for they decided independently and virtually simultaneously that they should meet. Thus, Penelope had no sooner hung up with Samantha after agreeing to a lunch date, than Nora called with the same idea.

They met at a coffee shop outside Empty Creek where they would be unlikely to meet anyone they knew. Samantha and Nora were still excited at their part in rescuing the horses.

"I can see why you like this so much," Samantha said. "It's really quite a break from the usual routine."

"So," Nora said clapping her hands. "What's next?"

"Perhaps we should consider," Penelope said reverting to the Master once more, " 'the curious incident of the dog in the nighttime.' "

" 'The dog did nothing in the nighttime,' " Nora said.

" 'That was the curious incident,' remarked Sherlock Holmes.' " Samantha contributed the conclusion.

"Very good, class," Penelope said. "I'm glad to see we've all been studying the Canon. Unfortunately, there was no dog."

"Well, there should have been."

"At least, a cat. Big Mike would have known what to do."

"Only a horse."

"And the horse did nothing in the nighttime."

And that, Penelope thought, is also curious. Why didn't Beauregarde do something? More to the point, why didn't the killer do something?

And that was the answer! At least, it was the right question.

There were more than a few loose ends to gather up, of course, but . . . it was a starting point—at last. Penelope sat back in her chair and smiled somewhat smugly.

"What?" Samantha asked.

"Yes, what?" Nora added.

"I don't know what you mean."

"We mean," Samantha said, "that you look just like Big Mike confronting a bowl of lima beans."

"A very big bowl."

"Oh, it's nothing," Penelope said striving desperately for a suitable distraction. It wouldn't do to get Sam and Nora involved in this little scheme. Unlike a confrontation with Mattie, this one might really be dangerous. Stymied for something plausible, Penelope turned to an old reliable. Sex was always good. "I was just thinking of Andy last night," she said. "He was worried because I was so late and I felt so awful that I hadn't called . . . well . . . you know."

Samantha did know and blushed. "Never mind."

Nora, who didn't know, at least not at firsthand from last night, turned a bright red as well. Anthony Lyme-Regis certainly had a way with words.

That afternoon, Penelope pretended to order books while she was sitting at her desk in the back room of Mycroft & Company. Business was brisk, but the continuous tinkle of the bell announcing each new cash customer didn't distract her in the least. Scheming and plotting was too much fun.

The fact that her plan might get her in a great deal of trouble didn't bother Penelope in the slightest. It was a risk she was willing to take on her own. If he knew, Dutch would try to dissuade her and if that didn't work would probably have her tossed into a cell until it was over. Tweedledee and Tweedledum would only call her crazy and upset the timing somehow. But since she didn't plan to tell them, it really didn't matter all that much.

The plan was quite simple. Of course, if any of the premises were false, Penelope would wish she had completed that long-ago class in logic, instead of bailing out at the first syllogism.

Premise #1: The killer hadn't been watching Mattie at all. She had scared him off before he could take Beau.

Premise #2: The killer didn't know who had the horse but desperately wanted that information because he was still going to blackmail Horace Melrose somehow.

Premise #3: The likeliest suspect now that Horace had an alibi for the time of his wife's murder was Arguing Man.

Premise #4: The killer—and the blackmailer—would contact Horace again soon.

Therefore, Premise #5: When the blackmailer—and the killer—called Horace again, have Horace tell him that Penelope knew where the horse was.

That might be a little dicey for Horace if the killer-blackmailer tried to torture the information out of him, particularly since Penelope had no intention of telling Horace of Beau's present whereabouts.

Penelope didn't like thinking about the possibility that the killer-blackmailer might bypass Horace Melrose and try to torture the information out of *her*. But in either scenario, the killer ultimately had to come to her. Since the killer seemed fond of telephone booths as a means of communication, Penelope had already picked out her own where she would take the message.

She hoped that everyone else who knew the little secret would have the good sense not to say a word to anyone.

She had already briefed Horace who was less than enthusiastic about the scheme but, as Penelope quickly pointed out, "What other choice do you have?"

"None, I guess. The police still think I'm involved. That's why I didn't tell them about the blackmail call. You're the only one who knows."

"Let's keep it that way," Penelope said, although she promptly went over the strategy with Big Mike, who seemed to approve. In the retelling, however, Penelope discovered a flaw in Premise #2. What if the murderer had already accomplished his purpose in killing the erstwhile lovers and didn't care about Beauregarde at all? In that case, the killer was gone and the murders would be carried on the books, probably forever, as unsolved. Except that Maryanne had denied knowing Loper in Arkansas. If Arguing Man was Dr. Wendell P. Oliver's brother and if he sought only revenge for his sibling's incarceration and death . . .

Well, with luck, it *was* possible to get away with murder. Still, the blackmailer's call indicated that Beauregarde was involved. That was the only thing that made any sense whatsoever.

Right?

"Damn, Mycroft, your namesake's family was much better at this," Penelope said.

Big Mike had been on the desk the entire time imitating Mycroft Holmes in the silence of the Diogenes Club where speech was forbidden except in the Stranger's Room. Now, he merely yawned and stretched to show his approval.

"Mr. Richard Raymond," Kathy announced.

"Oh, bother, what does he want?"

Kathy shrugged. "Shall I ask if he has an appointment?"

"That would be out of character. No one around here ever makes an appointment. They just barge in, like me."

"Andy used to make appointments to see you all the time."

"Well, yes, but that was just Andy." In the early days of his courtship Andy did, indeed, make appointments to come by Mycroft & Company where he stammered and blushed and knocked things off the shelves. Penelope had thought he would never work up his nerve to ask her out. Smiling at the memory, she stuck her head through the curtain and said, "Come on back, Richard."

"So this is what the back of a bookstore looks like," he said. "I always wondered."

"Very much like the front of a bookstore," Penelope said. "Filled with books."

"Yes, I can see that now. Most illuminating."

Penelope thought it was most cluttered but let it pass. "Where's Susan?" she asked.

"She's resting, the poor thing. The strain is getting to her. I'm not sure she's cut out to be an investigator."

"I suppose these things take time."

"Oh, she passed her probationary period, of course, but she lacks stamina and staying power. It may be that she's suited to another aspect of the business. Still, time will tell. It always does."

"How can I help you?" Penelope asked, not wanting to pass judgment on Susan Vaughn's aptitude for snooping. It was not an acquired trait to Penelope's way of thinking. Either you were born a snoop or you weren't.

"I'm afraid my excursion into the computer files didn't turn up anything. I was hoping to find something, anything, that might provide some slight hint of what was going on." Raymond spread his hands helplessly. His pencil-thin mustache twitched, reminding Penelope of the bunny rabbits at the barn.

"Well, you tried."

"It's Lora Lou on the phone. Says it's important."

Penelope picked up immediately. "Warren, Homicide," Penelope said in her best TV cop imitation.

"He's here!" Lora Lou whispered.

"Who's here?" Penelope asked. "Or there rather."

"The man I saw arguing with Jack Loomis."

"Are you sure."

"I'm positive. He's out back loading feed into his pickup right now."

"Keep him there. I'm on my way."

On her way past the counter, Penelope told Kathy to call the police. "Tell them there's an armed robbery in progress at The Tack Shack."

"Really?"

"No, there's a man loading feed in his pickup, but they won't come for that. Tell them they better surround the place just in case there are hostages."

"Who takes hostages to load feed?"

"Never mind, I'll explain later. Just do it."

Penelope ran out the door with Big Mike and Richard Raymond right at her heels.

Reporting an armed robbery was certainly an effective way to get everyone's attention. By the time Penelope and Big Mike reached The Tack Shack—Raymond was running a poor third—black and whites from all over town were rolling to screeching halts at Lora Lou Longstreet's place of business. Unconcerned at the sight of so many police officers leaping from cars with shotguns, Penelope calmly strolled right through the front door ignoring Sam Connors who hissed at her to stop. While his sharply whispered commands went unheeded by Penelope, Big Mike stopped to pay his respects and show there were no hard feelings on his part over that long-ago incident. Connors scooped the cat off the sidewalk and plopped him on the front seat of the police car. "Stay!" he said.

Yeah, right, and miss all the fun? Mycroft scooted right out the other door and into The Tack Shack.

"Is he still here?"

"Out back," Lora Lou said, falling in step next to Penelope who was heading for the back door. "My God, what did you do?"

"Reported an armed robbery in progress."

"Here? And they believed you?"

"Well, a cowboy could have been stealing a saddle or something."

"At gunpoint?"

As they passed through the back room of The Tack Shack—filled with miscellaneous tack naturally and an oil painting of a very nude Lora Lou Longstreet—Penelope said, "Nice rendering."

"Thank you."

"Hi, Leia." Lora Lou's big white dog looked mournfully at Penelope.

"Freeze!" Peggy Norton's cup of police vocabulary verily runneth over.

"Not us," Penelope said calmly. "Him." She pointed to the man in the doorway of a storage trailer holding a fifty-pound sack of feed.

Peggy and Sam Connors swung to point their weapons at the cowboy who promptly dropped the bag to the ground where it landed with a resounding thud. He flung his arms in the air. "Don't shoot!"

"Him?"

"That *is* the man?" Penelope asked Lora Lou.

"That's him."

"He's the one," Penelope said.

"What's going on?" Sam Connors asked. He was growing

very suspicious of another Penelope plot. "He's stealing feed? Where's his gun?"

"No," Lora Lou said. "It's paid for. He doesn't have a gun. That was Penelope's idea."

"Figures."

"What's going on?" the cowboy asked plaintively. "Can I put my hands down?"

"No," Penelope said. "He's the man who was seen arguing with Jack Loomis shortly before he was murdered."

Sam and Peggy looked at the cowboy with new interest. "Is that so?" Sam drawled.

"Assume the position," Peggy said curtly. It didn't take long to pat him down. Peggy had been getting some practice lately. "He's clean."

"What's going on?" Richard Raymond asked as he emerged from the rear entrance of the establishment.

Penelope was tired of answering that particular question so she asked one of her own. "Where have you been?"

"I stopped to admire a very nice painting. Is it for sale?"

"No," Lora Lou said. "Who are you and what are you doing in my shop?"

"I'm with her," Raymond said. "Them," he amended as Big Mike arrived on the scene. Apparently he had stopped to meditate on the painting as well and say hello to the shy wolfhound.

"What about me?" the cowboy asked from his position against the black and white. "Can I get up?"

He was answered with a resounding chorus. "No!"

"Well, fiddely foo."

What kind of cowboy—or killer for that matter—said fiddely foo? Penelope wondered.

"What's going on?" The police chief had arrived.

"Yeah, what's going on?" The Robbery-Homicide Bureau had now been heard from.

Penelope sighed. That was what came of too many video games in the world. Originality and creativity had been sent packing. She explained once more.

Eventually, the confusion was sorted out and the cowboy was allowed to stand without the assistance of a police car while Dutch delivered a stern lecture about the impropriety of falsely reporting an armed robbery in progress.

"It worked, didn't it?" Penelope believed truth was the best defense against one of Dutch's lectures.

Dutch sighed and turned to the cowboy. "What's your name?"

"Elmer Goymes."

Elmer Goymes? Penelope was beginning to have a bad feeling about the situation, particularly since Big Mike had ambled over to check him out and had apparently anointed him with the honorary title of Cat Person.

"You sure your name isn't Oliver from Arkansas?"

"Arkansas? I was born in Arizona. I've never even been to Arkansas."

"Why were you arguing with Jack Loomis?"

"He owed me money. Twenty bucks."

Oh, oh! Penelope edged backward toward the door.

"Don't take another step," Dutch said.

"I have to get back to work."

"Freeze."

Penelope froze.

"I just started working here," Elmer said. "I was down in Tucson for a while. Figured I'd work my way north. See what it's like up here." Surrounded by police officers wearing serious frowns on their faces, it looked like Elmer Goymes was thinking of moving back to Tucson without bothering with the rest of his feed order.

Tweedledee compared the artist's sketch with Elmer. "Doesn't look anything like him."

"Don't blame the artist," Lora Lou said, "blame me. I just didn't give him a very good description."

"You're the Arkansas expert," Penelope said turning to Richard Raymond. "What do you think?"

"Doesn't look anything like the Wendell Oliver I knew."

They checked him out anyway. Using a battery of telephones and radios, they ascertained that Elmer Goymes was, indeed, Elmer Goymes of Tucson.

Fiddely foo was right!

As the gathering slowly dispersed, most of the men found an excuse to pass through The Tack Shack's back room and take a furtive glance or two or three at Lora Lou Longstreet starkers. She was, after all, a very attractive young lady, with or without her clothes, in real life or on canvas.

"Are you sure you wouldn't like to sell it?" Raymond asked again.

"Pete the bartender wants to hang it in the Double B," Lora Lou said. "I think it would be very good advertising."

"It's a good likeness," Penelope said, "at least as far as I can tell, not having actually seen you in your birthday suit."

Lora Lou laughed. "The rest of it's pretty good, too. A little flattering, but close to the real thing. You should let my little sweetie paint you. Pete would have a matching set then."

"Don't even think about it, Penelope," Dutch said.

"Why not? I think Lora Lou's right. It *would* be good for business."

"And we could have postcards done up for the snowbirds."

"Show the artistic side of Empty Creek."

"With Stormy and Laney, too."

"Don't forget Nora."

Dutch groaned and fled just as Samantha Dale wandered in.

"What's going on?" Samantha asked.

"How would you like to pose in the nude?"

"Show the business side of Empty Creek, so to speak."

Penelope and Lora Lou broke up laughing and Samantha never did completely understand what was going on although she did think Big Jake wouldn't mind having a portrait of her, but not behind the bar of the Double B.

While making Dutch blush—and Samantha for that matter—was fun, it didn't bring the case any closer to a conclusion, particularly since Arguing Man had now been dismissed as a suspect. There was nothing left to do but wait for the real killer-blackmailer to call.

And Penelope was tired of waiting.

The cuckoo bird danced out of its home and announced the hour. There was just time to drive out and ensure that Horace Melrose knew exactly what to do before meeting Andy. And there was always the slight possibility that the killer would call while she was there.

"Come on, Mikey, let's go visiting," Penelope said as the little bird retreated and the door closed protectively behind him. It did occur, albeit briefly and much too late, to Penelope that the cuckoo bird knew what it was doing. But then its role in life was strictly defined and did not allow for a great deal of initiative. Penelope imagined it was rather like working for the United States Postal Service.

Driving out of town, Penelope did a double take when she saw Ms. Susan Vaughn scurry from the biker bar and hurry off in the direction of the Lazy Traveller. Watching Susan recede in the rearview mirror, Penelope realized that poor Ms. Vaughn must have received the shock of her young life when she wandered into that particular watering hole by mistake. Although the bikers were aging and fairly harmless, they did show a ferocious front with their beards, leather jackets, and chains. Doubtless, Ms. Vaughn was now on her way back to the motel for another rest period.

Oh, well. Penelope smiled as she visualized the expression on Susan's face when confronted by a dozen or more imitation outlaw bikers.

The expression on Horace Melrose's face was sickly in comparison as he answered the door warily, peeking through a crack before releasing a newly installed chain.

Penelope looked just as warily at Horace when she saw the 30–30 Winchester in his hand. "Is that loaded?"

"Of course, it's loaded."

"May I?" Penelope asked holding our her hand. Horace relinquished the rifle reluctantly and watched as Penelope pointed the rifle to a far corner of the ceiling and worked the lever action quickly and expertly, ejecting cartridges on the floor. "Loaded rifles make me nervous."

"What if he comes and knocks on the front door?"

"Then, we'll reload the rifle before we open it. Besides, he's going to call. He doesn't want you to see his face."

"He could wear a mask."

"That's true, I suppose, but unlikely." Penelope handed the rifle back to Horace and knelt to retrieve the cartridges from the living-room rug. Big Mike was sniffing at one of them.

"What did you find, Mikey?" He turned and wrinkled his nose distastefully at Penelope. Apparently, he didn't like the smell of cordite.

Five of the six shells on the floor were gleaming in pristine condition. The sixth had been fired. Penelope picked it up carefully and smelled it. She did like the smell of cordite, but on the firing range, not under this particular condition. "Did you fire the rifle recently?" she asked.

"No. I just got it out from under the bed after you called."

"You didn't check to see if it was loaded?"

"I always keep it loaded."

Horace Melrose had obviously not been a Marine with all of the safety instruction that came while earning the title, even before the recruit touched a weapon for the first time.

"That could get you killed," Penelope said.

"So could hanging around with you."

He had her there.

Penelope was about to say something reassuring when the telephone rang.

CHAPTER
NINETEEN

I t rang a second time, and a third.

"Answer it," Penelope said.

Horace approached the instrument much as he would a coiled and buzzing rattlesnake, so Penelope finally plucked the phone from its receiver and handed it to him.

"Hello?"

Penelope waited.

Horace listened for a long time before saying, "No, I already subscribe to the *News Journal*."

Damn!

"Why didn't you interrupt?" Penelope asked.

"I don't like to be impolite."

"You wasted his time. He could have been calling someone else who doesn't subscribe."

"I never thought of that. Besides, it was a woman."

"Man, woman. Let them get on with their job."

The phone rang again.

This time Horace picked up immediately and said, "I already subscribe."

Penelope nodded approvingly until she saw Horace blanch and grab for a piece of paper.

"I don't have him," Horace read from what appeared to be a prepared script, "but I know who does . . . No, the person involved won't do that . . . I'm telling you . . . This is the way it has to be . . . I don't know and I can't find out," Horace cried rather plaintively. "If you want Beauregarde, follow these instructions exactly. Call this number at eight o'clock tonight. You'll be told what to do then . . . The person involved was very specific. That's all I can do." Horace slammed the phone down.

"Good," Penelope said. "You were very convincing."

"I was nervous. I'm not cut out for this sort of thing."

The telephone rang again. Horace grabbed it. "I told you what to do!" he hollered. "That's it . . . Oh . . . No, I already subscribe to the *News Journal*. Sorry."

"Was it the same man?"

"I told you. It's a woman."

"The blackmailer?"

"Oh, I thought you meant the subscription lady. Yeah, it was the same guy."

"What did he sound like?"

"Some guy. I don't know. He had a deep voice. Like he smoked too much."

"You didn't recognize his voice?"

"Just like last time. Somebody I never heard before. He sounded a little like Boris Karloff."

Some help that was. Penelope could just imagine calling

Dutch and telling him to put out an APB on some guy who
sounded a little like Boris Karloff. "Can I use your phone?"

"Can I have my rifle back?"

"After we leave. By the way, did you happen to take a shot at
the insurance investigators?"

"No. Why would I do that?"

Penelope could think of any number of reasons, but let it
pass. "Did you fire it recently?" she asked. "For any reason."

Horace shook his head, looking at the spent cartridge. "I
don't know how that happened unless Maryanne . . ."

"Why would Maryanne shoot at them?"

"I don't know."

"Did she know where to find it?"

"I kept it under the bed."

"On second thought, I'd better take that rifle to the police.
The lab guys can check the ballistics."

"How am I going to protect myself?"

"You only have one weapon in the house?" Penelope questioned, conveniently ignoring the fact that she only had one
rifle.

"I've got a twenty-two, but it's loaded with snake shot."

"We're dealing with a snake. Use the twenty-two. Now can I
make a couple of calls?"

"Go ahead."

"What's Abigail's number?"

"Why are you calling her?"

"None of your business. The less you know the better."

Penelope dialed as Horace recited her number.

"I already subscribe," Abigail shouted. "I've told you that."

"It's Penelope."

"Oh. I'm sorry. That person just keeps calling. I was ready to take the phone off the hook."

"Do that after I hang up. Would you mind if we stopped by for a few minutes?"

"Not at all. Who's we?"

"Just Mycroft and me."

"I thought you meant Horace."

"How did you know where I was?"

"I'm an FBI agent. Remember? Besides, I can see your Jeep from my window."

Penelope chuckled. "See you in a few minutes." She depressed the receiver with her finger. "One more call and we're out of here."

"Newsroom, Anderson."

"You sound a little like Boris Karloff. Did you know that, sweetie?"

"Where did that come from?"

"Never mind. I have some things to do. Can we meet at the Double B about eight-thirty instead of dinner at home?"

"Sure, no problem."

"By the way, did you know your telephone solicitors are bothering people all over town?"

"It's a trap," Abigail Wilson said scratching Big Mike's neck. He had claimed her lap without being invited.

"Yes."

"And you're the bait."

Penelope nodded. "And you're the backup."

"Why not involve the police?"

"Dutch is too protective of me. He'd have a SWAT team out there to say nothing of every cop in town. Scare every murderer in Arizona away. Right now only three people know the plan."

"Four. Don't forget the killer."

"Yes, four. Five, really. I told Mycroft all about it."

Abigail looked down at Big Mike and gave him another scratch. "I like it. Did he approve?"

"He purred. Of course, he was eating at the time."

"He's purring now."

"Then, he must like the plan, too."

Abigail nodded. "I really want to catch this guy."

"Is it personal?"

"A little."

"I wondered. Were you and Jack lovers?"

"You knew?"

"I suspected."

"I liked him and we were together a lot. It just happened. I didn't plan it. And then . . ."

"Never mind. We're going to get his killer."

"And Maryanne's," Abigail said. "I owe her that much."

The Empty Creek Police Department was nearly deserted after hours. The evening watch was already on the streets.

Penelope dropped Horace's Winchester off at the desk to be logged in as potential evidence. Fortunately, Dutch and the homicide detectives had already gone home so she didn't have to answer any questions, although she did leave a note for Dutch explaining the rifle's presence and requesting a ballistics check.

Maryanne Melrose. She added one more unknown aspect to a case in which nothing was as it appeared and the main players seemingly changed names and identities as often as they changed clothes. If the ballistics test came back showing that

Maryanne fired the shot at or near the insurance investigators, why then . . .

"Thank you, Maryanne," Penelope said. "Rest in peace."

Choosing the very same telephone booth at the Lazy Traveller used by the shooter satisfied Penelope's sense of irony very nicely, indeed. She could have chosen a more obscure location, but figured the killer had access to telephone locations through one source or another. If not, however, Penelope didn't want to make it too hard.

She glanced up at the Lilac Suite and thought she saw the curtain move. The insurance investigators had probably ordered room service as a prelude to whatever erotic activities were planned for the evening. Penelope didn't begrudge them a final Empty Creek fling. With luck, everything would end tomorrow.

The telephone rang precisely at eight o'clock. Penelope picked it up and said, "Yeah."

"All right, I'm tired of messing around."

The go-between did sound a little like Boris Karloff.

"Then, do exactly as I say."

"That ain't the way it works. You do what *I* say."

Penelope hung up.

"Did that get your attention?" Penelope asked after picking up again.

"Jesus, I hate pushy broads."

Penelope hung up again. This time she let the phone ring several times before answering.

"Stop doing that."

"Say you're sorry."

"Jesus!"

"Say it!"

"Wait! Don't hang up. I'm sorry, all right?"

"Say you're really, really, realllllly sorry and that you'll be a good little Boris Karloff from now on."

"Huh?"

"Do it."

"I'm really, really, realllllly sorry with sugar on it. What was the rest of it?"

"Oh, never mind. Do you want Beauregarde or not?"

"Yeah, but . . ."

"But me no buts," Penelope said. "You're going to do exactly as I say or else there's no payoff. Got it?"

"I got it, but . . ."

Penelope interrupted again, curtly issued instructions, made him repeat them once, and hung up abruptly, feeling rather pleased with herself. "If we ever want a second career," she told Big Mike, "I think we have a future as blackmailers."

With the Plan now bubbling right along, Penelope and Big Mike went to the Double B to meet Andy.

Red and Mattie were seated at a secluded table in the far corner of the dining room. My God, Penelope thought, another first. She had never seen Red anywhere but at his usual bar stool. If this kept up, Red would have to light out for the Territory soon. Like Huckleberry Finn, civilization was nipping hard at Red's heels. Red was oblivious but Penelope caught Mattie's eye. The older woman gave a slight nod. The horses were under guard.

Good old Plan.

Penelope was tempted to order a glass of champagne but decided that a celebration was just the teeniest bit premature so when Debbie came by the table she asked for her usual white wine.

"Any news on Chardonnay yet?" Debbie asked.

Penelope hated lying to Debbie but frowned anyway as she shook her head. She tried to squeeze out a tear or two, but she was unable to cry on cue like Stormy.

"Too bad, but it'll work out." Debbie patted Penelope's shoulder reassuringly.

"I'm sure it will," Penelope said.

Penelope was equally evasive when Andy came in and sat down after the obligatory greeting to Big Mike who was a little lonely without Red on the next bar stool.

"There's nothing new," she stated flatly.

They ordered dinner and Penelope tried not to think of the Plan as it gurgled merrily along. At least, she hoped it was gurgling and not disappearing down a sinkhole.

As they entered the house, Penelope said, "Would you pour the wine, dear? There's something I have to do. I'll be right out."

Penelope went to the bedroom closet and took a magazine for her AR–15 from the top shelf and loaded ten rounds. When the civilian version of the military's M–16 was loaded and the safety clicked on, Penelope placed the rifle carefully under the bed where it would be close at hand during the night. There was no use taking chances at this stage.

"What are you doing?"

Caught in the act, Penelope jumped guiltily. "Just a precaution."

"You're up to something. You never load that thing unless something is about to happen."

"No, really," Penelope said jumping up, "it's nothing but a precaution."

Andy looked dubious, but Penelope took her glass of wine and clinked glasses. It was distraction time and Penelope knew how to play that game to perfection.

While distracting Andy at night was one thing, Penelope found that repeating it in the morning was quite another thing entirely. When she awakened at her usual hour and sluggishly fought for consciousness, he was still there, a beaming apparition bearing coffee. "I thought you'd be at work by now," Penelope mumbled.

"I thought I might take the day off."

"Well, I'm going to work."

"Good. I'll write a feature on a day in the life of my favorite bookstore owner."

"How boring."

"Oh, I don't think so. An inside look at an independent bookstore, competing and surviving against the threat of the big chain stores. I should have thought of it sooner."

Penelope stumbled to the shower. Think fast, she told herself, think fast. The Plan was in motion and she didn't want any deviations. Last-minute changes were always disastrous. The hot water streamed over her, clearing her mind, but not enough to come up with a plausible excuse short of telling him to buzz off.

"Andy. . . ." She smiled seductively.

"Forget it," he said with a grin. "That's not going to work this morning."

Damn. Penelope slipped into her bathrobe. It was time for Plan B—whatever *that* was.

Plan B apparently consisted of Andy keeping an eye on Penelope while she dressed—fun—while she sullenly drank coffee at the kitchen table—not so fun—and while she drove to Mycroft & Company, keeping a safe distance between the vehicles—exacting because Andy thought she might just take off and he would be in a high-speed pursuit.

In short, Andy stuck to Penelope like Krazy Glue, even in the relatively small confines of the bookstore, prompting Kathy to ask, "What's going on?"

"Ask Penelope," Andy said.

"What's going on?" Kathy repeated, turning to Penelope.

"I hate that question. People keep asking it."

"That's because you never answer it."

"All right," Penelope said. "I give up."

"Are you finally going to tell me *what's going on?*"

"When you get back."

"And just where am I going?"

"Back to my place." She sighed with resignation. "Get the rifle, but hurry. We have to be on the road soon."

"Where are *we* going?"

"*We* are going to catch a killer."

"We *are?*"

"Yes, *if* you get going."

"What are you going to do?"

"Call Dutch," Penelope lied. "We may need backup."

"Promise you'll wait. I don't want to miss anything."

"Of course."

"I'll be back in a flash."

"Be careful. It's loaded."

As soon as he was out of sight, Penelope told Kathy, "We'll be back later."

"Aren't you going to wait for Andy?"

"Tell him I'll meet him behind The Tack Shack."

"Okay, but where are you going? I thought you were going to call Dutch."

"To The Tack Shack, of course," Penelope said. "I'll call Dutch from there."

She bundled Big Mike into the Jeep and drove off down the alley behind the storefronts, heading away from The Tack Shack without so much as a By Your Leave. She felt terrible about deluding Andy like that, but this was all her idea and she didn't want him getting hurt.

There were two choices now as Penelope saw it. Borrow a gun or buy a new one. Borrowing might take too long and require explanations. With all of the federal paperwork involved in a firearms purchase, buying a new one would take some time, but it would require no explanations.

Heading for the Gun Emporium, however, Penelope found a third option. She could always steal one. It wouldn't exactly be stealing, however, since she fully planned to return it. It was like borrowing without the explanation.

She cut the Jeep's engine and glided to a stop beside the black and white parked behind Mom's Do-Nuts. The cops always parked behind the donut shop, rather than leave the citizens with the impression that they were always on a coffee break at Mom's.

Penelope looked up and down the alleyway.

Perfect.

"Keep an eye out, Mikey," she said.

She opened the passenger door of the black and white and went to work on the lock of the shotgun rack.

Yes!

One police shotgun.

Dutch was going to be really angry. So were two unsuspecting police officers who should have kept a closer eye on their car while consuming jelly donuts and coffee. Oh, well. It was for a good cause.

If all went well, another hour or two would see Richard Raymond in jail charged with double homicide. Never trust a man with a pencil-thin mustache.

CHAPTER
TWENTY

Quiet.
    Deserted.
    The old one-room shack was perfect for a clandestine meeting with a blackmailer and a murderer. Abandoned years ago by the last in a long series of squatters and desert rats, it had not yet been reclaimed by the desert but the winds and sand and scrub were trying. Penelope had found the place during a ride with Laney when they decided to explore a territory away from their usual horseback haunts.

    Driving down the dusty desert track, Penelope noted with satisfaction that the photograph of Sir Beauregarde was attached to the trunk of the saguaro cactus she had specified, telling Boris Karloff's sound-alike that it would mark the way. The marker served a second purpose as well since Abigail Wilson had posted it, a signal telling Penelope that her backup was in place and ready.

    At the saguaro, Penelope swung the Jeep into a barely visible turnoff and was immediately swallowed up by the desert. Half a mile later, she saw it and her heartbeat quickened. Despite knowing that Abigail was in position, Penelope cautiously skirted the deserted shack, driving beyond, well out of anybody's revolver range, before pulling the Jeep off the corrugated dirt track. She got out, shotgun first, and jacked a round into the chamber. The ominous clatter carried in the quiet desert air. That would get anybody's attention—if he was already there.

As Penelope slowly approached the back of the old shack, Big Mike caught the mood and went into stalk mode, abbreviating the process slightly to match his friend's pace because she wasn't nearly as patient. She would have a hard time surviving if forced to subsist on the fruits of *her* stalking techniques. The poor thing would be hard-pressed to catch a bird or a lizard unless they keeled over from sunstroke at her feet or came prepackaged with a terminal case of stupidity. It was a good thing that Big Mike was around to take care of her.

But, if asked, Mikey would admit that she was pretty adept at stalking humans. It was probably all that good Marine Corps training. Penelope approached the shack from a blind side, sidled around the corner, and suddenly poked the shotgun through the empty window while providing the smallest possible target of herself.

Empty.

It was a good thing, too. Penelope had been prepared to fumigate the place with buckshot at the slightest indication of hostile habitation.

So far Boris Karloff was following her instructions.

Penelope and Big Mike went around to the door and settled in to wait.

While Penelope sat in the broken easy chair, the shotgun

across her lap at the ready, Big Mike explored the one-room shack, making friends with a lizard on one wall, sniffing distastefully at an old paint can, batting at a none-too-bright horsefly in search of a horse, before settling into the dark cover provided by a cabinet with an askew door. It was the kind of hidey-hole any self-respecting cat would commandeer as a headquarters.

Despite the broken window, the air was thick and warm and smelled of dust accumulated over the years of neglect. With a good hour to wait *if* Boris followed his instructions to the letter, Penelope regretted not bringing a book and refreshments to while away the slowly passing minutes. After all, she could read and listen at the same time.

That was Andy's fault. If he hadn't been so persistent in playing Macho Man Protecting Helpless Damsel, she would have thought of a few amenities. It served him right if he had to sit around waiting for her to show up at The Tack Shack. Of course, when *he* got bored, he could always go in and admire Lora Lou in the altogether. Maybe sending him there wasn't such a good idea after all, Penelope thought. Lora Lou *was* pretty damned cute and didn't need a Super Bra. It would also serve Andy right, Penelope decided, if one of Empty Creek's finest happened by to ask him what he was doing sitting in an alley with a loaded rifle.

"Oh hell," Penelope muttered, "I should have let him come along. We could have played literary twenty questions."

Big Mike, having already noticed a lack of snacks and entertainment, was asleep in his hidey-hole. Besides, being a cat more suited to action, he wasn't all that good at twenty questions, literary or otherwise.

She peeked at her watch. Fifty-five minutes to go if . . .

Penelope listened intently. Apart from a scattered chirp or two from birds going about their business, the desert was quiet.

Fifty-four minutes. . . .

Penelope rose and moved quietly about the room looking for something, anything, to read amongst the litter left behind by the cabin's last inhabitant. Nothing. What kind of desert rat took off without leaving something behind for the next guy?

She finally found an old Campbell's soup can in a corner. The can had once contained Oyster Stew. Obviously, a gourmet had once lived here. The colors of the label were faded, but the information was readable so Penelope returned to the chair and read the nutritional information per serving and moved on to the ingredients. The ingredients sounded okay, but she didn't know what most of them were and decided to look up Oleoresin Paprika when she got home, thinking it might be like a Greek wine flavoring. Then, she savored a recipe for Deep Sea Potage that sounded good. Finally, she moved on to the directions. She even read the fine print that guaranteed satisfaction or money back.

She carefully placed the old can on the floor beside the chair before glancing at her watch.

Good God! Fifty-two minutes to go. That's what came of reading too fast.

By the time Penelope had memorized the recipe for Deep Sea Potage and replaced the can on the floor, time had raced by, leaving only forty-seven minutes to zero hour.

Next time, Tweedledee and Tweedledum can do this part, Penelope decided. This is entirely too boring. Of course, things would liven up considerably when Mr. Richard Raymond arrived. While more than ready to march Raymond off to justice, Penelope actually felt a little sorry for poor Susan Vaughn who would have to find someone else to share the next Lilac Suite with, but there was nothing for it. Having eliminated the *impossible*, the *improbable* Mr. Raymond remained.

It was Raymond who had the Arkansas connection.

It was Raymond who had put suspicion on Arguing Man, the hapless drifter Elmer Goymes.

And, although the ballistics results were not yet in, Maryanne Melrose had fired a shot at Raymond.

There were unanswered questions Penelope knew, but once the elusive Mr. Raymond arrived all would become clear. She resisted glancing at her watch and then said to hell with it. Forty minutes left. Damn, this is really, *really* boring. She recited the recipe for Deep Sea Potage once again, thinking that it better be good after all this trouble. At that precise moment, however, tedium fled at the sound of a soft footfall on a creaking step.

Too early! Penelope raised the shotgun and tensed. Damn Boris anyway. I wanted time to get psyched up for this. She worked the action on the shotgun. It just sounded so damned mean and deadly. That was enough psych for anyone, herself included. She quickly picked up the ejected shell and slid it into the loading port.

"Penelope."

"Abby? What's wrong?"

The door slowly swung open.

A handcuffed Abigail Wilson was framed in the doorway.

"You!" Penelope exclaimed. So much for *that* improbable.

"Don't even think about it," Ms. Susan Vaughn said from behind Abby, "this gun makes me ten feet tall." Her left hand was intertwined in Abby's hair while her right hand held what looked very much like a cocked and loaded .44-caliber revolver stuck in Abby's ear. "Put it down very carefully and kick it over here."

Penelope hesitated, realizing somewhat belatedly she should have arranged backup for the backup, but he was now sitting in an alley ten miles away, probably getting pretty damned mad at her.

"Do it, or I'll kill her. One more won't make any difference at this point."

Slowly, very slowly, looking for an opportunity to do something, anything, Penelope put the shotgun on the floor and pushed it away with her foot.

"Okay, where's the damned horse?"

When in doubt, stall for time. "Where's Raymond?" Penelope asked. "Are you in this together?"

Susan Vaughn laughed harshly. "That fool. He's sleeping off the pills I put in his drink. That's why I came early. I need to get back before he wakes up. He thinks he's just tired."

"Where's Boris?"

"Who?"

"The guy who made the calls. He sounds like Boris Karloff."

"He's nobody. Just somebody I found in a bar."

Penelope remembered Susan leaving the biker bar. Boris won't be hard to find when we get out of this. *If* we get out of this. . . . Right now, however, Penelope had to admit, things looked pretty bleak.

"Why are you doing this?"

"All of the usual reasons. Money, revenge."

"What's *your* real name?"

"Susan Oliver."

"Wendell Oliver's daughter?"

"His wife. We were married while he was in prison."

Now, why didn't I think of that? Penelope wondered. That's the most *improbable* thing I could have imagined. "Did you have conjugal visits?"

"None of your business."

"I just wondered."

Mrs. Susan Oliver pushed Abby over to stand next to Penelope.

"I didn't hear her coming," Abby said. "I'm sorry."

"That's all right. I didn't hear her coming either. I'm afraid I was memorizing a recipe."

"Enough. Where's the horse?"

Penelope shrugged.

"You're not going to be stubborn, are you?"

"You need me as long as I know where Beau is and you don't."

"That's going to put your friend in a rather awkward position." Susan reached behind and pulled the door closed.

"Why is that?" Penelope smiled. Susan Vaughn . . . Oliver . . . whatever her name and marital status was, had just made a mistake. At least, Penelope hoped it was a mistake.

"Because I'll shoot ner in the kneecap. If you don't tell then, I'll shoot her other kneecap. I'll keep doing it until I know where that stupid horse is."

"Go ahead," Penelope said. "She only has two kneecaps and I hardly know her anyway."

"Penelope!"

"Just kidding, Abby. I thought a little levity was in order."

"Where's the horse?" The revolver lowered just enough to point at Abby's right kneecap. "I'm going to count to three."

"Don't tell her," Abby said. "She'll kill us anyway."

"Oh, I'll tell her, but I'm going to make her wait until three."

"One."

Penelope thought she detected a slight twitch in old what's her name's nose.

"Two."

Yes! A very definite twitch.

"Thr . . ."

"He's at . . ."

No one would ever dissuade Penelope—not Andy, not Dutch, not Samantha, not even Doctor Bob—that Big Mike did not possess the uncanny ability to shed hair at will, particularly when confronted by a crazed woman waving a .44 revolver around. Penelope not only believed that Big Mike could shed hair whenever he wanted, but she was also firmly convinced that he could fire it across a room at a target, hitting the X ring of the bull's-eye with unerring accuracy. Penelope firmly believed Big Mike was the cat with the invisible flying fur. Of course, she was the only person who believed such a thing was possible, but it didn't really matter since . . .

Susan Vaughn sneezed.

And sneezed.

"Where is he?" Susan Vaughn screamed between sneezes. "I'll kill him."

Big Mike growled, deep and raspy, the guttural warning of an aroused African lion.

Susan Vaughn sneezed again. Then, she found her target. The blast was deafening in the small room, but another sneeze—and a Campbell's soup can punted with unerring accuracy—drastically affected her aim and a most startled lizard on the wall nearly left his tail behind while getting out of Dodge.

Penelope tackled Susan Vaughn, incidentally throwing a shoulder right into her belly, eliciting a most satisfying, "Ooofff."

Even though she was handcuffed, Abby leaped into the fray by kicking the revolver away and yelling, "Belt her again!"

Penelope was happy to oblige.

Just for good measure, Big Mike sent another barrage of invisible flying fur in the murderess's direction.

Sitting astride the prostrate and red-eyed woman, Penelope was not at all sure she had the authority to read Susan Vaughn her rights, but she did so anyway while rummaging through her captive's pockets until she found the handcuff key and freed Abigail. "You have the right to remain silent. You have the right . . ." Penelope thought she had covered them all.

Susan Vaughn sneezed. "I need a tissue."

"I don't think you have the Constitutional right for a tissue," Penelope said. Shoot at my buddy, will you?

Susan Vaughn was hauled rudely to her feet and forced to stand spread-eagled against the wall to be searched and handcuffed.

"You should have stayed in Arkansas," Penelope said.

Susan Vaughn Oliver sneezed all the way back to Empty Creek because of the seating arrangements. Penelope drove. Mrs. Oliver was curtly ordered into the passenger seat and Abby climbed into the back seat where she was ready to pounce on the now handcuffed and soon-to-be former insurance investigator at the slightest provocation. Big Mike checked it out and decided to ride on Mrs. Oliver's lap.

Served her right.

When the foursome entered the Empty Creek Police Station, they could hear Andy in the back shouting and demanding a search party be mounted.

A relieved officer on the desk waved them back without so much as a question about why one of their party was handcuffed and had red eyes and a puffed cheek.

Four jaws dropped as Susan Vaughn Oliver stumbled through the door of Dutch's office propelled by an energetic push from a still-pumped special agent of the Federal Bureau of Investigation. "Sit," Abby ordered.

Tweedledee and Tweedledum sat.

"She meant her," Penelope said pointing to Susan Vaughn Oliver.

"Oh."

Andy was so relieved to see Penelope that he forgot to be angry—until later. Dutch and the two detectives were also pleased to see Penelope, but they weren't about to admit it.

There were to be a great many rather heated recriminations during the remainder of the afternoon with a whole bunch of stuff about missing shotguns, wild-goose chases, dangerous situations, both of you ought to know better, how could you do such a thing, where did you learn to pick locks, dumb, dumb, dumb. . . . It was enough to make Big Mike turn to the remains of a jelly donut for solace. Penelope was almost ready to join him.

But through it all, they managed to book Susan Vaughn Oliver for the murders of Jack Loomis, aka Jim Loper and Maryanne Melrose, aka Emma Snyder, etc.

With that accomplished, Dutch growled and complained

some more. "When I agreed to keep the horses hidden, I didn't agree for you to go running around alone, damn it."

"I wasn't alone. Abby and Mycroft were with me. Besides, you didn't say I couldn't."

Dutch groaned. "You're supposed to be smart enough to figure that out all by yourself."

"Look, do you want to hear this or not?"

"I do," Andy said with notebook poised and pen at the ready.

"Well, let's go somewhere, sweetie, and I'll tell you all about it."

"Sit," Dutch commanded.

Penelope sat.

"Talk."

Penelope talked.

"It was easy once I found out Maryanne could have fired the shot. With that information, I reached the conclusion that she wasn't attempting to frighten away insurance investigators, but rather to scare away . . ."

"Or kill," Dutch interrupted. "The bullet matches, by the way."

Penelope nodded. "Or kill a blackmailer attempting to cut into her fortune. We'll never know which for sure now. Susan fooled me though," Penelope admitted. "I thought it was Raymond. The pencil-thin mustache threw me off. I forgot all about women with thin pinched lips."

"What are you talking about?"

"Oh, never mind. It just shows that one shouldn't have preconceived notions. Anyway, I thought it was Raymond doing a Boris Karloff imitation. It made sense because of his Arkansas connection, particularly after Lora Lou identified poor old

Elmer. I should have taken it another step further, but who would have thought little Miss Prissy . . ."

"They called from the hospital, incidentally," Dutch said. "Raymond's a little groggy, but he'll be all right. She damned near added a third homicide to her record, to say nothing of you two."

"Don't start that again," Penelope warned, "or I'll tell Stormy to start rehearsing *Lysistrata.*"

"What's that?"

"A classical Greek comedy by Aristophanes in which the women refuse to have sex with their men until they stop fighting wars. Stormy would be perfect as Lysistrata."

"No, she wouldn't and it sounds like a tragedy to me."

"Don't think I won't do it," Penelope said, "and don't think Stormy wouldn't cooperate for her big sister."

"Why did Maryanne call Susan?" Abby asked. "That's what I don't understand."

"I think Maryanne must have believed it was Raymond also, particularly since Boris was making all the calls. When Maryanne couldn't reach me, she probably felt safe in calling Susan and meeting her later," Penelope said, "because she was a woman and an insurance investigator officially connected with the case."

"She would have suspected Raymond because it was a man who called her."

"That's right, I think. Ironically, Maryanne might have wanted to warn Susan. Instead . . . Maryanne would have no reason to suspect that Mrs. Oliver was killing the people she blamed for her husband's death. That part must have been purely revenge."

"What about Horace Melrose?" Andy asked. "What did she have on him?"

"Nothing," Penelope replied. "Nothing at all. She planned to give Horace a simple choice. Either he cooperated in the plan to kill Beauregarde and split the insurance money with her or, if he didn't, Susan would kill Beauregarde anyway and Horace would be ruined. No money. No potential national champion. No ranch. And, by bilking the insurance company that was instrumental in sending her husband to prison, her revenge would be complete. To his credit, Horace told me about the blackmail attempt."

"Maybe, I should have dinner with him after all," Abby said. "He's not as bad as I thought."

For Penelope, it ended almost as it had begun, with an impromptu party. Laney got the desert drums to talking and soon the house was filled with Penelope's friends toasting her success.

As the hero of the day, he of the invisible flying fur was also suitably pampered. Alexander gave his friend one good slobbery lick and then sat back. Demanding little Kelsey, on the other hand, looked as though she might issue a protest at all the attention shown Mycroft, but once shown a rolled-up issue of the *Empty Creek News Journal* she was quickly disabused of that notion and sulked until Stormy offered her lap.

Dutch grumped about until Penelope slipped over and whispered in his ear. "Cheer up," she said jokingly, "or . . . *Lysistrata.*"

That took care of Dutch, but Andy wasn't ready to forgive her yet.

During a lull in the celebration, Penelope caught Samantha's eye and nodded toward the kitchen. Together, they made up a feast for the little rabbits and then walked down the path to the stables. Mattie and Red had brought Chardonnay home in time for the party.

"I have to make it up to poor Andy. I really wounded his pride today, but I didn't want him to get hurt."

"I know. Jake wasn't too pleased when I told him about our little adventure out at Mattie's. Men are always so protective."

"What did you do?"

"Let him win at strip poker."

Penelope laughed. "Does your board of directors know about that?"

"I'd rather we kept that our little secret. What are you going to do?"

"Oh, I'll think of something."

"You always do. I'm really grateful for what you've done. Big Jake is, too. The loan is solid now and the show will go on. People have already started calling Jake to cancel their cancellations. And it's all because of you and Big Mike."

Penelope sighed. "I'm just glad it's finally over."

It took a very long time to cajole Andy back into a good humor. Even the promise of an exclusive interview for the *News Journal* wasn't quite enough to restore his spirits. But when the last guest departed, Penelope got out a deck of cards and said, "Cut for the deal."

Well, one thing just naturally led to another. . . .

EPILOGUE

The President's Ball was a happy affair.

With all forgiven now, Penelope and Andy snuggled close as they danced. Andy had accepted her apology and her promise that next time—if there was a next time—she would take him along on whatever adventure it might be. He didn't even mind her postscript to that particular conversation. "You'll be sorry," she had said, wondering if they still shouted that cry at poor unsuspecting boots entering the United States Marine Corps Recruit Depot. Penelope had certainly been sorry until that proud graduation day when she marched with her platoon, passing in review as the band struck up the "Marine's Hymn." But she wasn't sorry about having Andy in her life, not one little bit.

They weren't the only ones snuggling at the President's Ball either.

Samantha and Big Jake danced cheek to cheek during all of the slow tunes. Still-slick Red kicked up his heels with Mattie during the fast tunes. Nora, despite wearing the highest heels she could gracefully manage, was forced to dance cheek to chest with Anthony Lyme-Regis, but what the hell. . . .

Reggie was quite happy in the company of a certain quarterback until they had to meet their respective curfews for training purposes at which point she dramatically announced to her mother, "This stage of my life is over. I'm ready for college now."

Abiding by the curfews, however, achieved their designs; Reggie went on to win her event at the Great Empty Creek Horse Show and Dirk led the Gila Monsters to the championship title. (By the by, the San Diego State Aztecs beat the BYU Cougars and all was right in Penelope's football world.)

A much subdued Horace Melrose attended the ball with Abigail Wilson, soon to be reassigned to the Phoenix office of the Bureau.

Poor Richard Raymond was distraught over the events and did not attend the ball, but his broken heart was somewhat alleviated by Lora Lou finally giving in and selling him the portrait. After all, she was already posing for another.

By the time the obligatory fistfight broke out well after midnight, the happy couples in attendance at the President's Ball had already slipped away to other pursuits.

The Great Empty Creek Arabian Horse Show was deemed a tremendous success as well. Jake introduced Penelope and Big Mike during the awards ceremony on the last day, embarrassing the one and satisfying the other, particularly since he was rewarded with a full case of lima beans.

Sir Beauregarde Revere of Dunbarton Oaks was duly crowned champion of the show. It turned out that his sojourn with Mattie Bates had included some training according to her own precepts and it was Mattie who took Beau through his paces in the center ring to great applause and cheers.

The Super Bra commercial was a big hit as was *Vanessa Diamond, P.I.* when it premiered. As a result, Stormy was offered a role in an Off Broadway play.

Even better from Muffy and Biff's point of view, Stormy and Dutch set a wedding date.

Anthony Lyme-Regis became a frequent visitor to Empty Creek and Nora and Reggie took turns grounding each other for various offenses.

A certain poet reached Book VI of a certain epic poem.

Cackling Ed talked his doctor into giving him a hormone shot and he successfully pursued a younger woman of a mere seventy-six years.

The city council lured a minor league baseball team to town that would join the Arizona–New Mexico League in the spring as the Empty Creek Coyotes.

Penelope and Stormy spent a day together, shopping, having lunch, going to a movie in the afternoon, and dinner afterward while their guys actually went fishing.

When all was said and done, however, Penelope did not have the heart to check into the Lilac Suite. She had no intention of following in the murderous Mrs. Oliver's footsteps. The Chrysanthemum Suite was quite another matter entirely.

Thus, Big Mike was duly sent to spend the weekend with Alexander and Kelsey where he had a pretty good time scarfing down the liver crunchies and lima beans, romping with his pal, and giving their Kelsey nemesis another lesson in manners.

Penelope and Andy spent the weekend basking by the pool, ordering room service, and watching naughty movies while complaining about the overwhelming pink decor of their suite.

And Penelope never did receive a telephone call from Josephine Brooks about Big Mike, Murphy Brown, and another litter of little Mycroft look-alikes.

This time.